BEHIND the SCENES

Dahlia Adler

Spencer Hill Contemporary / Spencer Hill Press

Contact: Spencer Hill Press, PO Box 247, Contoocook, NH 03229, USA

Please visit our website at www.spencerhillpress.com

First Edition: June 2014
Second Printing: June 2014
Dahlia Adler
Behind the Scenes: a novel / by Dahlia Adler - 1st ed.
p. cm.
Summary: A girl takes a job as her best friend's assistant on a hit teen TV show and begins a relationship with one of the actors that sends her deeper into the world of Hollywood than she ever wanted.

Cover design by Christa Holland (Paper & Sage Design)
Interior layout by Jenny Perinovic

ISBN 978-1-939392-97-8 (paperback)
ISBN 978-1-939392-98-5 (e-book)

Printed in the United States of America

To my *family*,

for always assuming the writing I wouldn't share were the greatest stories never told

IF MY PHONE BUZZED ONE MORE TIME, I was going to pull it out of my backpack and hurl it at the linoleum.

Dammit, Van. It was definitely her calling, even though she knew I was in school. She'd had an audition that morning for a teen dramedy show, and I swear she seemed more desperate to land the role of Ditz #3 on *Daylight Falls* than she'd been to play Brad-freakin'-Pitt's stepdaughter three years ago.

I couldn't turn my phone off—not with my dad in the hospital—so when it finally shut up, I said a silent prayer that she wouldn't try again. I hated when Vanessa interrupted me during class. Little-known fact: Girls who pick up the phone during French do *not* get to keep their shiny new acceptance letters to Columbia.

Just when I was finally sure Van had gotten the message, my bag began vibrating for a third time.

"Hey, Duncan, I think your bag is buzzing."

"I know," I whispered back to Nate Donovan without turning around, "but what am I supposed to do about it?"

"Have you considered, I dunno, answering it? Man, and to think I actually needed *you* to tutor *me* a few months ago."

"Funny, Donovan. Anyway, it's just Vanessa. She can wait. *Le subjunctif* cannot."

"Vanessa, you say." Even in a whisper, he sounded obviously intrigued. I rolled my eyes. Nate always got a hard-on at the mere mention of her name. As far as I knew, he'd never had trouble landing a girlfriend, but the only girl he'd ever expressed interest in to me was my utterly unattainable BFF. "I could get that for you if you like."

"*Monsieur Donovan et Mademoiselle Duncan, est-ce qu'il-y-a quelque chose que vous voulez partager avec la classe?*"

No, I definitely didn't have anything I wanted to share with the class. I was not there to share. I was there to learn, to get an A (or A+, I really wasn't picky), and to make myself fluent enough that—combined with two and a half years of French at Columbia—I'd be able to get around the country when I studied abroad in Paris for spring semester of my junior year.

"*Non, Madame Boulanger*," I replied for both me and Nate. "*Excusez-nous.*"

She nodded and turned around, and I resumed my forceful focus on the board...for about thirty seconds, until my phone buzzed yet again.

"Un-freaking-believable," I muttered, refusing to take my eyes off Madame Boulanger.

"Just take it," Nate whispered. "I'll get the notes. I promise."

Clearly, I didn't have a choice; she wasn't going to let up any time soon. I snatched the phone from my bag, slipped out of the classroom, and dashed around the hallway corner to the ladies' room.

"I could kill you," I whispered fiercely the second I picked up. "You know not to call me during class—"

"I know, I know," she interrupted, "but I promise, Ally, my news is totally worth it."

"Does this mean you got the part?"

"I have so much to tell you, but I can't talk now. Can you meet me at the Lunchbox after school?"

I rolled my eyes. This was so typical. Still, she'd piqued my curiosity, and I didn't have anything else after school today. "Fine, but my BLT's on you, and don't even think about refusing to split fries with me."

"Deal. Gotta go. See you later!"

She hung up without waiting for me to say goodbye, which was also typical, but it's hard to blame Van for her flightiness when she's in a profession that forces her to be fake on a daily basis. I don't know how she does it, but acting's been her dream for as long as either of us can remember. Definitely *not* something we have in common.

I palmed my phone and headed back to class with what my father would call "a spring in my step." Despite my annoyance at the poor timing of her insistent phone calls, I was happy for Van, who'd obviously gotten the part. Plus, free BLT. Everybody wins. It was shaping up to be a great day, and I hadn't had one of those in a while.

★★★★★

Vanessa beat me to the diner, but it took me a minute to realize it because she was decked out in full hidden-star mode: sunglasses, dark hair tucked under a baseball cap, and an unassuming outfit of Gap jeans and a striped tee.

"I'm surprised you didn't toss on your old Raggedy Ann wig just to *really* throw off the paparazzi." I slid into the seat across from her in our usual booth and smiled when I saw that she'd already ordered me an Arnold Palmer.

"Oh, A, mock if you must." Vanessa sighed dramatically. "But when one is the star of Hollywood's hottest new teen drama, one must take special precautions." She leaned over and took a sip of the raspberry iced tea in front of her, her enormous aviators blocking the coffee-brown eyes I knew must've been twinkling behind them.

"You got it!" I jumped up from my seat and squeezed Van around her shoulders, knocking her cap to the ground. "Congrats, Van. I know this was a big one for you."

"Oh, but I haven't yet told you just how big." She reached down and grabbed her hat, set it on the table next to her tea, and glanced around quickly as I sat back down before taking off her sunglasses as well. "I mean it when I say I'm the star. You're looking at Bailey Summers, baby!"

Van's squeal was so high-pitched I was sure I'd heard her wrong. "What are you talking about, V? I thought you were auditioning for a character named Grace."

"I *was*," said Van, pausing for a sip of her drink, "but they loved me so much that they asked me to try out for the lead instead. And I got it!"

"I thought they wanted some tall, blonde babe to be the lead," I said, still confused. I could swear I'd been listening closely to Van when she'd described the show to me, but maybe I'd been in a bigger studying haze than I'd thought. "Didn't you say—and I quote—'that bitch Zoe Knight totes has it in the bag'? I distinctly remember wanting to vomit that you used the word 'totes' in real life."

"That was the original plan, but I guess the acting talents of Miss Vanessa Park were enough to convince the powers that be that Bailey Summers—love interest of the super-hot Tristan Monroe, played by none other than the super-hot Liam Holloway—was meant to be a petite Korean chick." Van's smile was so bright it practically lit up the entire interior of the Lunchbox, and I couldn't help mirroring it. "They've already cast my parents, so they're just going to capitalize on how hot foreign adoption is right now." She airquoted that last bit and rolled her eyes, but it barely detracted from her gleeful expression.

"That's so, so awesome, Van. You deserve it, and I'm glad they were smart enough to see it! Now where is our freaking waiter already so we can order you something celebratory? I skipped lunch to work on my article about the talent show, and I am starving."

"Already ordered," Van said proudly as a waiter emerged with two plates, one holding the promised BLT and the other containing Van's signature salad. (Literally. The Lunchbox named it after her because she got it so often and she's by far their highest-profile customer, though she and I were such regulars that no one even blinked at the sight of her anymore.)

"I'll be right back with your fries," he said, nodding slightly before disappearing back into the kitchen.

"Vanny, you are not only a TV star, you are totally the star of my heart." I lifted my Arnold Palmer. "Can we toast to your success now or what?"

She must've been excited because she absolutely hated when I called her Vanny, but she didn't so much as stick out her tongue. "Definitely!" She lifted her iced tea, and I clinked my glass against hers.

"To Vanessa Park, the hottest teen actress Daylight Falls—and Hollywood—has ever seen."

"Hear, hear!" Vanessa flashed another megawatt smile and then tossed back a long swallow of tea.

"I can't wait to tell my parents," I mused, after taking a sip of my own drink. "They're gonna be so ridiculously proud."

"Oh, crap, I am such an asshole," said Vanessa, all traces of her smile disappearing from her face. "How's your dad? I'm so high on myself today I completely forgot to ask."

I immediately felt awful for raining on her parade, even though it hadn't remotely been my intention. "Please, Van, you are definitely within your rights to be self-obsessed today! Besides, this is exactly the kind of thing that will make my dad's day. As he's constantly pointing out, it helps to keep fighting when you have major things to live for."

"How's the treatment going? And what's it called again? It's not chemo, right?"

I shook my head. Chemo had been my assumption, too, when he told me he'd been diagnosed, but apparently it had even crappier odds with stage IV melanoma than the relatively new treatment my dad *was* getting.

"It's called immunotherapy," I managed around the lump that magically appeared in my throat whenever I recalled that conversation. "Bolsters the immune system instead of killing cells like chemo does." The waiter returned with our fries, and I immediately snatched one up and popped it into my mouth, as if the grease would make that lump slide right out. "It's still too early to tell if it's working, but I'm going to visit him in the hospital straight from here. The official

Duncan family party line is that we're cautiously optimistic, so I'm trying to roll with that."

"Do you want me to come with you? I'd love to say hi, and I can totally reschedule my meeting with John."

This was exactly why I loved Van. No matter what was going on in her life or how swelled her head should be, she was always grounded enough to be there for me. When I got into Columbia early, she took me out for an awesome celebratory evening, even though she was presenting at some award show the next day, and when I called to tell her about my dad, she'd left the audition she'd been at and raced right over.

"Thank you for offering, but trust me, it's better for both of us if you meet with your agent ASAP. Besides, he'll probably fall asleep after ten minutes while I just sit there researching melanoma on the Internet."

Vanessa groaned. "A, what'd I tell you about doing that? It'll only make you crazy."

"I think it's a good thing to be informed," I countered, prodding at the sandwich I was starting to lose my appetite for. "I just wish websites would stop informing me that only something like six percent of people with his cancer live longer than six months."

"And I wish *you* would have a little more faith and a little more self-control," said Van, chewing thoughtfully on a fry. "Are you sure you don't want me to come?"

"Yes," I said firmly. "Vanessa Park, you are about to become an even bigger star, and you need to focus on—"

"Excuse me, did you just say Vanessa Park? Oh my gosh, are you Vanessa Park??"

I stopped mid-sentence, and Van and I both looked up to see a timid tween with huge, blue eyes looking down at Van in awe. As Van smiled and graciously agreed to an autograph and a picture, I couldn't help but wonder just how big a star she was about to become. She was gonna be in for some serious coverage and publicity as soon as the news broke that the main character of *Daylight Falls* had been rewritten to accommodate her. I was thrilled for Van, but selfishly, I couldn't help but wish she'd be around more, now of all times.

"I love having young fans," said Van as soon as the girl was out of earshot. "Do you think I'll have a lot more now that I'm actually on a teen show instead of playing 'the daughter' or 'the medical student prodigy' in movies for adults?" (Believe it or not, Van's played "the med student prodigy" on multiple occasions. As hard as it is for Asian-Americans to get cast in Hollywood, she never seems to have any problem landing roles like those.)

"I'll tell you what I think." I nabbed a piece of avocado from her plate. "I think you're about to become America's newest teen idol."

She laughed. "I think those are usually guys. Liam Holloway's got that job in the bag."

"Well then, whatever it is girls are, I think you're about to become that." And as I said it, I knew in my gut it was true; Van was about to become huge, and I could only hope that didn't change things between us, especially now when I needed her most. Despite the goofy smile that spread over her face, I couldn't help the tinge of anxiety that danced like a butterfly down my spine.

"HI, I'M HERE TO SEE A PATIENT—Ezra Duncan. He's in room 1028." I signed in with my left hand and held up my school ID in my right like the seasoned pro I'd become after a couple of months.

"Right down the hall and make a left, sweetheart."

"Thanks." I hitched my backpack higher on my shoulder and swung around the reception desk, heading down the hall until I found the correct room. I was surprised to see that the door was wide open, even though my dad was in bed, a pajama-sporting bump on a log covered by one of those thin white blankets that couldn't keep a fire warm.

"Hey, Dad," I greeted him warily, trying to keep my voice down as I took a cautious step into the room. "How are you feeling?"

"AlGal!" He waved me in with an IV-filled arm. "Come in! Sit!"

I couldn't help but laugh. Even in a hospital bed with a bunch of tubes sticking out of him and a bag full of rust-colored pee hanging down the side, my dad was cheerful. His straw-colored hair—so much like my little sister Lucy's and so *unlike* the auburn mane I'd inherited from my mom—was graying a bit, but otherwise, he looked...like himself. I exhaled with relief as I plopped down on the chair next to his bed. I guess I hadn't realized how much I'd expected cancer to change him.

Then again, it had only been a few weeks.

"So how's it going?"

"Actually," I said, drawing out the word, "I have some *very* exciting news, though it's not exactly mine. And speaking of which, Van wanted to come visit, but she has a meeting with her agent."

"Aw, that's nice, honey. Please tell her thank you for me. So I take it she's the one with the news?"

"As usual." I smiled, relaxing back in the chair and dropping my backpack to the ground. "Get this. Van's going to be the star—like, the actual lead role—in TV's newest teen dramedy, *Daylight Falls*!"

Dad laughed, and I couldn't help joining in. It was so nice to be able to make him happy in his current state, and I knew that, despite his laughter, he was every bit as proud of Van as I was. She and I had been friends since sand was our idea of haute cuisine, and she was nearly as much of a daughter to him as Lucy and I were. The fact that Van couldn't stand her own parents only strengthened her bond with mine.

"That's fantastic," he said, shaking his head and laughing again. "Have you told Lucy yet?"

"No, but I know she'll flip when I do. Don't worry—I won't let her anywhere near the set."

"Good girl." He smiled and reached for the cup of water on the small table next to him, then took a tiny sip. "And how are you feeling about Vanessa's potentially impending superstardom?"

I shrugged. "I'm happy for her. I'm always happy for her. I just hope she doesn't disappear."

"She won't," he said confidently. "The two of you have been friends for so long, it's incredible. When she first started getting real jobs, your mother and I were afraid things between the two of you would fall apart, but that crazy sci-fi movie was, what, eight years ago? And the two of you seem just as strong as ever."

I curled my legs underneath me and eyed the untouched Jell-O on his tray. Despite having just consumed my weight in beef and bacon, the jiggly red cup was calling my name. "Wanna know the secret?"

He smiled knowingly. "Is the secret that you want my Jell-O?"

"I'm not taking your food," I said defensively.

"Don't worry, I can always get more if I want. I'm just having a hard time stomaching anything right now. Go ahead, have at it."

He certainly didn't need to tell me twice. I grabbed the Jell-O and plastic spoon from the tray and dug in. "The secret," I informed him, as I took a bite of the first jiggly spoonful, "is that neither of us is remotely envious of the other's life. You couldn't pay me ten times Van's salary to have to smile for strangers' cameras or sign a zillion autographs a day, let alone have to look perfect all the time and get chased by paparazzi. And don't get me started on how *nice* she has to be to everyone all the time, even when people are being jerks." As for Van, let's just say she had zero regrets when she left school. Hayden High was the last place she'd ever wanna be.

"So you really have no interest in stardom?"

"Really. None," I said firmly. I'd spent enough time both in public and on set with Van to know that I did not want her life. I liked both my privacy and my alone time, thank you very much, not to mention that I was utterly incapable of waking up in time to put on a full face of makeup before I had to start my day. "The occasional event I attend with her is plenty. Which reminds me that there will definitely be some sort of red-carpet thing coming up." I groaned. "Fantastic."

"Is that your way of hinting at money for a new dress?"

I grinned. "It wasn't, but I wouldn't say no if you're offering."

He laughed, but it was weaker this time and I could tell he was growing sleepy. "Sounds like a job for the emergency credit card," he mumbled, adjusting his pillow.

He was passed out in moments, but I stuck around anyway, figuring it was as peaceful a place as any to do my homework. Despite frequent interruptions from nurses and my dad randomly waking up to have three-minute conversations before falling asleep again, I didn't realize how long I'd been there until my ringing cell phone jolted me from my textbook and I saw that darkness had settled outside. I glanced at the screen; it was my mom, undoubtedly concerned about my whereabouts, especially since I'd biked today instead of driving. *Whoops.*

"I'm at the hospital with Dad," I greeted her without preamble. "Not lying in a ditch somewhere, I promise. I just lost track of time."

"Do you want me to come pick you up?"

Hmm, no lecture about not having called? Interesting. "A ride would be great, thank you."

Twenty minutes later, I was affixing my bike to the rack of my mom's SUV before climbing into the passenger seat. "Thanks for picking me up," I said as I buckled my seatbelt. Only then did I see that Lucy was in the backseat. "Hey, Luce."

"Jason Creeley tried to kiss me today," she greeted me, making a disgusted expression.

"Jason Creeley has excellent taste," I informed her. "But next time he tries coming at you without your consent, you should really go ahead and kick him in the—"

"Ally!"

"I was going to say 'shin,'" I lied. "Anyway, I have some fun news that will clear the gross image of Jason Creeley's lips right out of your head." I filled them in on Van's exciting day.

"No way!" Lucy's face lit up. "That's supposed to be the best new show *ever*. I can't believe I know a TV star! I can't wait to tell everyone at school!"

"I think you should probably wait for the casting news to be officially released," I told her gently. "I know that being the envy of the fifth grade is super-important, but hold off on the major revelations until I get the all-clear from Van, 'kay?"

"'Kay," she mumbled. "When's she coming over? I'll ask her myself."

"I have a feeling it's gonna be a while, squirt, but I'll send her your love."

"How's your dad doing?" Mom asked. "I stopped in during my lunch break, but I had parent-teacher conferences after school. Was he awake when you left?"

"Tossing and turning, but definitely not coherent." I watched the lights of Hayden Heights, the L.A. neighborhood I've lived in all my life, whiz by as we drove. I was about to ask why she hadn't just come in when she'd picked me up, but then I remembered that she and my dad were still iffy on whether or not it was a good idea for Lucy to see him in the hospital. "I just hate leaving him alone, even when he's asleep."

"I do too," said Mom, "but it's just impossible to be everywhere at once. Besides, your dad has Steve's entire DVD collection."

"As if even half of the Edelmans' collection would fit into a hospital room."

The car fell quiet, and I glanced at the rearview mirror to see if Lucy had fallen asleep. She hadn't; she was staring glumly out her window, her chin balanced in her palm.

"Everything okay, Luce?"

I was instantly sorry for saying it; I realized what she was about to say an instant before she even said the words. "I want to visit Dad."

I glanced at my mom. "Maybe I'll take you later this week," I hedged as we pulled into the driveway. I was suddenly very, very tired. "I'm gonna head up to bed. Thanks again for the ride, Mom." I gave her a kiss on the cheek and hopped out of the car.

It was still pretty early, but I didn't feel like talking to anyone, I'd finished my homework at the hospital, and I didn't have the energy for yet another practice Advanced Placement exam. Instead, I went to the bathroom, turned on the shower, and stripped off my clothes. As the white-tiled room filled with steam, I proceeded to examine every micro-inch of my body, from in between my toes to whatever scalp I could manage to view before the mirror fogged over. Once I was temporarily convinced that no new or growing moles graced my skin, I stepped into the spray and let the hot water rinse me clean.

★★★★★

There was one more person I knew would be interested in Van's news, and when I told Nate the next morning, his grin could've lit the entire football field.

"So *now* do you think she'll go out with me?" he promptly asked.

"Not following your logic there, Donovan," I said as we walked down the hall toward my physics lab. "More famous plus hot costar does not equal, 'Hey, *now* I'll grab a slice with high school boy.' Not that Van's a snob," I added quickly. "Just curious about your making this particular leap. Besides, why Vanessa? You could easily get a girlfriend at Hayden if you wanted one." In fact, I had at least one friend who was quite interested, but when I'd mentioned Dana Mitchell to Nate, he'd dismissed the idea of dating her without a second thought.

"Maybe that's why I don't want one," Nate said matter-of-factly.

I rolled my eyes. "She texted me last night to ask me to go shopping with her after school. You're welcome to join, as long as you've got an opinion on asymmetrical hemlines."

"On what now?"

"I'm guessing that's a pass."

He sighed. "Women. Later, Duncan." He turned and walked off to his own class with a 180-degree flip of his hand over his head as some sort of dismissive wave.

As I walked up to my desk in lab, I couldn't help feeling a little bad that I hadn't even pretended Nate had a shot. I pulled out my phone and texted Vanessa.

Hey, what are you doing this weekend?

"Hey, Ally."

I looked up. Speak of the devil—Dana Mitchell and her favorite tagalong, Lenore Akers, were headed my way. I wasn't really in the mood for either Dana's inevitable gossip or Leni's automatic agreement with everything Dana said, but with Van off in Hollywoodland, they were what passed for my good friends at Hayden. "Hey, guys. Cute skirt, Len."

Leni opened her mouth to respond, but as usual, Dana quickly steamrolled her. "Are you still going to insist there's nothing going on between you and Nate Donovan? The two of you are together like every day."

"There is definitely nothing going on with me and Nate," I assured Dana. "He just has a little crush on Van, and he's trying to get me to hook it up. Don't worry," I added quickly, "it's never going to happen."

Dana sighed dramatically. "Of course. How am I supposed to compete with a little Hollywood princess?"

"Dane—"

"Maybe next time he asks you about Vanessa, you could tell him to drop the fairy tale and pay attention to the reality in front of him," Dana suggested, trying and failing to keep her voice casual.

"I'll be sure to," I said, although I didn't think I'd have any more success on a second attempt.

"What are you doing after school?" Leni asked.

"Going shopping with Van." I glanced at the door as our teacher entered the room. "Hey, Bowinger's here."

They started to shuffle off to their shared desk, and I knew they were waiting for an invitation to join me and Van, but they weren't going to get it. I likely didn't have much BFF time left, and I wasn't about to give any up.

★★★★★

"What do you think of this one?" Van asked, emerging from the dressing room wearing a one-shoulder dress with a crossover hemline in a blinding shade of purple satin.

"It's a little...extreme."

"Hmm," she said thoughtfully. "I'm not sure extreme is bad in this case, but okay. Hand me that black leather one."

I did as she asked and then watched her recede into the dressing room. "Hey, Van?"

"Mmhmm?" She was clearly pulling the dress over her head, muffling her response.

"Any chance of your giving Nate a break and actually going out with him this week?"

Her sigh floated under the dressing room door. "Al, even if I was interested in Nate, I don't have the time. Filming starts next week and I need to spend the weekend learning my lines and working on my tan. Plus I already have a little cast party to go to. A meet-the-costars thing. No plus-ones allowed, or I'd totally invite you."

I laughed. "Thanks for thinking of me, Van, but considering what you've told me of Zoe Knight, I'm not sure I want to meet your costars ever."

"Yeah, right." She snorted. "Tell me you don't want to meet Liam Holloway."

"I don't know a thing about Liam Holloway," I countered.

"You've seen a picture. What else do you need to know?"

"Um, maybe that he's not a self-centered walking six-pack?"

"Ouch, harsh much?" Van stepped out of the dressing room. "What do you think?"

"Tough but hot," I responded, nodding with approval at her selection. "And I'm not being harsh. The guy gets work because he has a ridiculously good body and eyes bluer than anything found in nature. He's asking to be pre-judged."

"Come on, A. How would you like it if someone talked about me like that?"

"No one would," I responded instantly. "You've proven you have talent in a variety of roles. Liam's work mainly consists of Abercrombie ads and that embarrassingly bad movie you made me watch on your fifteenth birthday."

"The movie was bad, but *he* was good," said Van, examining herself in the mirror from all angles. "Anyway, it'll be nice to spend some time with everyone outside of work. I just have to make sure I actually find time to learn my lines before we film."

"Nate could help you practice," I offered, inexplicably feeling the need to make one last-ditch effort.

"But that's what I need *you* for," Vanessa said cheerfully, slipping a chunky brass crucifix on over the strapless leather sheath. "You know you're the only one who can make me focus."

I shook my head at the crucifix and watched her try on a long strand of misshapen pearls instead. "My dad's supposed to come home on Friday and he'll be pretty out of it, so I need to help my mom get him settled back in, but I can come over on Sunday."

"I have a better idea," said Vanessa, slipping on a pair of lace open-toe booties and checking out the whole look. "How about I come over on Saturday, and that way I can visit your dad *and* you can help me out?"

"I should warn you—if you come over, Lucy's gonna be all over you. She was practically foaming at the mouth when I told her you got the part."

Van laughed. "That's just fine with me. You know Lucy's like the little sister I never had."

"Or wanted," I pointed out with a smile. Van had never made a secret of the fact that she was glad to be an only child. Hard to blame her, since she barely got any attention from her parents as it was.

"Regardless, it'll be excellent practice for handling the tween mobs that are sure to be all over me once *Daylight* airs."

"Ah, we're just calling it *Daylight* now?"

"It's my show; I can be on a first-name basis with it."

"Fair enough. So, Saturday?"

"Saturday," she confirmed. "And I am totally getting this outfit."

I watched as she practically danced up to the counter to pay for it all, dropping her plastic like it was nothing. Not that I was jealous. Like I'd told my dad, jealousy didn't factor into our friendship; it never had. And I wouldn't let it start now.

She was still my best friend. She was still coming over and hanging out with my family. And just because she didn't want to date Nate didn't mean she was getting too big to hang out with "the little people" in her life.

I knew all this, and yet, as I followed her out of the store, a thousand bucks' worth of new stuff in the shopping bag swinging from her fingertips, I'd never been more aware of our differences.

"I'M GOING TO MAKE YOU SORRY YOU were ever born."

"Aaaand cut!" I dropped Van's pages–sides, whatever–on my bed and stretched out my legs. We'd been reading the scene where she first meets Zoe's character, Grace, for what must've been hours, and I'd listened to her read the lines as sweet, angry, sarcastic, fearful, and everything in between. "We have definitely earned a snack break."

We scrambled off the bed and headed downstairs to the kitchen, but I paused on the stairs when I heard my dad's voice float out of the dining room.

"Hey, he's up," said Vanessa. "Let's go say hi."

We slowed our pace, not wanting to make too much noise in case he had a residual headache from a week's worth of poison being pumped into his body, but when his actual words became clear, I froze.

"How do you want me to do that, Pam?" he demanded of my mother, his voice rising. "'Sorry, Al–I know you busted your butt to get accepted early to Columbia, but when we inevitably hit my insurance cap, we're gonna have to use up your entire college fund on my medical bills'?"

I don't know what happened first—the dizziness, the feeling of my stomach bottoming out, or the rush of heat through my body—but suddenly I felt on the verge of both collapse and throwing up. I didn't even remember that Van was right behind me until she reached out and took my hand.

"Don't," I whispered fiercely, pulling back. I instantly felt bad for snapping, but I needed a minute to process what I'd just overheard and having Vanessa react simultaneously made it hard to focus.

Van simply nodded and trudged back upstairs. Meanwhile, I had no idea how to fix this. All I knew was that inside that room, my dad felt like shit for trying to save his own life, just because I had a stupid dream of going to a stupid college. Fresh off my acting practice with Van, I took a deep breath, wiped the tears that had been pricking at my eyes, and plastered a smile on my face.

"Would it help if you just did?" I asked, trying to adopt a joking tone and hoping that the shaking I heard in my voice was only in my own head.

Dad jumped up, and I could tell from his immediate recoil that he was still dizzy. "Oh, no, Ally—"

"Dad, please." I walked over to give him a hug and gently push him back into his chair. "It's okay. Really. There's still plenty of time for me to apply elsewhere regular decision, and I've been thinking that it makes more sense for me to go somewhere local anyway."

I don't know how the lies flowed out of my mouth that easily, but as soon as they did, I realized that maybe they weren't really lies...or at least, they shouldn't have been. Well, okay, that bit about having time to apply regular decision was—that ship had sailed weeks ago—but with my dad's prognosis being six months and it now being February of my senior year, had I really failed to consider that I'd be going to college across the country just as my mother became a single parent to Lucy? How selfish was I that I'd never even considered giving up my Columbia dream until just this moment?

"Ally," my mom said delicately, "this isn't a decision to be made lightly. I'm sorry you overheard that, but we're really just figuring things out right now."

"I know, Mom." I shifted from one foot to the other, trying to keep my composure. My mother—both my parents, really—just looked so...exhausted, both physically and mentally. I had a hard time even making real eye contact with my mother these days. Every time I looked at her, I saw a new layer of sadness and concern etched on her face, as if she'd just figured out yet another way her life was going to change for the horrible once the cancer took its course. Lord knew I'd seen it on my own face enough times. "I just don't want to be an added source of stress. Whatever happens, I'll be fine."

My mom opened her mouth to say something, but then she closed it again. "Of course you will, sweetheart," she said instead of whatever she'd originally wanted to. She stood up, kissed me on the forehead, and let herself out of the room, mumbling something about needing to help Lucy with her homework.

My dad gestured for me to take her seat. "Alexandra Mabel Duncan, listen to me," he ordered, his voice taking on a determination I hadn't heard since he'd informed us he was going to pursue aggressive treatment despite the low survival odds. "You are *going* to Columbia. It's going to be a little trickier to make it happen now, but I *will* do everything in my power to make sure that we get you there."

I opened my mouth to tell him again that it wasn't necessary, but the words got stuck on their way out. Everything from my throat to my skin to my eyeballs felt prickly, and I could barely breathe, let alone speak. Because all I could think was that, even if he succeeded, he wouldn't be around to see the fruits of his labor.

"AlGal, one of the biggest things keeping me going right now is the thought of getting to see you fulfill your Columbia dream," he said, his voice low. His words came out thick, and I wondered if he felt the same thing in his throat that I did. "Promise me you won't give up."

I remained silent. What was I supposed to say? *Yeah, Dad, I know you're dealing with a literal life-or-death situation right now, but could you please expend whatever energy you have left on being concerned about paying for my ridiculously overpriced education?*

"Promise me."

"I promise," I managed, unable to deny him that, and as I forced the words out of my mouth, the tears started to fall.

As my father hugged me close, I realized that his face was wet too.

★★★★★

After a couple of minutes, I cleaned myself up and went upstairs to apologize to Vanessa for biting her head off when she'd been trying to be nice. Before I could even say a word, she immediately said, "Ally, I could lend you—"

"No," I said abruptly. I should've guessed she would offer. Like I said, she was my best friend for a reason. "I mean, thank you, and I love you for offering, but I have no idea how I would ever pay you back, and money just makes friendships messy. So thank you, but no. I'll figure it out."

"Well, how about getting a job? I bet if we spoke to Ramon—"

"Waitressing at the Lunchbox wouldn't make me even a fraction of the money I need." I collapsed next to her on the bed and curled into the fetal position in an effort to soothe the leaden feeling in my stomach. "It'd barely cover my textbooks."

"Maybe you could get your old babysitting job back from the Andersons, too?"

I laughed bitterly. "Ah, yes, because *that* will bring me up to 50K."

"Well, nothing's gonna bring you up to 50K," Vanessa reasoned, "but at least it would make a dent, and then you can get loans for the rest."

"Even if I got loans to cover actual tuition, just a dorm, books, and meal plan would be more than I could afford on a waitressing-and-babysitting salary. Thanks for the help, Van, but my brain is fried and I just need to chill in front of a mindless movie or something. Is it all right if we pick up where we left off tomorrow?"

"Sure," she said softly, getting up. "You sure you're okay?"

"I'm fine. Or, at least, I will be tomorrow."

"Call me later." She gave me a quick squeeze around the shoulders and let herself out.

I waited until I heard the front door close behind her and then turned on my little TV and checked the movie channels. Go figure—the aforementioned Stupid Liam Holloway Movie, aka *The Rules of Ethan*, was coming on in five minutes. I sighed. It may have been terrible, but it was exactly the kind of terrible I needed.

Besides, his eyes were really, really pretty.

★★★★★

The movie was a good distraction, but nothing was going to help me sleep that night, not even my usual cure-all of the Beatles' White Album on repeat. Worrying about my dad, paying for Columbia, and money in general rendered the odds of falling into a blissful slumber somewhere between slim and a snowball's chance in the Valley. I needed something to take my mind off of things, but when I tried to shift mental topics, all I came up with were my scholarship applications, a paper I had due for my history class next week, and the fact that I had zero article ideas to pitch at this week's meeting of the *Hayden High Herald.*

I flipped over for the millionth time, grateful that at least I had soft sheets, when suddenly I heard my phone beep with a text. I slipped out of bed and checked my messages. It was from Vanessa.

They just asked me 2 come in 4 a fitting tom. Can u come??

I smiled. Yes, it was an obvious distraction tactic, but hardly an unusual request from her. She was forever asking my opinion on clothing, despite the fact that I had zero fashion sense. She always said she didn't trust anyone else—which was true in many areas of life—but you'd think she'd at least be confident about a professional on-set stylist. Especially since said stylist wasn't going to give a damn about my opinions anyway.

Still, I agreed to go, just to have something else to focus on for a morning. I wondered if the stylist had had to come up with a whole new wardrobe to accommodate the fact that their new lead didn't remotely embody the original look they'd had in mind. It was still hard to believe just how much things had gone Van's way, especially considering how often they hadn't in the past. Sure, she'd done okay for herself, getting secondary roles in some decent projects, but for every time she crowed about a successful audition, there were a hundred other times I'd had to say, "Whatever, they suck. You'll kick ass next time." It was brutal, watching her go through that day after day, but nothing compared to the times she'd come back crying because the critiques had effectively amounted to, "We're looking for someone more...Caucasian."

It amazed me every time she picked herself up and did it again; Lord knew there was no way in hell I could have. But Van loved Hollywood, loved acting, loved all of it. So I just had to go ahead and hate it all enough for the both of us.

This time, though, things actually had the potential to be different. I'd seen her act plenty of times, but I'd never seen her be the star, the one in control. Her new costar, Zoe Knight, was a notorious on-set diva, but Van was by no means a Hollywood princess; she was way more sensitive than she let on. I just hoped she'd enjoy this new role as much as she expected to.

I texted her back, saying I'd be happy to come, and groaned out loud when she responded that she needed to be at the studio at 9:00 a.m. She *did* sweeten the deal by saying she'd pick me up—she has an awesome BMW convertible that she bought with her first high-five-figure paycheck—so I reluctantly agreed to wake up at what I considered to be the crack of dawn for a weekend, set an alarm, and went back to bed.

★★★★★

I managed to fall asleep after only an hour or so of tossing and turning, but I still looked like complete crap by the time Van showed up. Neither a long, hot shower nor concealer could fully hide the fact that I'd spent much of the previous day crying and stressing. However, the fragrant vanilla latte in the passenger cup holder looked as if it could go a long way toward fixing that.

Van grinned. "Yes, dear, that's for you."

"Vanny, you are my BFFFFFF." I emphasized each F as I picked up the cup and inhaled the sweet vanilla scent.

"You're so easy," she teased. "Besides, I had a feeling you weren't going to get much sleep last night."

"You felt right." I waited until she pulled up to a red light before taking my first delicious sip. "And yet you still asked me to come to a 9:00 a.m. fitting."

She laughed. "Come on, you know I can't go onscreen without you approving my look. Besides, I figured you could help me run lines some more during breaks."

"Breaks? How long is this going to take?"

"They're fitting the whole cast today. The producer was dying for Tina Smalls to do our styling, but she only works by the day and this was the only day she had free before we start filming. I'm really excited to meet her. She's supposed to be a crazy genius."

"How big a genius do you have to be to pair skirt X with top Y?"

"You're kidding, right?"

Traffic had slowed enough that I could safely take another sip. "Maybe?"

She rolled her eyes. "You're ridiculous, you know that? How's it possible that you're even more jaded about Hollywood than I am? You've never worked on a set a day in your life."

"Yes, but I've been to plenty of them, thanks to you, and it seems like a bunch of people who pretend to be nice and intelligent for interviews and are actually moronic assholes in real life. Not to mention all the people who get paid to do things you can do better yourself. Remember your hair that time you guest-starred on that show? The one by the *Lost* guys that wasn't *Lost*?"

"Okay, yes, that was awful, but you're totally underestimating what these people do, and you're totally *overestimating* my own talents with my hair, makeup, and clothes. Besides, if I could style myself, would I need you to come with me?"

"You don't *need* me to come with you," I pointed out. "You like the company because you don't like to be alone."

She didn't respond, and I wondered if I'd crossed a line. It was no secret to either Van or me that her parents had done a number on her—making it clear that they thought both she and her career were pointless. I even remember the exact moment they told her she was a mistake, the result of a contraceptive malfunction.

I remember it because I was there when they told her.

I certainly didn't *mind* that Van kept me around as a reminder that at least one person in this world loved her unconditionally, but for her sake, I hated the fact that she needed me for that reason. I don't know if it made it better or worse that her parents really liked me. Either way, she was counting down the days until she turned eighteen, and I was pretty sure that once she did, she'd be out of her house with the speed of a lightning bolt, never to return. I never really understood why they let Van audition for anything in the first place.

"Nobody *likes* to be alone," Vanessa said finally. Then she turned on the radio, as if to preempt any further conversation, and searched through the stations until she found a song she could sing along to at the top of her lungs.

BY THE TIME WE RAN INTO THE FITTING, ten minutes late thanks to some bumper-to-bumper, I was wired from the coffee and my eventual joining in with Vanessa's out-loud singing, which had inspired an impromptu sing-along with other convertible drivers. I could feel actual beads of sweat forming along my hairline, which of course meant I would bump into Liam Holloway almost immediately.

He didn't say anything, though. Just glanced briefly at Vanessa and me and moved on to a small table on the side where he picked up whatever magazine he'd been reading and took a sip from his coffee.

"Good Lord, he's even better looking in real life," I muttered at Vanessa as we headed over to the rack with her name on it. "How is that humanly possible?"

She laughed. "I know, right? I try not to let it get to me." She started rifling through the clothes; Tina was busy fitting Carly Upton, who played Bailey Summers' best friend, Gwen. "Ooh, I like this."

"Any chance of something happening there?" I asked. Normally, I'd assume Van would have already told me if there were, but considering their respective gorgeousness, it was hard to imagine they weren't a perfect fit.

"Nah, he's weird." She pulled a funky belt from the rack and looped it around her tiny waist. "How cool is this?"

"What do you mean, he's weird?"

She shrugged. "He's really quiet, and he seems pissed off a lot of the time. I feel like he kind of hates being here. But then, like, dude, what are you doing here? A zillion guys would kill to have your job."

That *was* kind of weird, although considering my feelings on Hollywood, I couldn't really blame him for not being into the whole thing.

"I've even seen him spend his free time studying. He has that same SAT book you have, the enormous red one. So bizarre, right?"

"Very," I murmured, unable to stop myself from glancing over again. Somehow, knowing he actually cared about things like the SATs made him even hotter. Thank God he was obscenely off-limits to me as an Average Person or I might've been striking up a serious flirtation right about now.

"I got it!" Van clapped a hand to her mouth. "I know how you can make the money to send yourself to Columbia!"

I raised an eyebrow. "Selling that SAT book as firewood?"

"No, silly! Become my on-set tutor!"

Van looked so excited that I hated to shoot her down, but I couldn't help pointing out the obvious. "I'm pretty sure you need actual experience for that, and tutoring underprivileged kids in math last year doesn't really count. You probably even need special certification."

"Well, you wouldn't be my *actual* on-set tutor," Van explained, still in full-force excitement mode. "I have Michael for that. But my parents would be *thrilled* if you tutored me for the SATs on top of that, and I bet Liam would totally hire you too. You could help Carly with her French for that movie she's in this summer, and Lord knows Zoe could use some etiquette lessons."

I couldn't help laughing out loud at that last one, even if the whole idea was crazy. "Van, they would never–"

"And you could be my assistant!" Van steamrolled on. "The studio wants me to hire one anyway, and they would totally pay you–it wouldn't even be coming out of my pocket. You already know how I like my coffee, my sizes in absolutely everything, every conceivable way to reach me... Who would be a better choice than you?"

I started to protest again, but Vanessa cut me off one last time with the argument she knew I couldn't beat. "It would pay way, way better than anything else you could get, and you know I'll work with your schedule."

I gnawed on the inside of my lip. She had a point–it was by far the easiest, fastest, and most convenient way to make much more money than I would waitressing or babysitting, which would take a lot of stress off my parents. And it was hard to beat a boss who'd be cool with me taking time out to visit my dad in the hospital. Plus, I'd probably get plenty of downtime on set to study, and even get to hang out with Van, whom I otherwise rarely saw when she was filming.

"Fine, we'll try it, but if for *any* reason it's not working out, whether it's because I suck at it or because it's in some way detrimental to our friendship, you find yourself someone new. Deal?"

Her smile lit up the room, and I couldn't help flashing one of my own to match. "Deal."

★★★★★

The studio wouldn't have the necessary paperwork for the assistant job ready for another few days, and I had newspaper after school on Tuesday, so that Wednesday marked my first tutoring session with Vanessa, and it was not going spectacularly well.

The thing was, Vanessa wanted to help me. What she really, really didn't want to do was study for the SATs.

"Is it time for a break yet?" she whined, starting to pull on a perfectly styled curl until I smacked her hand away. Her hairstylist, Isaac, would kill her if he saw her doing that. "I need a drink."

"I'll go grab you an iced tea from craft services," I offered, figuring I should get some practice being her assistant.

"Not that kind of drink," she replied wryly.

I rolled my eyes. "This is *not* that bad, Van. I studied this stuff for months before I took the test. You've barely been studying it an hour."

"Yeah, but you *love* school," she shot back. "And–"

"Park, you need to sign these."

Irritated at the interruption, I looked up at the gum-snapping blond chick who had just dropped a stack of black-and-white photos of Van on the table between us. "We're studying," I informed her.

"What the hell for?" the girl muttered. "Anyway, these have to get done. You can fight with Jade if you don't like it." She slammed a black permanent marker down and glared at me.

I didn't respond; Jade was Van's publicist and she terrified me, not least because she hated me since Van wouldn't make any big decisions until I okayed them first. Satisfied that she had won, the blonde turned on her five-inch heels and stalked off.

"Sorry," Van apologized with no trace of apology, clearly pleased to have gotten out of tutoring for the day. "Work calls, and you know how Jade is."

"What are these for, anyway?"

"Who can even keep track?" she replied, shrugging as she picked up a glossy eight-by-ten and scrawled her familiar loopy signature. "Half of these are just gonna end up on eBay anyway."

I laughed. "How much does your autograph go for, exactly?"

"Used to go for thirty, but it'll probably be up to fifty now that the casting news is out. People are cray-cray."

"Man, I should really sell off your old birthday cards." I gathered up the SAT stuff so it wouldn't land in the way of her flying permanent marker.

The idea hit both of us at the same time. And no, it wasn't to sell the birthday cards. "I'll ask for more pictures," Van said quickly, "but I bet you could get even more money if I signed some of my actual stuff. You know I never look at anything three months after I buy it anyway."

"Van..." My protest was not even a protest. I was already mentally combing the contents of Van's closet and wondering how much I could get for the red snakeskin boots she *never* wore, especially if she autographed the soles.

"It's about damn time you stop even pretending to fight me on this one," Vanessa said smugly. "I bet the others would chip in too." She looked up. "Hey, Liam, come here for a sec."

"Van!" I whispered fiercely.

"What's up, Bailey?" he asked, shuffling over.

"They like us to keep in character by calling each other by our names on the show," she explained with a roll of her eyes. Liam was dressed half as his character, Tristan, in a pair of board shorts, and half as himself in a worn navy Henley that lent a sexy, smoky quality to those beautiful blue eyes and clung to his toned pecs in an annoyingly attractive fashion. "You haven't met my best friend, Ally, yet, have you?"

"Nope." He nodded. "Liam. Or Tristan. Or whatever."

I couldn't help smiling. Vanessa was right; he practically oozed *oh my God, this is so stupid* from every pretty pore. "I'll stick with Liam. I'm just the hired help."

To my surprise—and obviously Vanessa's—he cracked a smile of his own. "What are you hired to help with, exactly?" He looked down at the bright-red book in front of me. "Are you guys studying for the SATs?"

"Ally's tutoring me," said Van before I could answer. "And she's really, really good. And way cheaper than Michael. She could help you too. You're studying for them also, right?"

Before I could jump in, Liam shrugged and said, "Yeah, I guess. I asked Michael and he said, and I quote, 'I never want to think about that fucking test ever again.' I'm pretty sure he'd change his mind for a thousand bucks an hour, but he's not *that* good. Plus, it was a totally different test when he took it. No writing section."

A thousand dollars an hour. Jesus. I would've been able to pay for a semester at Columbia in no time with that kind of cash. Even if Liam were going to pay me a fraction of that, it would've been completely dishonest to take it. I was no SAT tutor. It was one thing to let Vanessa pay me for tutoring—I knew it was killing her that I wouldn't take any money from her, and she was happy to give it this way—but I'd taken the test less than a year ago; how could I possibly take money for teaching it?

"I'm not really a tutor," I admitted to Liam. "We're really just helping each other out a bit. I'm short on cash, and Van's—"

"Van's lucky to have a best friend who was accepted to Columbia early, whose GPA is like a 12.0, and who happens to have aced this test on her first shot," Van cut in.

"Indeed she is." Liam flashed me another smile that could've melted the entire North Pole. Was that a tiny dimple? Why, God, why? "Let me know when you've got some time. I'm happy to pay."

"Great!" Van answered for me. "Also, I'm giving Ally a few autographed things to sell on eBay, since my closet is basically overflowing with crap I never use anyway. Got anything to spare?"

I could feel some serious heat flaming in my cheeks at Van's brazenness. "You don't have to—"

"Tristan! Bailey! We need you!"

"Whoops, duty calls," said Van, jumping up. Liam turned to follow her when suddenly he pulled off his shirt, grabbed Vanessa's marker, scribbled his autograph, and tossed it into my frozen hands.

"Hope that helps," he said, and I didn't know if the grin he was flashing was at his own cleverness or the fact that I was blatantly staring, mouth wide open, at his beautiful shirtless form with its finely carved pecs and six-pack. Before I could recover and close my jaw like a normal human being, he was gone.

★★★★★

The shirt smelled ridiculously good—faint traces of cologne and deodorant mixed with that guy smell—and I hated to sell it, but bidding went up to four hundred bucks within two hours and I reasoned that if Liam and I were going to study together, I'd probably have many more opportunities to inhale his scent.

Not that I was planning to sniff Liam Holloway.

Van had actually underestimated her fan base; two of the autographed photos she'd snuck me were going for seventy-five each. (I saved the third for Nate; I had a feeling he'd appreciate it.) I had to hand it to her. The girl may have had no desire to go to college, but she sure knew how to build a college fund.

"What are you doing, Ally?"

I spun in my desk chair to face a very inquisitive-looking Lucy. "I'm just selling a couple of things Vanessa gave me online."

"You're selling presents from Vanessa?" My mom joined Lucy in the doorway. "Ally—"

"It's not what you think," I said, holding up one of the glossies. "Van gave them to me to put up on eBay. Her costar Liam gave me something too."

Mom sighed. "Luce, go brush your teeth, okay?"

Lucy shrugged and danced off to the bathroom. Mom closed the door behind her and sat down on the bed. "Ally, I'm sorry you overheard me and your father the other day, but I'm really not sure this is the best way to make up for a bad situation."

"Why not? This is the easiest money I've ever made." Never mind that it was a miniscule fraction of what I needed. "Now you and Dad don't need to worry about a thing. Well, besides the obvious," I added, realizing how stupid I sounded.

She seemed to be searching for the words to respond, but I couldn't take another chat about money with my parents this week. I was well aware of how hopeless the whole situation was, but my dad had made it pretty clear that I couldn't give up. If Van and Liam were willing to help me without literally having to empty out their wallets, why shouldn't I take them up on it?

"What about the newspaper?" she asked finally.

"We met yesterday. Van knows I can't come to set on Tuesdays."

"And the debate team?"

"Only has one meet left for the rest of the year, and it's a small one, so Dr. Phillips wants to use newbies. I'm off the hook."

"What about—"

"Mom! Relax. School is under control. My APs aren't for three months and I've already put in plenty of studying time. I'm working on my scholarship applications. The closest thing to assistant work Van's had me do is get her coffee. I'm basically getting paid a decent amount of money to hang out with my best friend I'd never get to see otherwise and a really hot guy, plus tutor them in stuff that comes easily to me. I'd think you'd be happy that I'm working extra schoolwork into my new routine," I added, a tiny edge creeping into my voice. I was seriously trying here, but it was only a matter of time before her doubts that I could handle it all would start causing me to have my own. There was no room for that in my life right now.

"Okay, no more questions," she conceded, standing up. Then she walked over, gave me a hug, and started to leave, but stopped just short of the door. "Everything's going to be all right, Ally."

I couldn't tell from her tone of voice whether she was asking me or telling me, so I simply nodded.

"BON WEEKEND!" Madame Boulanger trilled over the sounds of the ringing bell and twenty kids shoving books into their bags. Frankly, I couldn't wait to have a *bon* weekend; the day before had been incredibly long, and now I was headed back to set again. Not that it'd been a bad day. Tutoring Vanessa was kind of a pointless task, but it was fun to hang out. She'd also found a few more assistant tasks for me to do, and by the time I'd finally gotten home around ten, I'd been in no mood to work on the history paper I hadn't even started yet.

"Fancy togs you've got going on there, Duncan," Nate observed as we filed out of class along with everyone else.

Trust Nate to call me out on the fact that I'd dressed up a bit for another day at the studio. "Togs? Really? Has anyone said that in the last seventy years?"

"I'm gonna bring it back," he vowed. "And hey, thanks again for that picture of Vanessa. It's, uh, getting a lot of use."

"Gross. Now I'm just sorry I gave it to you." I stopped at my locker and swapped my books for the weekend while Nate disappeared with his surfing buddies. A quick examination in my locker mirror revealed just how obvious it was I hadn't gotten much sleep the night before. I dabbed a bit of concealer under my eyes, touched up my eyeliner, and smoothed on some lip gloss before heading out to my car.

When I got to the studio, Vanessa was filming, and judging by the impatient jut of her hip, the number of takes for the scene was reaching the high double digits. Liam, on the other hand, was sitting peacefully at his usual table, reading a book whose cover I couldn't see but which definitely didn't contain SAT tests.

I was about to sit down at an empty table when Liam looked up and waved briefly. Taking it as an invitation, I strolled over and sat down next to him. "What are you reading?"

He picked up the book to show me the cover. It was *Catch-22*, aka one of my favorite books of all time.

"I freaking love that book. When Major Major—"

"Spoiler alert!" he yelped with genuine panic, and I laughed and mimed a lip-zipping motion. "I know I shouldn't really be reading it with all these stupid lines to learn and SATs to study for, but every now and again I need to get my mind on something normal." He stopped, looking surprised at himself for his admission.

"If you don't mind my asking, why *are* you studying for the SATs? I mean, Van's pretty much just pretending so she can slip me money, but considering the buzz for the show, I have a feeling you guys are gonna be just fine, career-wise, without college."

"If you know Vanessa's just having you tutor her so she can pay you, why are you letting her?" asked Liam, dodging my question. "Just take her money. Whatever it is you need it for, she seems perfectly happy to give it to you."

"You obviously understand the importance of taking them if you're studying for them yourself."

He quirked an eyebrow. "So you're letting her think she's just giving you money when in fact you're trying to prepare her for a fallback lifestyle?"

It sounded so awful the way he said it, like I was trying to be her babysitter. All I wanted was for her to be able to do the normal college-and-job thing if acting didn't work out. Was that really so bad? It's not like I had no faith in her; I just had no faith in Hollywood or its casting directors, and I hadn't ever since Vanessa's first audition, when she'd come straight to my house in tears after they told her they weren't looking for someone "ethnic."

"Is that what you're doing?" I retorted, hoping to turn the heat on him instead. "Preparing for a fallback lifestyle?"

He seemed startled by my response, and I wondered if I'd crossed a line, but I didn't have much time to think on it because just then, Liam was called to set.

"Later," he muttered, leaving me alone with Yossarian and the ghosts.

★★★★★

I was still on set many hours later when they finally broke for the night. I'd managed to tune them out and get a decent amount of homework done, and Van was too busy to need anything from me.

"Lady, I am exhausted," she muttered as she flopped down in the chair next to me. "Can we go out? Preferably somewhere with an IV drip of either coffee or beer; I don't even care which."

I laughed. "You just said you're exhausted. Wouldn't you rather just chill at home? Or come over and watch a movie or something?"

"Anything sounds better than being here." She yawned. "I'm gonna go to my trailer to clean myself up. Would you mind getting me a cup of coffee?"

I was about to make a joke that I wasn't her lackey when I realized that, yeah, actually, I was. I went to get her a cup, and found that Liam had already beaten me to craft services.

"Hey," I greeted him cautiously, remembering how I'd snapped at him earlier.

"Hey." If he had any feelings about it, they certainly didn't show on his face. *Well, of course he doesn't,* I reminded myself. *He doesn't care about you. Look at him, for God's sake.* "S'up."

"Just getting Van some coffee," I mumbled, feeling a bit embarrassed about that fact. I wasn't crazy about the idea of being viewed by Liam as an assistant. The last thing I wanted was for him to get on board with that and start having me pick out the blue M&Ms from the bowl in his trailer or something.

He grunted and stepped away from the urn to make way for me. I filled Van's cup almost to the top and debated filling one for myself too, but decided that drinking caffeine so late was a bad idea. Then I moved over to the milk just in time to see Liam dump what looked like a cup of sugar into his black coffee and then take a sip of the undoubtedly scalding liquid.

"Seriously?" I couldn't help asking as I poured soy milk into Van's coffee.

"What?" he asked defensively.

"Black coffee, pound of sugar, and not even going to wait for it to cool. What kind of crazy coffee daredevil are you?"

The smile was small, but it was there. "I like to live dangerously."

"Clearly!" I reached for the nearest artificial sweetener and sprinkled a much more conservative amount into Van's cup.

"That's your idea of safe living?" he asked, eyebrows raised. "That stuff could take the rust off a car."

"I think you're thinking of cola."

The corner of his mouth lifted just a bit. "You always have to know the most about everything, don't you?"

Naturally, the best response I could come up with was, "Do not."

"Yes, you do. But it's oddly unannoying on you."

"How flattering," I said, trying to keep my voice sarcastic even though I could feel the semi-compliment bringing a blush to my cheeks. He didn't say anything, so I started to turn and walk toward Van's trailer with her coffee when he called my name. I turned back around. "What's up?"

"I'm heading to a party at my friend Josh's house as soon as I get showered and change into something a little less...surfer-douche chic." He took another sip of his coffee, blowing on it slowly first, allowing me a moment to admire his mouth as he did. He really did have nice, soft-looking lips, and pursed like that, I could almost imagine—oh, dammit, he was talking again.

"Sorry, what?" I could feel that flush creeping into my cheeks hardcore now, and I wondered if I'd been caught staring.

"I asked if you and Vanessa wanna come."

To a party? With Liam? That sounded...awesome? Terrifying? I actually had no idea. I'd never been much of a party person, but it was nice of Liam to include me when inviting Vanessa.

"I'll ask her," I replied, then rushed out as quickly as I could without spilling, to avoid saying anything else stupid.

★★★★★

"Mmm, thank you," Vanessa said gratefully as she took her first long sip. She'd already removed her excess makeup and changed back into jeans and a silky T-shirt with a bright, funky pattern. "So, movie at your place?"

"Actually..." I dropped onto the plush red loveseat that lined one wall of the trailer she shared with Carly Upton and plucked an after-dinner mint from the small dish on the end table. "I bumped into Liam at craft services, and he invited us to a party."

"Ooh, now you're talking." Van's eyes lit up. "Whose party?"

I shrugged. "I think he said his friend Josh?"

She laughed. "You know who that is, don't you?"

"Am I supposed to keep track of Liam's friends now?"

"Um, hi, even Alexandra Duncan, Jaded Queen of Hollywood, knows who Josh Chester is."

My jaw dropped. "*That's* whose party it is? Liam's friends with him?"

"Best friends," Vanessa confirmed. "How do you not know this? Their best friendship definitely falls under the category of 'common knowledge.'"

"Pardon me for not assuming that Liam's BFFs with a guy who's been to rehab more times than Lindsay Lohan, not to mention been in the tabs for mooning paparazzi more than once."

"Maybe Liam's not the class act you think he is." Van put her drink down to rummage around for her hot-pink heels. "And by the way, don't think I haven't noticed that you have a huge crush on him."

I rolled my eyes, though I could feel myself blushing again. "Please. He's hot; that's it. Whatever... *admiration* I have for him is no greater than the rest of the free world's."

"If you say so," Van replied, trying and failing to hide the smirk on her lips. "So are you coming to the party with me or what?"

"Definitely not. My parents would absolutely kill me if I went to a party at Josh Chester's. He probably gives everyone a free bump upon entry."

"As if you ever have to worry about me doing drugs," said Vanessa. "I'm not an idiot."

"You say that now..."

She huffed a sigh. "You're impossible. Fine. I'm going without you, and I will gladly report back about every awesome thing you missed so that the next time a fun opportunity like this arises, you will strap on a pair and join us."

I didn't anticipate there being a next time that would include an invitation for me, but it was pointless to say so to Van. "Have fun," I trilled, "and *don't* call me at 4:00 a.m. looking for a designated driver."

"Deal." She grabbed her lightweight scarf, and the two of us walked out. "Come on, let's go tell Liam you're being a loser."

"Um, maybe you could just tell him yourself?" Yes, it was ridiculous, but while I was used to it from Van, I didn't think I could handle Liam telling me how lame I was just then. "I gotta get back home. History paper's not gonna write itself."

"History paper. Seriously. How are we even friends?"

"G'night, Van." I started to walk out to the parking lot.

"Hey," she called after me, "as my assistant, can't I demand that you drive me to and from or something?"

I stopped and turned. "Yeah, I guess you could. Do you really want to?"

She stuck her tongue out at me.. "No. I just want you to get out and have some fun. You've earned it."

"I'll have earned it when I can afford my first semester's tuition," I replied, turning around and walking out into the night.

★★★★★

I changed my mind a hundred times on the drive home and continued to do so for the next bunch of hours as I alternated working on my history paper, studying my carefully made flash cards for the Physics Advanced Placement exam, and reading the Wikipedia page on melanoma for the millionth time while studying the mole on my left thigh. All were half-assed efforts, my mind constantly wandering to the party and what I might have been missing. I finally passed out on top of my books at some point around dawn.

I woke up to a phone call from Vanessa a few hours later. Snaking my hand out, I grabbed my phone from where it lay on my desk amid a pile of pencils and highlighters.

"Hey, Van." I yawned hugely. "What's up?"

"Man, I thought you went to bed early last night." She sounded annoyingly awake. "Why do you still sound like death?"

"I went *home* early," I corrected her. "Then I did work for about a zillion hours."

"Man, you really *should've* come out with us last night."

I rubbed my eyes and sat up fully. "How was it?" I asked, stretching my free arm over my head and yawning again.

"Fun. And crazy. You would've absolutely hated it. It was basically a bunch of celebs sitting around getting trashed."

"Oh, but think of the cash I could've gotten for selling pics of that to the tabs," I mused.

Vanessa laughed. "You could probably *buy* Columbia with photographic evidence of some of the shit I saw last night, not that most of it would surprise you."

For reasons I did not care to contemplate, the idea that Liam was a part of this crowd—and probably every bit as much of a bad boy as Josh Chester—turned my stomach. Or maybe I could blame that on the lack of sleep. "Well, I'm glad you and Liam had fun," I said weakly.

"Ha, Liam is almost as big a homebody as you are. We were there all of ten minutes when he made some comment about how you had the right idea. You guys are so alike, it's gross. He even mentioned something about it being cool that you're so good at French, so I suggested he ask you for tutoring."

"Van!"

"What? You don't need the money?"

"Of course I need the money, but I also need you to stop passing me off as being qualified to teach things I'm not. No one wants a high school senior who's never even been to Europe to teach him French!"

"Actually, Liam does, smartass, and you'd better be willing to do it because I just gave him your number and said I knew for a fact you're free the rest of the weekend."

"You're a ridiculous human being, Vanessa Park. You're basically bullying him into giving me money for nothing." I was being unfair—she really *was* trying to help—but the thought of Liam Holloway even putting my number in his cell phone, let alone calling me, was making me so nervous and nauseated I could hardly think straight.

"Not for nothing, and I'm not bullying him!"

"Fine, charming him with your dazzling beauty then."

"As if. Anyway, Shannah Barrett was there, and I'm sure she's more his type. Not that I'm interested in him," she quickly clarified.

Of course. Shannah Barrett was tall, blond, insanely stunning, skinny as a bobby pin, and made major bank as both a model for some handbag line and a star of one of those family shows where everyone ends up hugging in the last five minutes. I could just imagine him taking a shot off her praying mantis-like body. She was like a Thinsperation poster girl.

"Shannah Barrett's every guy's type," I muttered, feeling another yawn coming on. "She—"

Beep. Oh God, call waiting. *Liam.*

"A?"

"Sorry, Van, it's just call waiting. I'll ignore it."

"No, don't. It's probably Liam, and I have to go anyway. Bikram yoga. I'll call you later, 'kay? And try to have some fun today."

"You're the boss," I replied before clicking over to the other call. "Hello?"

"Hey, Ally?"

Definitely Liam. Why did the sound of his voice make me so nervous? It's not like I'd never spoken to any stars before. Thanks to Van, I'd met about a zillion of them. So maybe they didn't all have fantastic abs and eyes so beautiful they could probably stop a moving train in its tracks, but so what?

I must've hesitated for way too long because he spoke again. "Is this Ally? It's Liam."

"Liam," I repeated dumbly.

"Holloway," he elaborated, which would've made me laugh if I hadn't been so anxious. The fact that he thought I could confuse him with anyone else was ridiculous. I wondered if he'd continue, "from *Daylight Falls*, the guy with the brown hair," if I stayed silent long enough.

"Hey, yeah, it's me," I replied, finally finding my voice. "Or 'I,' if we're being grammatically correct." *Oh my God, Ally, you are such a dork.*

He laughed like the polite gentleman with the cute butt he was. "I think you're safe. Pretty sure there's no grammar on the SATs."

"You never know when they'll throw a curveball."

"I suppose. Anyway, I mentioned to Vanessa that I've always wanted to learn French, and she–"

"She told me," I said. "Listen, Liam, it's sweet that you guys wanna help me, but you've got resources–you should get yourself a tutor who's actually been to the Eiffel Tower, or something."

"I've been to the Eiffel Tower. It's not that great, if you wanna know the truth."

"No, don't tell me that! In my mind, Paris is perfect, and I would like to keep that illusion intact until I can go and shatter it for myself."

"I see. Well, I was just trying to make you feel better. It's actually the greatest landmark on Earth."

"Really?"

"Not even close."

I laughed. "Thanks for trying. Like I was saying–"

"Is tonight okay?" he broke in.

"Okay for what?"

"Teaching me French."

Suddenly, my bedroom felt like a sauna. It was an innocent request, but the combination of a nighttime invitation and the fact that my brain kept adding "kissing" to the end of that sentence was making me so hot I wanted to crawl out of my own skin. "Sure," I croaked.

"Great. I'll text you my address. Is seven okay?"

"Yeah. Great. Sure."

"Great. See you later."

We hung up, and I realized that all traces of my sleepiness were gone, replaced by a frightening rush of adrenaline. What the hell was I going to wear? What should I teach him? Should I practice my accent, listen to tapes, *something*?

First things first–I needed a shower. An ice-cold one.

IT WASN'T UNTIL I WAS ACTUALLY on the road to Liam's apartment that I started thinking like a sane human being.

"What am I doing?" I asked aloud as I flipped through the radio stations to find something that might calm my nerves. "What if he's an ax murderer and I'm going straight to his apartment?"

My mind shifted to potential images of his abode. What if his "apartment" was actually some drug den and he tried to shove piles of coke at me while he answered calls on four different cell phones? Or what if he decorated with animal carcasses, like this guy I once saw on an episode of *Hoarders*? What if *he* was a hoarder, and I had to sit on a pile of old headless Barbies and takeout containers from In-N-Out Burger?

At least the outside of the building looked reasonably decent, I noted as I pulled into the gated underground parking lot. It wasn't too flashy, although it did come complete with a beautiful pool area that looked like the perfect place to lounge with a piña colada on a Saturday afternoon.

The doorman let me up without a fuss—apparently, Liam had put me on his "OK" list. I traveled up to his ninth-floor apartment with the same fistful of fear in my gut that I'd had on my first day of high school, though I was beyond determined not to show it.

My tension finally abated a bit when Liam opened the door, dressed to chill in jeans and an old Bob Dylan T-shirt. He smiled and stepped aside to let me in. "Welcome to, uh, Chez Holloway. Is that right?"

I laughed. "Yes, that's right. You're practically fluent already."

I glanced around at the living room and felt my anxiety drain even further. No visible drug paraphernalia; no bearskin rug. In fact, the entire place was decorated pretty much exactly as I'd do it—posters on the walls and mostly neutral colors with the occasional splash of brightness. Plus, the couch looked like the absolute comfiest thing in the world.

And was that pizza I smelled?

Liam must've noticed me sniffing. "I didn't know if you were a vegetarian or not, so I got half-carnivore, half-plain."

"Mmm, carnivore." I hadn't even realized how long it'd been since I'd eaten until I felt my stomach rumble at the mere mention of meat. "That sounds perfect, thank you. *J'ai une faim du loup.*"

"Jay wha?"

I grinned. "It's a French expression for 'I'm starving.' It basically means 'I have the hunger of a wolf.'"

He tried repeating it, then laughed when he failed miserably. "Maybe we'll save that for a more advanced lesson." He went to grab a couple of slices from where he was keeping them warm in the oven. "Sit, make yourself comfortable."

So far, Liam had done a decent job of proving he wasn't a creep, so I put my bag on the large glass coffee table and sat down in the corner of the sectional, which turned out to be every bit as comfy as it looked. If I'd actually been here to hang out and not just to teach some spoiled actor French on his random whim, it would've been pretty nice.

"Here you go." He placed a plate of pizza in front of me and then handed me a bottle of water. "Sorry, I don't have anything else to drink. Must keep the whites pearly and all."

"Water's great, thanks. So," I said, eager to get down to business and be professional, "where should we start?"

He shrugged, his mouth already full of pizza. "You tell me," he said as soon as he'd swallowed. Then he looked down at his plate. "How do you say 'pizza'?"

"*Pizza*. But maybe we should go a little more basic."

"More basic than a direct translation?"

I laughed. "More basic than random foods. Put it this way—what is it you want to learn French for?"

He shrugged. "To not be a stereotypical American d-bag who thinks English is the only language that matters?"

It was the sexiest response he could've possibly given me. "Excellent answer." I took a big bite of pepperoni and meatball. "In that case, let's start with some basic greetings and stuff that are the bare minimum you should know if you ever go to Paris and want to avoid getting a death stare from a waiter. Or so I hear," I added quickly, not wanting to sound like an even bigger fraud than I already was for being paid to give lessons in a language I'd only studied in a classroom setting. "I've never actually been to Paris."

I felt like a loser for saying it, but he simply replied, "I've only been once, for a lame press event for a movie, and I've never gone back."

"Really? How come?"

He shrugged. "Never really had both the time and a travel buddy."

"You never travel alone?"

"Nah. Too afraid of death stares from random French waiters." The glint of mischief in his eyes made me laugh. "What about you? How come you've never been?"

"My family vacations were pretty Disneyland-centric." I took a small sip of water. "I plan to go in college, though. Study abroad in Paris junior year, eat lots of delicious French food and see the Louvre from top to bottom, travel around the country on the weekends. I'm dying to see southern France, too—Nice, Marseilles. Then for spring break, I'll spend the week in Italy, dividing the time between Florence and Rome..." I trailed off as I realized that I was really just babbling now. "Anyway, I plan to go," I said hastily, then took another bite of pizza in the hopes it would shut me up.

If Liam thought I sounded like an idiot, he certainly didn't let on. "That sounds awesome. I've only been to Italy for press events, and it was just one day each in Venice and Rome. I'd love to go to Florence, see Michelangelo's *David* in person."

I swallowed so excitedly I nearly choked on a piece of pepperoni. "Yes! How cool would that be? Can you imagine standing in front of a statue carved by Michelangelo himself? And it's supposed to be huge and so perfectly detailed it's incredible. And the Vatican, oh my God—what could be more incredible than seeing the Sistine Chapel in person?"

"Why don't you just go to Italy for the semester?" he asked.

I shrugged. "I've taken French for so long that I'm dying for a chance to use it on a regular basis.

But believe me when I say I plan to go to Italy every weekend possible."

"I'm sure it'll be nice to get around by your own fluency," he said. "It's awesome that you're so good at French."

"Just you wait," I said. "We'll get you there too."

"I'll believe it when I see it," he said with a smile, "but okay, we should get started then. Lesson one: How not to be a d-bag in Paris. Go!"

I laughed. "Well, first and foremost: please and thank you."

"Thank you is *merci*, right?"

I winced slightly at his pronunciation, which was way too close to the English *mercy*. "Emphasis is on the second syllable, actually," I said, repeating the word. "And please is *s'il vous plait*."

He repeated after me, and I was pleased to note that his pronunciation was way better on the second try.

"Excellent," I said. "Now you can already put together a sort-of sentence." I was about to say it, but Liam beat me to it.

"*Pizza, s'il vous plait?*"

"*Merci!*" I replied instantly.

He laughed. "That doesn't even make sense."

"I know, but it's like we just had our first French conversation!" I know, I'm a dork, but I lived for that moment in tutoring when it felt like something clicked. "I'll get into this more later when we do subject pronouns, but actually, because I'm a friend, you would use the less formal '*s'il* te *plait*,' although you'd be correct using '*s'il* vous *plait*' when talking to a waiter. But don't worry about that now."

He took another bite of his pizza and followed it up with a swig of water. "So," he said thoughtfully. "We're friends, huh?"

I immediately felt a blush rise into my cheeks. "I didn't mean—well, you know what I meant."

"So we're *not* friends?"

I glanced into his eyes for a hint of the teasing I'd seen there before, but there was none. He seemed to be asking a genuine question. "Are you *trying* to fluster me?"

"Am I flustering you?" He sounded even more confused.

"What am I supposed to say?"

He shrugged. "I thought we were friends. You're the one who snapped at me the other day and then bailed on the party."

"I didn't *bail*. I just didn't realize when you first invited me that it was going to be some drug-fueled orgy."

At that, Liam threw his head back and laughed. "Wow, Josh would wet himself with joy if he heard you describe his parties that way."

"How'd you guys become friends, anyway?"

"I met him at my first modeling gig. We're not completely...into the same things, but he's a good guy."

I'll bet. "Do you still model?"

"Every now and again. It pays the bills." He took another long drink of his water. "What about you and Vanessa? How'd you guys become friends?"

"Oh, same old story as everyone else. Girl meets girl in playgroup. Girl and girl share blocks. Guy asks one girl why she has slanty eyes and other girl makes guy eat dirt. Instant friendship."

Liam laughed. "So you guys have been friends for a long time, huh?"

"Going on sixteen years. I haven't had to make many guys choke on sand since then, but we're still pretty good at sticking up for each other when necessary."

"I'll bet. Kind of funny, though. You guys don't seem to have much in common."

"Neither do you and Josh," I pointed out. "At least, you don't seem like you do."

"Yeah, but he's loyal and consistent, and for me, those are the most important things. My life hasn't exactly been...stable."

I waited for him to elaborate, but it quickly became clear he wasn't going to, and I was afraid it was too invasive to ask. "Loyal and consistent are definitely words I'd use to describe Van." I took a sip of water. "And we do have *some* things in common. We both love the Beatles, and back when we were kids we used to love reading my mom's ancient Nancy Drew books and camping out in our backyards. I guess those are silly kid things now, for the most part, but we had a lot of fun together back when we used to spend time on things other than studying for standardized tests and memorizing scripts."

"Sounds like it," he said with a smile. There was no trace of sarcasm in his voice, and I wondered what his childhood had been like—if he and Josh had ever fruitlessly looked for stars in the sky over L.A. while sharing a thermos of root beer and sitting on a ratty fleece blanket. Judging from the slightly wistful expression on his face, the answer was no. I tried to think of a way to change the subject, but then he said, "So, are we friends?"

I decided on the easiest response. "*Oui. Nous sommes amis.*"

He grinned. "*Oui* means yes, right?"

I couldn't help but smile back. "*Oui.*"

★★★★★

The rest of the evening was surprisingly fun, and when Liam asked if I wanted to stick around and watch a movie, I immediately agreed, despite the fact that I had scholarship applications to work on and my history paper definitely needed revisions.

Liam had every Al Pacino movie known to man, and once he found out I'd never seen *Scent of a Woman*, he threw it in the Blu-Ray player faster than you could say *merci*. The movie itself was good, and Chris O'Donnell was adorable, but it was Liam who had me cracking up, doing random Al Pacino imitations and blurting out the French translation of every word he'd learned. When the auditorium full of preppy schoolboys exploded in applause at the end, I was so sucked in by my surroundings that I felt the urge to join in.

Until Liam opened his mouth and asked, "Are you ever gonna tell me why you're suddenly so hard up for cash?"

I exhaled sharply. "Wow, couldn't even wait for the end of the movie, huh?"

"It's basically over."

"That's not the point."

"Hey, I literally gave you the shirt off my back. How much did you get for that, anyway?"

"Five hundred bucks," I grudgingly admitted. "Apparently, the potential for inhaling a trace of Liam Holloway's sweat is just too much for some people to resist."

Liam rolled his eyes. "That's insane. I know I'm supposed to appreciate my fans and everything, but Jesus Christ."

"Tell you what. I'll tell you why I need the money if you tell me why you hate your career."

"Who says I do?"

"Every eye roll, every snort, and pretty much everything you've ever said on set that was neither a line nor something relating to the SATs."

He narrowed his eyes, and I was afraid he was going to yell at me, but he simply said, "You first."

"Fine. My father's dying of cancer and my college fund is going to pay his medical bills, so I've got to pay my own way if I want to go to Columbia. Happy now?"

Liam's eyebrows shot up. Guess that wasn't the answer he'd been expecting. "What about financial aid?"

"Apparently, my parents make too much money for me to qualify for it. Never mind that we can't afford to *use* any of that money for college," I said sourly. "And don't get me started on loans. Just thinking about paying them back with interest gives me hives. The last thing I need is to get stuck in raging debt when my mom's already struggling to make ends meet for my sister."

"I hear that." He was quiet for a moment, and then said, "My mom died of cancer when I was a kid. It's a bitch."

Now it was my turn to be surprised. "I'm sorry. I didn't know."

He shrugged. "How would you? And I'm sorry about your dad."

"Thanks."

"What kind of cancer?"

"Melanoma. Stage IV."

"Jesus. Where'd it metastasize to?"

Sick as it was, there was something oddly nice about being able to talk cancer with someone who already knew the terminology. "It's in his liver and lymph nodes. What'd your mom have?"

"Lung. She never smoked or anything, but she got lung cancer anyway." We both fell silent, and then he said, "Makes you feel like a hundred years older, doesn't it?"

"Sometimes. Sometimes it makes me feel even younger than I am, realizing how much I need my daddy." I plucked a red throw pillow from the couch and started picking at the tightly knit threads, just to have something to do with my hands. "I feel like I should be able to do something for my mom and sister but really I can't do anything but run away."

"You're not running away," Liam argued. "You're running *to* something. And you don't *have* to go to Columbia, do you? It's still early in the year; can't you apply elsewhere?"

"Not really. Maybe. I don't know. Honestly, I don't even really care anymore." I hadn't even realized how true that was until I spoke the words out loud. "I've wanted to go to Columbia forever. The idea of going to an Ivy League school *and* living in New York is just...I mean, how could I not want to go to school where I could walk to Central Park and listen to the Beatles *in* Strawberry Field? All while going to classes taught by some of the best professors in the world?"

"Oh, well, I didn't know about the Beatles thing," he teased.

I stuck out my tongue at him in an admittedly childish gesture. "Look, I know it sounds stupid, but that's just always been my vision. Go out on Long Island one Sunday and read *The Great Gatsby* where Fitzgerald wrote it; take a class on Impressionism and then go see *Starry Night* at the Museum of Modern

Art—that sort of thing. But now that all just seems so incredibly ridiculous and unimportant."

"So why are you still so intent on going?"

"Because it's something to focus on. And it's something for my dad to focus on. Which turns my work and achievements into things that matter, even though nothing fucking matters anymore." It probably should've hit me at some point that of all the people to spill my guts to, Liam "Buy This Cologne Because I Have Nice Abs" Holloway was probably the strangest choice. But while I was still weirded out by how attractive he was, the bluntness of his questions—and the fact that he actually seemed to care about the answers—compelled me to babble on endlessly about things I hadn't really discussed with anyone else, not even Van. "Whatever, it's all stupid. I'm so incapable of focusing on my own work at this point that I'll probably write awful scholarship essays and get ones on all my APs and then I won't be able to afford to go anyway."

"Ally, please. I've successfully uttered at least five French sentences that I'm pretty sure make sense, and you've only been tutoring me for a day. You'll ace them." The pizza was long gone, but Liam had made us popcorn for the movie and he popped one of the few remaining kernels into his mouth. "Besides, it's cool that it makes your dad happy to watch you succeed. It's not like he'll love you any less if you don't. It's just a nice bonus. If you wanna know the truth, the first thing I think when I get a part is that I wish my mom were around just so I could tell her." He made a face. "Not that I'd want her actually seeing any of this shit."

Despite the heavy conversation, that made me burst out laughing. "Okay, your turn. Why the hell do you do all this stuff if you hate it? Is it, like, in The

Rules of Being Attractive that you must become an actor-slash-model?"

He smiled slowly, my heart melting just a tiny bit with each new millimeter. "Does that mean you think I'm attractive?"

I rolled my eyes, hoping it was dim enough in his apartment to hide my blush. "You're just avoiding the question now." Though I was deliberately avoiding his, too.

He popped another kernel into his mouth. "See? You're brilliant. You're going to be valedictorian of Columbia."

I refused to rise to the bait. I'd spilled my guts, and now it was his turn. I told him as much.

He sighed. "Okay, okay. Yes, I hate all of this shit. Are you happy? I hate modeling–it makes me feel like a mannequin with an IQ to match. I hate acting, especially in stupid teen shows. I hate that everyone under the age of twenty-one recognizes me and waves a camera in my face every time I'm just trying to have a burger, and I hate that there are people out there who'll pay five hundred bucks for something just because I touched it. I'm a self-loathing, ungrateful, unappreciative asshole. Are you glad to know that?"

It was by far the most worked up I'd ever seen Liam about anything, and it was oddly intriguing. "I'm glad to know the truth, I guess. But then why do you do it?"

"Simple–emancipation."

"Come again?"

"My mother's dead. My dad's a dick. When she died, I had to move in with him. He didn't want me any more than I wanted to go to him, but it was either him or my crazy grandparents in Montana, so I promised him that if he took me in until I was old enough to be emancipated and then let me go, I'd start working and he could keep half the cash."

I was horrified. My dad might've been sick, but at least I'd had eighteen wonderful years with him. Liam had never even known what it was like to have a father worth missing. "Liam, I'm sorry–"

He shot me a hard, unblinking look, and I shut my mouth and let him finish.

"So I got into acting and modeling," he continued, his gaze no longer meeting mine as he looked down at the label he was peeling off his water bottle. "I was already getting asked to be in commercials and shit all the time. All I needed to do was work on a regular basis and my life would be mine as soon as I turned fourteen. Or at least I thought it would be, because I was a child and an idiot. I had no idea how soul-sucking this would all be."

"Can't you get out of it now? Aren't you legally an adult?"

"I'll be nineteen this summer, but what's the point now? A few modeling campaigns, some stupid movie roles and magazine covers, and now I can barely walk down the street. If I tried something else, I'd just look like some enormous has-been who couldn't get any more work. It's probably just my stupid pride speaking, but that seems worse."

"That *is* stupid pride speaking," I said firmly. "If you're not happy with your life, make a change. Aren't you studying for the SATs so you can go to college someday? Didn't you work for your freedom for the very purpose of being in control of your own destiny?"

"It's not that simple, Ally. This is my *life*. I can't turn it upside down just because I feel like it."

"But–"

"Look at you," he broke in. "Look how much your life has just changed and you're struggling to get your footing, and that's *with* everyone you know trying to help you out. I don't have 'people' like you do. I have costars and an agent. And Josh," he added, almost as an afterthought.

I didn't know what to say. I suddenly felt very naïve, and very, very young, despite the fact that Liam and I were almost the same age. "Don't forget a tutor," I said meekly and was relieved when he laughed.

"Right. *Nous sommes amis.*"

I whistled. "Not bad. Hey, maybe I really *am* awesome at this."

"I told you."

"That you did." I stood up, feeling like it was definitely time to go. Liam had politely ignored the foot I'd shoved down my throat, but the air around us had grown extremely charged in the last few minutes and I wasn't helping things by butting into his life. "Listen, it's pretty late and I should probably head out. I'll see you on set tomorrow." I got up and dusted off my jeans, taking my time to get myself together in the hopes that he would ask me to stay a little longer.

Instead, he nodded, got up, and walked to the door. "Thanks for the tutoring. Do you want cash or—"

"Keep it," I said firmly. "Consider it my half of the pizza." Not that my going rate for tutoring was equivalent to half a pie, but it felt cheap to take money after I'd had a good time hanging out at his apartment. He might as well have told me he was leaving the cash on the nightstand. "Have a good night, Liam."

"*Au revoir*, Ally."

He closed the door behind me, and I couldn't help feeling a bit relieved that he'd chosen the phrase for "goodbye" that actually meant "until we meet again."

"I'M GONNA SAY…C!"

I sighed. "Van, you've said C for the last seventeen questions. Are you even paying attention?"

"If C's not the answer, then what is it?"

I took an exasperated bite of my no. 2 pencil. "Okay, it *is* C, but that's not the point!"

She smiled triumphantly. "I believe it *is* the point. If I recall correctly, they don't ask you on the SATs how you got the answer."

"You're impossible."

"You're just jealous because I'm kicking ass." Vanessa took a sip of hot water with lemon from the mug in front of her. She was a little hoarse from yet another party Friday night and the director was *not* happy about it. "And speaking of tutoring, you haven't mentioned how it's going with Liam."

I glanced over to where Liam was practicing a scene with Jamal Cowan, who played his best friend, Malcolm, on the show. As Tristan, he often wore nothing but board shorts or a wet suit peeled down to reveal that V of muscle right below his six-pack; right now, it was the latter, and I quickly looked away. After the way our first session had ended, I was sure Liam would be done having me tutor him, but he'd called to ask me to come over again the next night—which ended in yet another movie, this time *Scarface*—and then again on Friday night, when he'd surprised me with *La Vie En Rose* and French macarons. If I didn't know any better—and if I weren't leaving his apartment with cash in hand at the end of each session—I'd say it was almost like we were dating. Which, of course, we weren't.

"Yeah," I said, hoping I sounded casual. "He's a quick learner."

"Yeah, I've noticed that on set too." She pushed aside her SAT book and picked up her sides. "Would you mind running some lines with me before my next scene?"

"Sure," I agreed, grateful to change the subject from Liam's attractive traits. "Where do you want to start?"

"The line where I'm slutting it up with the science teacher," said Van, flipping her hair over her shoulder. "Aaaaand go!"

We went through the lines a few times, and it was such a ridiculous scene that by the time we got to the end of the third read-through, I was actually kind of enjoying myself. It was fun to pretend to be someone else, at least for a little while. In fact, as we started read-through number four, I actually started to feel sorry for Liam that he couldn't seem to enjoy acting, even though he clearly had natural aptitude for it.

"Ms. Summers, I'm afraid I'm going to require some extra credit," I said in my best stodgy old man voice, even though the science teacher, Mr. Vasquez, was played by a hot actor named Marco Barone who was barely older than Liam. It made Vanessa crack up laughing, and suddenly I heard, "What's so funny?" and looked up to see Liam himself standing over us.

"Just a silly voice I was doing," I said dismissively, embarrassed to have been caught making a fool of myself. The amused quirk of his lips suggested he'd been listening for longer than a line. "Do you need Vanessa?"

"Yup. The fight scene's coming up, and they want to fix her makeup."

"Ooh, fight scene. Sounds like fun."

"As long as Vanessa remembers not to *actually* slap the bejesus out of me like she did in rehearsal," Liam said wryly.

"Um, I was *committing* to the scene. Hello? Acting?" She winked at me before prancing off to makeup with Liam in tow.

It was nice to see the two of them getting along well, but I couldn't help feeling a little envious of their newfound rapport. Van was exactly the kind of girl Liam should've been with—beautiful, smart, talented, and every bit as famous as he was. She was probably just the person to make him appreciate his career, too. Assuming he stayed away from Shannah Barrett, I was sure it was only a matter of time until he and Van hooked up.

God, how I wished that fact didn't make me want to hurl.

★★★★★

After an hour or so—which I spent working on a fluff piece I'd agreed to write for the paper after I hadn't been able to come up with any good ideas on my own—Vanessa returned for her sides, saying the writers wanted to make a couple of changes to the script.

"What are you working on?" she asked, glancing over my shoulder.

"Just a stupid article about spring break," I replied. "It has to be in tomorrow, and it's basically a piece of crap."

"Ooh, spring break! How are you spending it?"

"Um, at home? Because I'm broke?" Did she really need a reminder of that? "Plus, it's an 'on' week for my dad in the hospital, so I'm sure I'll spend a lot of time there."

"Oh, we can definitely help you have more fun than that. Right, Liam?" she called to him for reasons I could not begin to comprehend.

"What?" he called back.

"We're going to make sure Ally has a good spring break."

"Cool. Now get back here."

Van smiled. "See? Even Liam's in. It'll be fun, Al. We don't even have to go to any parties or anything. We'll go shopping and get fish tacos and watch a movie or two and it'll be cheap and perfect and totally chilled out." She kissed the top of my head and went back to set, leaving me slightly bewildered. I loved the way Vanessa always believed she could make things better, no matter how crappy the situation.

And I loved the way she managed to make me believe it too.

★★★★★

Still, my spring break didn't sound nearly as cool as the ones everyone else was planning. All around me, people were going on and on about the great times they were gonna have in Cabo or Cancun. Even Dana and Leni had fun plans.

"So, you're sure you can't come to Jamaica with us?" Dana asked me at my locker the next day, twirling a strand of flaming red hair around her index finger. "It's gonna be so, so awesome."

"So awesome," Leni echoed.

"Thanks, guys, but I really can't," I said as apologetically as I could muster. The truth—besides the fact that I had no desire to spend a week trapped on an island with them—was that I hadn't actually told Dana and Leni that I was no longer operating on the same budget I once was. "My dad's going to be in the hospital that week."

"Bummer," said Dana. "Guess you don't wanna come shopping for bathing suits after school then, either."

"Sorry," I said, not even bothering to fake it this time.

Leni shrugged. "Later," she said as she and Dana walked off.

As quickly as they had gone, Nate took their place. "Bummer? Seriously?"

I groaned. "Why on Earth are you eavesdropping on my conversations?"

"Because they're so utterly fascinating, Duncan. Can you please explain to me why you continue to hang out with chicks who refer to the situation of your father being treated for cancer as a 'bummer'? I thought you were a Columbia girl. Don't you worry about them killing all your brain cells before you even get to freshman orientation? I can't believe you even tried to set me up with one of them."

"They mean well," I said, which I was *pretty* sure was the truth.

Nate smirked. "You are so full of shit."

I laughed. "Shut up. I'm trying, okay? Van and I were so attached by the ass when we were younger that I kind of missed out on the friend-making boat. Filling the last three-and-a-half years with newspaper, the debate team, tutoring, and a zillion random clubs hasn't exactly left me with tons of time to shop and tan with the rest of the class. At least Dana and Leni try to include me. When's the last time *you* invited me to Jamaica?"

"I'm actually sticking around here this week to save some cash for a graduation trip, but I *am* going to spend the day with my Nana on Monday if you'd like to join."

"Kind of you to offer, but I have a whole bummer thing going on that week," I replied sweetly.

He laughed. "Okay, fine, point taken—I shouldn't make fun of your friends if I'm not going to be any better. So maybe we should do friendly things. Liiiike, for example, visit a TV set together."

"God, you have such a one-track mind," I said, rolling my eyes.

"I was just kidding. But really, you should come out with me and my friends some time. You could get to know some people who don't suck."

"Just in time for us all to graduate in three months?"

"Three months is three months, and besides, it'd still be more fun than hanging out with Tweedle Dee and Tweedle Bummer." He pulled out his phone. "Macy Easton's having a party at her house on Friday night, and I'm texting you the address right now. You should come."

"I'll think about it," I said, just as the bell rang.

"Good," he called over the noise as we each headed to our respective classes, but I could tell he knew as well as I did that I would never go.

★★★★★

I'd planned to go to set straight from school the following afternoon as per my typical Wednesday schedule, but Van texted me during lunch to ask me to run a few errands for her and drop by the set later. Since several of the errands involved making flight and hotel reservations online, I headed home to use my own computer and maybe even get my French homework done before I ventured out to the dry cleaners to pick up a dress Vanessa planned to wear to some event she'd just decided to go to.

Or maybe I should just save the French homework for Liam, I thought as I pulled out of the Hayden High parking lot. He'd been progressing at a rapid pace, obviously putting his actorly skills of memorizing lines and learning accents to good use, and I was curious to see just how good he was.

And, okay, it's possible I liked the idea of spending more time with him. I mean, he obviously wasn't hideous, and it was nice teaching someone who actually cared about learning. Plus, I had to admit that he'd introduced me to some damn good movies. And he always ordered really good takeout. And yeah, he was actually fun to hang out with, once you got him off set and into the comfort of his own home. And he definitely–

Honk!

Whoops–time to focus. L.A. drivers had no patience for girls who didn't watch carefully for light changes and developed ridiculous little crushes on guys who were way, way out of their league.

Kinda hard to blame them. I didn't have much patience for my ridiculous feelings either.

I was home less than ten minutes later and surprised to see Lucy sitting on the sectional in the living room, her feet dangling from the couch, her eyes glued to the TV. I hadn't seen my mother's car out front.

"Luce?" I closed the front door behind me and dropped my bag onto the kitchen counter. "Is Mom home?"

"Aunt Joanne's," Lucy answered dully.

"Why's she at Aunt Joanne's?"

Lucy shrugged.

"Are you home alone?" Lucy was never home alone. My parents' rule had always been that we weren't allowed to stay home alone until high school. Leaving her by herself for anything short of an emergency was unheard of, and if my mom's sister was having an emergency, we'd know it. Aunt Jo was the queen of blowing issues out of proportion; when she had a hangnail, we all got "911" texts.

"Yup."

Something was seriously wrong. It must've been. "Did something happen to Dad?"

"Nope. He just called to check in a few minutes ago."

"So they just...decided to let you stay home alone?"

"Yup."

"Ooookay." I grabbed an apple from the fridge before slinging my bag back onto my shoulder and heading for the stairs. Only when I got up to my bedroom door did it hit me that my little sister hadn't looked at me once.

★★★★★

I decided to give Lucy a little space; she was growing up, and maybe a little time with her own thoughts was exactly what she needed. I needed about an hour to deal with Van's errands anyway, but when I finished up and returned downstairs, it seemed Lucy hadn't moved an inch. Growing up or not, I couldn't ignore her weirdness anymore.

"Luce?" I hedged. "Is everything okay?"

"Uh-huh."

I sucked in a breath. Lucy was the sweetest, most overactive kid you could ever hope to meet. Something was clearly wrong here, and it was equally clear she didn't want to talk about it. Unfortunately, I still had to get to the dry cleaners and a whole bunch of other places—including the *Daylight Falls* set—and I didn't have time to sit around and try to coax information out of an ten-year-old. I could, however, prevent her from making a permanent butt imprint on the couch.

"Want to help me run some errands for Vanessa?"

"Run errands?" Lucy sounded like I'd asked her if she wanted to play with some gum from the bottom of my shoe.

"Some of them are fun," I promised. "She wants me to pick something up for her from Sephora—I'll buy you a yummy lip gloss if you keep me company. Plus, the dry cleaners are right near Pinkberry."

I wasn't sure exactly which one lured her off the couch, but I got a tiny smile and a practically whispered "okay" before she turned off the TV and joined me. I couldn't help giving her a spontaneous little kiss on the top of her pale blond head before grabbing the keys and shuffling her out the door.

Despite agreeing to go with me, she remained quiet, keeping her eyes on the scenery as we drove and answering my chatty questions with one-word answers. Even a scoop of mango yogurt with gummy bears failed to do the trick; she simply ate it in silence outside the store while I went into the dry cleaners to pick up Vanessa's dress.

Finally, I couldn't take it anymore. I pulled up in front of the house to drop her off before going to set and put the car in park.

"Luce, talk to me," I begged, turning to face her.

"About what?"

"About whatever's on your mind and obviously bothering you."

She continued to sit stone still, staring straight ahead, but a lone tear rolled down her cheek and it broke my heart.

"Did something happen at school?" I asked softly, afraid to find out what sort of situation I might be dealing with.

She shook her head, and more tears followed the first.

"Did you get into a fight with one of your friends? Did Abby say something to hurt your feelings again?" Stupid Abby—she was the worst of Lucy's friends, with a horrible mom to match.

"No," she said softly. She sniffled.

"Then what's going on?" I kept my voice as soft as possible; I couldn't shake the feeling that a loud noise or sudden movement might actually break my sister at that moment.

Finally, she turned to face me. "What's it gonna be like when Daddy dies?"

I should've expected that question. I don't know why it shocked the hell out of me, but it did. And despite the fact that I knew I should've had *some* answer, that I should've thought through this very same question from the minute my dad informed us of his diagnosis, I hadn't. It was just too much to think about, the after. Too scary. Too real. I had no desire to know what life would be like without my dad, and I sure as hell didn't want my ten-year-old sister to know. I didn't even like to know she'd been thinking about it, which was probably why my mind hadn't gone to the obvious question in the first place.

So, trying to hide the fact that I was shaking as I gave her a hug, I simply said, "It's going to be sad, but we're going to stick together." I prayed that she wouldn't ask exactly how we planned to do that when we were three thousand miles apart.

I WAS STILL FEELING RATTLED BY Lucy's question when I entered the studio half an hour later, laden down with bags of Van's requested items. Rattled and angry—at myself for not anticipating it, at my parents for not being the ones to handle it, at Lucy for making me think about it... Suddenly, all I wanted was to throw Van's stuff at her and run back to my house so I could curl up into a ball in my bedroom and never, ever leave.

Fortunately, Van was in mid-scene when I arrived, so I did in fact get to leave her things in her trailer without having a conversation, but I hadn't counted on bumping into Liam on my way out.

"*Bonjour, mon amie!*" The corner of his mouth lifted just enough to show that rarely seen dimple, and the mere sight of it improved my mood instantly, if only for a moment. "Are you heading out already?"

"Yeah, I just..." I trailed off, my brain completely devoid of excuses why I was dashing to my car like a bat out of hell. "I gotta go."

"Is everything okay?"

No, *everything is not okay. My father is dying, and I seem to keep getting distracted from that fact.* "Yeah, great. I just..."

"Gotta go," he filled in for me.

"Right."

He nodded, but he made no motion to leave. *I am too polite to call you out on the fact that you are feeding me complete bullshit right now* was written all over his face, and I gritted my teeth as I felt the first pangs of annoyed anger building. How dare he look at me like that? What the hell did he know about what I was going through?

And then I realized: pretty much everything. Everything that really mattered, anyway. How had I somehow failed to note that, of all the people in my life, Liam was the only one who'd been in this situation? Who'd watched a beloved parent slowly waste away while feeling utterly useless and incapable of doing anything to help?

"Okay," he said slowly. "So I guess—"

"Tell me what happens," I begged, suddenly desperate for him to stay and talk to me.

He furrowed his brow. "In this episode?"

I shook my head. "In life," I said, my voice raspy as the familiar fuzzy-throat feeling of oncoming tears surfaced. "What happens when one of your parents dies?"

"Oh, Ally..." He raked a hand through his hair. He must've had product in it from an earlier scene because it stuck up in tufts, the natural gold highlights glinting in the setting sun. "I can't—I mean, I don't—"

"Forget it," I said quickly. "It was lousy of me to ask."

I turned and walked briskly toward my car, the breeze my pace was creating blowing the rapidly flowing tears from my cheeks. It took me a full minute of fumbling with my keys to get the driver's-side door open; neither my shaking hands nor my blurry eyes were very helpful on that front. When I finally did manage to slip inside and slam the door behind me, I put my keys down on the center console and gripped the steering wheel, gulping in deep breaths in an effort to calm myself before starting the car.

A tapping on the passenger door made me jump up in my seat. I glanced over. Liam.

Reluctantly, I unlocked the door and watched him slide inside. "I'm fine," I said before he could open his mouth.

"I see that."

"I shouldn't have asked you that."

"Yeah, you should have." He set and unset his jaw a couple of times before speaking again. "Having no one to talk about it with when it was happening was really, really shitty. I don't want you to feel like you can't turn to anyone. I just don't want to be the person who tells you how much it sucks."

I nodded slowly. "Well, I can definitely understand that, seeing as I don't want to be the one who tells my baby sister that, either."

"I wish I could advise on siblings, but sadly, they are not my area of expertise." He tried to smile, but it didn't meet his eyes or make me feel better. We were both quiet for a minute, and then he said, "Ask again."

"I don't want to dredge up bad memories," I said, feeling guilty for my selfishness earlier. "Of course you don't want to talk about it."

"No, actually, I kind of do," he admitted. "No one ever asks me about it, about her. And, come to think of it, no one ever comes to me with their problems either. It's sorta...nice."

I couldn't help but smile, even as I sniffled loudly and wiped away a mess of tears with the heel of my palm. "So you like that I'm a bawling mess?"

"Love it," he replied with a smile of his own, a real one this time. He reached out and wiped a tear off my cheek with his thumb. The touch of his skin against mine nearly had me jolting out of my seat. I bit my lip, hard, as if that would keep me in place. "Ask again," he repeated.

"What's it like?" I whispered, feeling calmer now.

"It sucks."

And then we both cracked up. It wasn't funny by any stretch of the imagination, but it was as if both of us had been waiting for this worldly insight that just never came. When our laughter finally petered out, he fixed me with as earnest a look as he was able to manage and said, "Jesus, I'm sorry. I thought I'd be more eloquent than that."

"Well, I'm sure you're not wrong," I pointed out. "But does it suck every minute of every day? Or does it suck a lot at the beginning and then become sort of okay? And what does it mean for my family? Do I have to learn how to become a second parent to Lucy? How's my mom going to handle everything? She can barely handle things now—I always feel like she's two seconds away from falling apart, like she's already checked out of parenting. And will she remarry? Oh God, that would be so strange. I can't even imagine her with anybody else. Would he move into my house, or would we have to move? Will he expect me to call him 'Dad'? What if—"

"Ally!" Liam grabbed my forearm, which I'd been waving around wildly while the multitude of questions I hadn't even known I had bubbled out of my throat. "Take a deep breath, okay?" I did. "One thing at a time."

"I don't even know where to start."

"Haven't you... I mean, is this the first time you're thinking about it?"

"Of course not. It's just that lately I've been so focused on the immediate future, the college part and stuff, that I haven't really been thinking about the long-term. I mean, it just seems so...not possible."

"I know," he said softly. "Sometimes I still can't believe my mom is gone." He dropped his head back against the headrest. "You know what my first thought was when she told me she wasn't gonna make it? *Who's gonna cut the crust off my sandwiches*? I mean, seriously, can you believe that shit? How stupid do you have to be?"

"You were a kid!"

"I know, but still. Sometimes I wish I could yell at eight-year-old Liam, 'Who cares about a fucking sandwich, kid? You're never gonna go to the beach together again. She's never gonna see you in a movie. She's not gonna be at your wedding or meet your kids.' I would trade a whole lotta crustless sandwiches just to hear her pretend one more time that the broken shells I brought up from the ocean were the most beautiful things she's ever seen."

I had no idea what to say. "I'm so sorry, Liam." It sounded so pathetic in the sad silence of the car.

"Yeah, well." He shrugged. "I'm still standing. Hopefully I even make her proud every now and again. You'll do the same. So will your sister."

I cracked a small smile at that. "You don't even know Lucy."

"No, but I know her big sister, and I have a feeling the good stuff runs in the family."

For the first time since finding Lucy in my house that afternoon, I felt a calming warmth spread throughout my body, replacing the cold, uneasy feeling that had permeated every minute of that afternoon.

"Thank you," I said, reaching over to squeeze his hand. "For someone who doesn't get asked to listen a lot, you're awfully good at it. And it *is* nice to know that since you turned out semi-decent, there's probably hope for the Duncan clan."

He laughed and squeezed back. "Semi-decent, huh? Why do I feel like that's high praise coming from you?"

"Oh, come on. I'm not that bad."

He pursed his lips in a smug smile, and I whacked him on the chest with my free hand. "No, not bad at all," he teased.

We were both silent for a moment, and then I asked, "So what was she like? I mean, obviously she was pretty awesome if she cut the crusts off your sandwiches."

"Oh, she was beyond awesome," he replied, a tiny smile playing on his lips. "She used to leave notes for me in my backpack every morning. She even left a bunch of extras so I'd have some after she died. As hard as I cried when we buried her, I think I cried even harder when I ran out of those notes." He pulled his hand from mine and rubbed his eyes. "God, I sound so pathetic right now," he said ruefully.

"You do not," I argued, missing the consoling warmth of his fingers already. "You sound like a guy who really loves his mom."

"Yeah, well, my crying drove my dad nuts. He had no idea what to do with this little snot-nosed eight-year-old. Finally, he sat me down in front of *The Godfather* and explained to me that Michael Corleone was a real man, and I needed to stop crying and man up."

I whistled. "Wow. No wonder you wanted to get out of his house as soon as possible."

"The guy's a dick, no question about it, but for whatever reason, that always stuck with me. To this day, I still think Al Pacino is the biggest badass on the planet. All I wanted was to be just like his characters, to be able to take care of business without giving a shit about anything or anyone."

"That sounds...lonely."

He smiled wryly. "I prefer solitary, and yeah, my life's been pretty damn solitary, but it's how I like it. If you don't need anybody, you have a lot less to lose. Bonus points if nobody else needs you either."

"Well, I needed you tonight, and there you were," I pointed out. "Was it the worst thing ever?"

He shook his head slowly, as if it pained him to do so. "No," he said quietly.

His reluctant admission probably shouldn't have made me feel all warm and fuzzy inside, but it did. Suddenly, I wanted to yank his hand back and never let go. But I didn't, and after a moment, he glanced at his watch.

"Shit, I had to be on set like ten minutes ago. Will I see you tomorrow? I was thinking maybe we could squeeze in some SAT tutoring. It's been a while."

At that point, I probably couldn't have stayed away even if I'd wanted to. "Yup, I'll be here."

"Cool. Have a g'night, Ally."

I smiled. It felt really, really good. "*Bon nuit, Liam. À demain.*"

★★★★★

I took the long way home, and by the time I returned, Lucy was asleep. I trudged into my own room, changed into a T-shirt and shorts, washed up for bed, and lay on top of the covers, my brain working a mile a minute the entire time.

I wish I could've said that I was thinking entirely about my dad and the rest of my family, but the truth was, Liam was occupying a lot more of my brainspace than I would've liked. What had happened to the rational part of me who was able to compartmentalize "them" and "us"? The last thing I wanted was to end up like Nate, crushing on someone who was completely out of the range of possibility.

And speaking of "them," my phone began ringing, and I knew without a doubt it was Vanessa; no one else ever called me after ten. "What's up, V?"

"Hey, where'd you go? I thought you might stick around after you dropped my stuff off, but you totally disappeared."

"Sorry, hun. It's just been a long day. I felt like crashing." It wasn't technically a lie—I *did* leave with the intent to go home—but I just didn't feel like telling her about my conversation with Liam. It was too private, and worse, I knew she'd be on my ass in half a second with that "crush" crap again. "Where are you, anyway?" I asked, both eager to change the conversation and genuinely curious. "I thought you were going to that 'Save the Sea Otters' thing."

"I am; I'm in the limo, waiting for the rest of the cast to join me. Well, everyone but Liam. He handed me a check to pass along and mumbled something about not feeling well. I shouldn't be surprised, right?"

Not after the emotional wringer I put him through. "Well, parties aren't everyone's thing," I said lamely.

"I don't know. He seemed extra weird tonight. I asked him if he'd seen you around and he just kind of stared at me."

I wasn't quite sure how to take that, but it didn't matter, because before I could respond, Van was rolling again. "Are you sure you want to go to bed? I could definitely get you into this thing if you wanna join."

I laughed. "I am very, very sure. Please send my love to the sea otters."

"What about this weekend? Carly and I got invites to that super-cute Reese Witherspoon rom-com premiere Friday night. Wanna be my plus-one?"

"Did you actually get a plus-one?"

"No," she huffed, "but I'll bet you anything Liam would be happy to give up his ticket."

Liam again. On the one hand, I was dying to talk about him, and on the other hand, every time Van mentioned his name I felt sick to my stomach. Why was it that no matter how many times I ordered myself not to think about him, the universe seemed to have other plans? No chance I was subjecting myself to an evening of hanging out with his castmates. If I was going to get over my stupid crush, I was going to need to spend this weekend distracting myself with something completely un-Liam-related.

And then I remembered.

"Actually, I have plans Friday night." Not that Nate had actually mentioned Macy Easton's party again. "Just a little Hayden party, but I told Nate I'd go with."

"Nate, huh?" I could practically hear her eyebrows waggling over the phone. "You guys really are getting tight these days."

I snorted. "Please. Not only am I the furthest thing from interested in Nate Donovan, but you know as well as I do that his heart is otherwise occupied. Now *he* would love to be your date at the Reese Witherspoon premiere."

Van laughed. "I'll keep that in—ooh! Carly and Jamal are here. I gotta go. I'll see you on set tomorrow."

She hung up before I could say, "See you then."

NEITHER NATE NOR I BROUGHT Macy's party up once during the rest of the week, and by the time things wound down on set Friday evening, it was obvious he was going to be partying with Macy and the other cheerleaders on his own. That was the thing about Nate—he liked to talk big, but he kind of sucked at follow-through. Even if I'd managed to get him a date with Van, I had a feeling he would've dropped the ball on planning it and ended up partying at a friend's house instead.

Not that I was much better. Sure, I could've said something, but when it came down to it, pretending to be interested in Macy and Co.'s play-by-play of the last football game (and accompanying cheers, of course) didn't sound all that much more fun than wallowing in front of the TV while lamenting the fact that I was nursing a crush on a guy who was eons out of my league.

It was almost a shame about the party, though, because as much as I didn't feel like hanging out with a bunch of classmates I didn't really know, I also had zero other plans for the evening. Van was at the premiere, Dana and Leni were on a double date, and even Lucy was having a sleepover with her friends. How lame did I have to be to have a less exciting night planned than my ten-year-old sister?

I hoisted my bag onto my shoulder and headed out of Van's trailer, where I'd been simultaneously handling interview requests on my phone while answering her e-mails on the wafer-thin laptop she kept plugged in by her makeup mirror at all times. In my rush to get the hell off the set and into some comfy sweats for a night of TV watching, I nearly walked smack into Liam, who was walking toward the trailer he shared with Jamal.

"*Oú est le* fire, *mon amie*?" he asked, showing off his newly expanded vocab, compliments of yet another tutoring session the night before. "I'm guessing you've got some fun and exciting weekend plans."

If only I were a better liar—or actor—I would've loved to pretend to Liam that I was actually cool enough to have something to do tonight other than park myself on the couch. "*Le feu*," I corrected him automatically, "and nope, just heading home. You? Going to another orgy?"

He laughed. "Nope, just kicking back and learning my lines for a guest spot I have coming up on one of those CSIs. Almost as exciting, but not quite."

"Need help?" I offered. I regretted it instantly. That was *not* going to help my resolve to stop thinking about him. Not to mention that my tendency to say stupid things always seemed to kick in around Liam, and my habit of oversharing even worse. Now I was going to have to listen to him awkwardly make up a reason to reject my assistance.

"Sure, if you've really got nothing better to do."

Or he could say that.

"I just need to shower and grab a few things," he added. "Do you mind waiting in my trailer for a few?"

Waiting in his trailer...while he got completely naked. Yeah, I could probably handle that. "Sure," I croaked.

He must've noticed a trace of anxiety on my face because he said, "There's a comfortable couch, I promise."

Ha, yes, Liam, because that's what I was worried about—that the couch five feet away from where water will be spraying your naked body wouldn't be comfortable enough.

I followed him into the trailer and sat down on the couch, gratefully accepting the water bottle he tossed me from the mini-fridge. It was a nice trailer, though he hadn't added nearly as much décor as Van had. The only personal touches were a magnet on the fridge in the shape of a koala bear; a black iPod plugged into a pair of speakers; and two framed pictures—one of a woman I assumed was his mother and the other of Liam, Josh, and a third guy who looked vaguely familiar. I squinted at the picture. Was that Shannah Barrett in the background?

"Trying to figure out where you know Wyatt from?" asked Liam. "He's in that commercial with the dancing bottle of mustard. He's also Josh's cousin."

"Ah, gotcha. My dad loves that commercial. Dancing condiments always crack him up."

"How's he doing?"

Oh, yeah. I'd somehow managed to forget that Liam knew about my dad. "Fine, for now. He goes back in for round two of treatment in a week."

"Does he have to stay in bed the whole time between treatments?"

"Nah, he just needs a couple days to recover, and then he goes back to work. I mean, I'm sure he feels like crap, but it makes him happy to get out of the house."

"That's cool." He toed off his shoes and placed his watch on the small table next to the couch. He started to pull off his shirt, which probably would've sent me into embarrassing conniptions, but then he dropped the hem and grinned. "Can't risk you selling any more of the clothing off my back, now can I?" He winked and walked into the bathroom.

I exhaled sharply as soon as he was gone. Liam *had* to know that I had a, um, slight attraction to him. Was he torturing me to be a jerk? Or was he so used to turning on every woman in sight that he no longer even realized when he was doing it?

The shower turned on, and I tried not to focus on the fact that Liam had stripped down on the other side of the wall. Instead, I distracted myself by staring at the picture again, at how seamlessly Shannah Barrett blended into the background, how perfect and Hollywood she looked with her deep tan and stick-straight blond hair. My stupid red-brown mutt of a hair color was so freaking Anytown, U.S.A., and my skin could never approach that shade of golden in a million years. I made for a lousy California girl.

I was so busy seeing everything wrong with myself in that picture that I didn't hear the shower turning off or Liam exiting the bathroom. I didn't even realize he was standing a few feet away from me until he interrupted the silence in the room by asking, "You're really into that picture, aren't you? Lemme guess—you wanna bang Josh Chester like every other chick in the world?"

I had to bite my lip to keep from cracking up at that notion. "I can very, very safely say no to that question. I mean, no offense to your friend," I said quickly. "He's just...not my type."

"So what do you keep staring at?" asked Liam, sliding on his watch. "Don't tell me I have something in my teeth."

There was no non-awkward way to respond to the fact that I'd been caught staring, so I just went with the truth. "I was checking out Shannah Barrett, actually."

"Oh. *Oh*. I didn't realize you were, uh—"

"Stop right there," I cut him off. "Not a lesbian. Just envying her hair."

He snorted. "You could pay for that hair, too, you know. Also her tan, her nose, and her boobs."

"Wow." I whistled. "I thought you guys were friends."

"I'm not revealing anything that isn't obvious if you look at a picture of her from three years ago. But we aren't really friends, no. What made you think we were?"

Fair question. What I'd actually thought was that he wanted to sleep with her, just like every other living, breathing, heterosexual male in existence. I said as much.

He raised an eyebrow. "That's what you think my type is?"

I shrugged. "What, hot? Isn't that everyone's type?"

He shook his head slowly. "She's certainly not *my* idea of hot."

"And what *is*, then?" I challenged. "Zoe? Van?"

"Zoe doesn't look all that different from Shannah, and no offense to *your* friend, but I'm not into Van either." He leaned against the wall of the trailer and crossed his arms over his chest. "Do you think we're all just incestuous or what?"

"I think that when you're a Hollywood star, everyone else must look like a troll," I replied, trying and failing to keep the edge out of my voice. "You may not like what comes with being hot, but it's not always so fun being a normal person around Hollywood people either."

"Hey, I get—"

"No, you don't," I cut him off harshly. I knew I was being mean—unfair, even—but looking at him standing there, water droplets glistening in his hair, tan skin still slightly flushed from the heat of the shower, worn T-shirt clinging to his biceps, I felt all the frustration of the pointlessness of my attraction to him race through my body. "You don't even appreciate any of this. You're not remotely grateful about winning the genetic lottery. All you have to do is smile or lift your shirt and someone will give you every damn thing in the world. You don't have to worry about money, or not being able to get the girl you want, or having something to do on a Friday night. The world is yours and you don't even fucking want it."

"Wow, Ally, that's a lot of truth coming out at once. So not only do you think I'm a shitty actor, but you think I'm a spoiled brat, too."

I blanched, all the anger and frustration suddenly sapping out of my system. Jesus, I was a bitch. "Liam, I'm sorry, I didn't mean that."

"Yeah, you obviously fucking did." His beautiful eyes blazed with anger, and it was obvious from the set of his jaw that he was still holding back.

"I don't think you're a shitty actor," I said quietly. "And I don't think you're a spoiled brat. I'm just going through a seriously weird time and I keep waiting for something good to happen and it just...doesn't."

"What are you doing to turn things around?" he asked coldly. "Besides railing on the people who try to help you and get to know you."

I buried my head in my hands. "God, I'm sorry, okay? I'm an asshole. I don't even know why I'm being an asshole. It's just easier to get angry at you than to–" *Jesus, shut up, Ally!* My stomach suddenly turned at the realization that I'd almost admitted to Liam that I liked him. For the millionth time, it hit me what a stupid cliché I was, having a thing for Liam Holloway. "Sorry, I need to get out of here."

I started toward the door, but in a flash, Liam had blocked my way.

"Enough leaving, Ally. How is it that you're practically fluent in French but can't seem to finish a damn sentence in English? Do you hate me that much?"

I looked at him in disbelief. "Do I *hate* you? Are you kidding me?"

"You think I'm an ungrateful asshole who uses his looks to get what he wants, just because he can. Am I close?"

Yes, he was close–so close that his scent was making me dizzy. So close I could practically feel the heat of his skin. So close I seriously needed to get out of there before I did something incredibly stupid like lean forward three inches and close the space between our lips.

"Ally?"

Lord, I'd completely forgotten that he'd asked me a question. Not that it was my fault. He was the one flustering the hell out of me, as usual. "What do you even care what I think, Liam? There are about a zillion websites you could go to or magazines you could open that are full of disgustingly positive opinions of you. What does it even matter what I think?"

"It matters."

"Why?" I pressed.

"I'm still trying to figure that out."

My heart was pounding now. Yes, he still looked angry, but the anger in his eyes was mixed with something else, and I was dying to know what. "And what have you come up with?" I managed.

He was quiet for a minute, and then he said, "A theory."

"A theory," I repeated.

"Yes."

"About me? Or about you?"

He fixed me with a hard stare, and whatever it was competing with anger in his eyes took over; it looked strangely like lust. "About the fact that somehow, every time you yell at me, it only makes me want you more."

Heart. Pounding. "Liam—"

That time, it was Liam who didn't let me finish my sentence; his mouth was on mine before I could even finish breathing his name. I was so shocked by the kiss that it took me a moment to react, but only a moment. As my arms reached up to encircle his neck and pull him even closer, there was no denying that I'd wanted this for weeks.

After a minute, he pulled away, and I was sure he was going to put an end to it all, but then there he was again, gently sucking my lower lip between his teeth before slipping his tongue between my lips to claim mine. My fingers brushed his soft, damp hair before digging into his shoulders, trying to pull him impossibly closer, as if breathing each other's air wasn't enough. Finally, he pulled away, for real this time.

I could only imagine how I looked—hair a mess, eyes glazed over, lips swollen—and I prayed it somehow looked sexier in real life than it did in my head. Not that it mattered. Liam liked me. *Liam*. Liked *me*.

Maybe.

"So, that theory of yours..." I said slowly.

"Proven beyond a shadow of a doubt," said Liam, cupping my face and kissing me again, lightly this time.

"The theory wasn't that if you told me you liked me, I'd kiss you, was it?"

He cracked a smile that warmed me to my toes. "You're ridiculous, Ally, you know that?"

"But I've been a crazy, manic jerk," I sputtered. "And I *cried* in front of you. And I'm not—"

Liam kissed me silent. "Yes, you have been kind of a jerk. And I like that you cried in front of me. And I like who you are. And I definitely like who you're not. Will you just accept that I'm into you and give me some sort of clue as to whether or not it's mutual?"

"If I haven't given you any clues then I'm a lousy kisser."

He grinned and hooked an index finger through the belt loop of my jeans, pulling me closer. "You are most certainly not that," he breathed as he leaned in to kiss me again.

10

EVENTUALLY, WE GOT OURSELVES OUT of the trailer and moved on to Liam's apartment, where we preceded to talk and make out (but mostly make out) for another few hours. When we finally took a breather long enough for me to check my watch, I was shocked to see that it was almost midnight.

"Jesus," I muttered. "How the hell did it get so late?"

"Everything okay?" Liam asked, adjusting his jeans. He looked slightly dazed, which was unspeakably adorable. The idea that I could get a "teen heartthrob" all hot and bothered was an admittedly confidence-inspiring one.

"Yeah," I said quickly, raking a hand through my tangled hair. "Just hoping my parents aren't freaking out that I'm not home yet. Plus," I added with a smile, "we haven't actually worked on your lines yet."

"Forget the lines," said Liam, snaking an arm around my waist and pulling me into him as he leaned back into the corner of the couch. He kissed the top of my head, making my stomach do that fluttery thing it'd been doing a whole lot of lately. "You're my break from all that crap."

"You do realize you met me at work, right? And that I'll be there again on Monday?"

"Yes, and I'm very grateful and all that, but that's it. We wrap up shooting on the pilot next week, and then we can just be normal. Better than normal," he amended. "Awesome."

"I don't know if I can live up to awesome."

"You can definitely live up to awesome," Liam assured me, seeking out my hand with his free one and lacing his fingers through it. "Seriously, Ally, you make my day not suck, and that's no small thing."

I burst out laughing. "Is that what passes for high praise these days?"

"From me, there's no praise higher," Liam replied with a smile. "Actually looking forward to going to work because I know you'll be there? Having someone talk to me about things that have nothing to do with TV or whether I should say 'guys' or 'bros' in the cafeteria scene? Being able to say I want to prepare myself for the possibility of going to college one day and not having someone respond 'ugh, why?' These things are totally priceless."

He freed his hand to tuck a strand of hair behind my ear, lingering for a brief, delicate moment on the thin silver hoop that pierced my cartilage. "And I like that you try to push me to be my best self," he added, his voice softening. "You can be maddening, but at the same time, it's really...sweet."

I still couldn't process the fact that Liam actually liked me. "This is ridiculous, you know. You could get any girl you want."

"And so I did," he pointed out firmly, kissing me hard on the lips in a "stop talking like that" gesture. And I vowed I *would* stop. If he said he liked me—and he sure as hell kissed me like he did—he liked me, and that was that, impossible as it may have been to believe. After all, Liam had nothing to gain from being with me; what possible ulterior motives could he have?

We kissed for a little while longer, but eventually, guilt at making my parents worry crept up on me and I informed him that I had to get home.

"Fair enough," he said, nodding and pulling away. "Any chance you're free tomorrow for a French lesson?"

"*French* lesson. I get it. Funny." I tapped the end of his nose. "And yes, I'm free."

He smiled and kissed me one more time before standing up. "Good. I'll call you in the morning."

★★★★★

He didn't, though. I hadn't been able to fall asleep that night with both my mind and heart racing, so when I finally passed out around 4:00 a.m. or so, I made sure to keep my phone at my side. It didn't ring, and when I finally stirred at almost noon, I anxiously checked it only to see that I had no missed calls.

Okay, not a big deal, I told myself as I slid out of bed and began my morning routine with my cell phone at my side. *It's still basically morning, and anyway, just because he said "morning" doesn't mean it actually has to be morning. Stop being a freak.* I even forced myself to take a shower, despite knowing I could potentially miss his call.

I didn't, but I *did* have a rather scary text waiting from him when I emerged from the steam.

We really need to talk. Call you later.

Ugh. Not only were those the worst words in the English language, but this was probably the fastest breakup in history. I almost wished he'd just done it over text so I wouldn't sit around waiting for him to call and do it.

What had changed since last night? Had he gone out after I'd left? Gotten a phone call from someone he was more interested in? Gotten a fan letter with a naked picture that made him realize there were hotter peons out there?

I had no idea what to do now. Sit around and wait? Or come up with something to get my mind the hell off of the horrible impending phone call? Before I could decide, my phone rang, and I grabbed it like a wild animal. I took a breath before I picked up, not wanting to sound too crazed, and saw that it wasn't Liam calling, but Vanessa.

"Hey, Van," I said, hoping the disappointment wasn't obvious in my voice.

"A, listen to this craziness. I can only talk for a minute—I totally just ducked out of a meeting so I could call you."

"You have a meeting on a Saturday morning?"

"Jade had a brilliant idea and you know how she is—the second she says jump, everyone in her world says 'how high?' She's terrifying."

"So what's the brilliant idea?"

I could hear Van being called back to the meeting, so I knew she'd have to be quick. Jade did *not* like to be kept waiting. "Jade wants me and Liam to pretend to date to drum up some press for the show before it airs. How funny is that?"

Hilarious. Hy-freaking-sterical, Vanessa. It was obvious from her tone that she had no idea anything was going on between me and Liam, and how could she? I'd envisioned filling her in tonight over a cup of Pinkberry after I saw Liam again and confirmed there was something to tell, but there was obviously no way I could do that now.

"Liam's there too?" I asked lamely.

"Yeah, there are a whole bunch of people here, and everyone's on board. Anyway, I really have to run, but you know I always like to run my moves by you so you can keep me grounded if I'm being completely crazy. Is this so incredibly stupid? I mean, we're both single, and it might even help us become friends, so, whatever, right?"

"Right," I said, feeling myself choke on the word. The truth was, it *was* a good idea, as much as I hated to admit it. Fans adored when love interests had relationships both on and off the set; it made them see good chemistry between the stars whether it existed or not, and that made them think they were watching great performances.

Of course, the only problem was that Liam *wasn't* single, or at least, I hadn't thought he wanted to be. But he was in the meeting and he'd obviously agreed to go along with it and date Van instead, so where did that leave me?

The same place you were yesterday, an annoying little voice in my head pointed out. How could I have been so stupid as to think I was capable of being more than a hired hand and fashion consultant? Or naïve enough to believe a guy like Liam would want an actual relationship with me? Obviously it was all fun and games until it was time for the stars to shine.

No matter. I was at *Daylight Falls* because I needed the money and because I wanted to hang out with Vanessa. Even if there *was* something real between me and Liam, there was no way I would jeopardize either my job or her career for some guy, no matter how incredible a kisser he was or how sexily he said my name or how good it felt when he gently stroked my jawline with his fingers–

"A? Earth to Ally."

"Go for it," I replied weakly. "It sounds like a great idea."

"Okay, cool. And I'll totally need your help, because you are definitely better friends with him and I still have zero idea how to talk to him about anything other than the show." There was a muffled sound as she covered the phone and yelled, "I'm coming, dammit!" Then, "I gotta go, A." She hung up.

I stared at my phone for a good five minutes afterward, wondering if that had seriously just happened.

★★★★★

I was out of my room and deep into a Ben & Jerry's bender when my phone rang again, and this time, it *was* Liam. My stomach clenched, but I knew I had to deal with it.

"Hey," I greeted him, peeling myself off the couch in the den and walking into the kitchen to put the ice cream away.

"Can we meet up?" he asked without preamble.

I was tempted to stop him there, but I wanted to see him one last time before I had to deal with his face being mashed next to Van's in every single tabloid imaginable. I agreed, and we made a date to meet at the Lunchbox in half an hour. I figured that sitting in Van's and my favorite lunch spot would help strengthen my resolve to do what was best for her.

I searched frantically through my closet for something that screamed, "Remember how much you like me, even though the entire country will soon think you're dating my gorgeous best friend." Sadly, that wasn't something they sold at The Grove, so I settled for a cute jean miniskirt and the funky polka-dot top Van had given me last Christmas.

Judging by the appreciative way he looked me over when I strolled up, my outfit was just fine. He looked so annoyingly good in jeans and a button-down—even with a Lakers cap and sunglasses obscuring his handsome face—that I almost lost my resolve, but I reminded myself that I was at the home of the world's best peach pie sundae, so if it came to a second round of ice cream therapy, at least I was in the right place.

He started to stand when I approached, but I motioned for him to sit down. If he so much as touched me, I wasn't sure any amount of ice cream would make things better. I decided the best thing to do was just get down to business. I slid into the seat across from him, and when he opened his mouth to greet me, I held up my hand.

"Listen, Liam. I already know. Van called me. It's fine."

"It's not *fine*, Ally," he said, surprising me with his tone. "I don't want to follow through with this stupid plan, but I couldn't say anything because I didn't want to be the one to tell Vanessa about us. So are you gonna tell her so I can get us out of this mess?"

I nibbled on my lip while I got my bearings and the busboy came over with water. At no point in the hour since I'd spoken to Van did it even occur to me that Liam would rather be with me than follow Jade's orders. And I knew I couldn't let him—not if I wanted what was best for them, and not if I wanted to keep my job. I'd always kept my distance from Jade whenever possible, but if she found out I was behind the destruction of her publicity plan, she'd make sure even the Lunchbox wouldn't hire me.

"I'll tell Vanessa," I said slowly, "but you need to go through with Jade's plan."

"But Vanessa's your best friend," he replied, obviously confused. And hurt. "You want me to publicly date your best friend? Publicly *kiss* her?"

"Better someone I can trust than someone like Zoe, right?" I said with a cheerfulness I didn't remotely feel. We paused our conversation while a waiter came to take our orders (cheeseburgers with fries for both of us) and then I made sure the waiter was a safe distance away before I spoke again, taking care to keep my voice low. "Whether we like it or not, this *is* a good career move for both of you, and if I get in your way, not only will I feel awful about it, but Jade will probably make sure I don't get within a thousand feet of the *Daylight* set. Then I'll never get to see you *and* it's goodbye, Columbia."

He was silent for a full minute, and I was beginning to worry that he was going to get up and walk out when he said, "If I agree to the publicity stuff, do I still get to date and kiss *you*? Even if that confines us to takeout and movies in my apartment?"

My eyebrows shot up of their own volition. "Would *you* still want to date *me* if all that meant was getting takeout and watching movies in your apartment?" I returned. "And kissing, of course. There would definitely still be kissing."

He smiled softly, giving my sandaled foot a gentle nudge under the table with his sneakered one. "How could I not?"

I paused. "You are really, really good, Liam Holloway."

"No script or anything."

I put my elbow up on the table and balanced my chin in my palm. "I would really, really like to kiss you now."

"I would really, really like you to kiss me now," he replied, his voice husky.

"Should we get those burgers to go?"

He jumped up. "I'm on it."

★★★★★

The next few hours passed by in a lazy make-out haze, although I did make Liam run his lines with me once we eventually got down to eating.

"You're such a slave driver," he complained as he dragged one of his fries through our shared plate of ketchup.

"Isn't that what you like about me?" I asked innocently.

"Really, I just like the way you say *bonjour*," said Liam, eyes twinkling as he watched me watch him swipe a bit of ketchup off his lip with his tongue. "Something about the way you say it tells me I'm going to have a *very* good day."

I laughed and whacked him on the arm. "You've been spending too much time with Josh."

"I'm not kidding. Your French accent is super-hot."

I could feel myself blushing. "Super-hot" was not a description I was blessed with very often, but hell, I would gladly take it. "*Merci*," I mumbled, taking a sip of water.

"*Mon dieu*, you are cute," Liam said in an amazed voice that made me want to sink into the floor. "You would think no one's ever flirted with you before."

I shrugged meekly, unable to meet his gaze. "Maybe they haven't."

"Ally, that's not possible. You're hot and you're female. I guarantee you that guys have flirted with you; maybe you just haven't noticed."

I opened my mouth to respond that if he'd noticed who my best friend was, he might realize why I didn't get much attention from guys, but I really had no interest in making myself sound less desirable to Liam. Besides, maybe I'd grown up in Van's shadow, but I was out of it now. Judging by my "date" for the afternoon, I was doing just fine on my own.

"Maybe I just haven't been interested in responding to it until now," I replied instead, leaning across his little round table for a kiss.

I'd just been going in for a brief peck, but Liam immediately took the opportunity to bury his hands in my hair and kiss me so deeply it had my toes tingling. The burgers were instantly forgotten as we made our way back to the couch, but as soon as we hit the cushions, we were interrupted by the ringing of Liam's cell.

"Ugh." He sat up, smiling apologetically, and grabbed his phone from the coffee table. "What?" he grunted. Then he grew silent, apparently getting an earful from whoever was on the other end.

I decided to give him some privacy and went to the bathroom to swish some mouthwash and make sure there was no food in my teeth. When I returned, Liam was off the phone and clearly not a happy camper.

"Please don't kill me" was not the opening line I was expecting.

I narrowed my eyes. "What?"

He sighed. "That was one of Jade's people. They want me and Vanessa to go out and be seen. Tonight."

I exhaled sharply. Granted, I'd approved of the whole fake-dating plan, but I sure as hell didn't feel good about it. I thought I'd at least have a little time to get used to the idea. "Ally?" Liam walked over and cupped my cheek in his palm. "Are you okay?"

I nodded dumbly. "Yeah, it's fine."

"If you don't want me to–"

"Really, it's fine. I was just disappointed that we didn't get any French in today," I joked, interlacing the fingers of his free hand with mine.

"Oh, I would say–"

"The *language*," I cut him off, refusing to allow him to make that stupid joke again.

He grinned, and as my stomach did its usual flip-flop in response, I could barely fight the urge to beg him to stay. He must've noticed because he squeezed my hand and gave me a gentle kiss. "How do you say, 'I'll miss you'?"

"*Tu vas me manque.*"

"God, that sounds hot when you say it."

I whacked him on the shoulder again, but he caught my hand and brought it to his lips. "Promise me you'll stay away from the stupid tabloids and gossip sites."

I smiled. "Not to worry. Van's spent years ruining those for me with the truth behind the stories. I haven't read a gossip site in months, except for the articles announcing that Van got the part of Bailey."

"Good. Now let's spend the little bit of time we've got left doing something a little more fun than studying, because I don't want to *manque* you just yet."

★★★★★

I kept my word to Liam and stayed away from the gossip sites, but unfortunately, I couldn't stop everyone *else* from looking at them and coming up to me in the halls on Monday to ask questions about Van and her new boy toy, with whom she'd been photographed having a romantic dinner at some Italian restaurant.

"They're really cute," I said for the millionth time that day when Jennifer Chastain and Mia Prager practically chased me down in the hall to demand I tell them *everything*.

"So you've met Liam?" Mia's eyes grew wide. "Oh my God, is he as hot in person as he is onscreen?"

"He's so hot," Jennifer gushed. "Remember when I saw him at Fred Segal last year?"

"Jen, that totes wasn't him," said Mia.

No, *it definitely wasn't*, I thought. *Talk about a place Liam would never, ever shop for himself.*

"I'm telling you, he had red hair *for a role*," Jennifer whined, which only further cemented the fact that whomever she saw had *not* been Liam. But, with her and Mia arguing about Liam's doppelganger, I managed to escape and get myself to lunch. Not that I planned to sit—not unless I wanted to be bombarded by questions with every bite—but there were fish tacos on the menu, and I never, ever missed fish taco day.

"Exciting news about your friend today, huh?"

I whirled around, prepared to not-so-politely inform this newest gossip-hound that all I wanted was a damn fish taco, and found myself facing a grinning Nate. I breathed a sigh of relief, and then informed him that all I wanted was a damn fish taco.

We resumed the walk to the cafeteria. "So, is this why she doesn't want to date me? She's already got herself a boyfriend?"

"Yes, Nate," I said dryly. "That is the only reason that Vanessa—a girl who hasn't seen you in almost ten years—does not want to date you."

"Pretty impressive get as far as boyfriends go," he observed.

"Thank you," I replied without thinking.

He raised an eyebrow.

"On her behalf, obviously," I said quickly.

"Are you sure? Because you kind of sound like a lying liar right about now, Duncan."

I glanced at him. "You think I'm dating Liam Holloway?" I asked, curious if there was anyone on earth who would find it at all believable that we were together.

He laughed. "Obviously not. I do think you had something to do with the publicity stunt of their getting together, though."

Ouch. I grabbed his arm and pulled him aside. "For your information," I whispered tightly, "I *am* dating Liam, so shut the hell up. And if you tell anyone, I will tell the entire school that you still sleep with your baby blanket."

Nate's eyes searched my face, and I could tell he was trying to decide if I was telling the truth. I didn't so much as blink.

"No shit," he whispered.

"None at all," I replied. "But seriously, you can't tell anyone. I shouldn't have even told you. Hell, I haven't even told Van yet."

"Wha? How did you *not* tell Vanessa?"

I exhaled sharply. "She and Liam have been attached to each other—and to the cameras—this entire weekend. I want to tell her in person but I don't seem to be able to make that happen."

"Then just tell her over the phone," Nate suggested. "She's going to be seriously pissed at you if she finds out from someone else."

"Trust me, I know." The truth was there was a tiny part of me that didn't *want* to tell her. I was too afraid that it was just some sort of ridiculous dream and, in about five minutes, he was going to realize that he was about as interested in me as Van was in Nate. Then going to work would not only mean suffering through seeing him but enduring looks of pity from Vanessa as well. Not that I was going to tell any of that to Nate.

"I'll call her after lunch. Come on, let's go."

"Just call her now, Duncan. What are you waiting for?"

"I'm not calling her now just so you can bug me to get on the phone with her."

He grinned. "Am I that transparent?"

"Yes. Now come on. I want a damn fish taco."

THE ENTIRE WEEK WAS A bizarre and confusing mess. I continued to help out during their last week on set and pretend I didn't want to hurl when I listened to Vanessa recount all the funny and crazy things that happened on their "dates." I even managed to have the occasional conversation with Liam and even more occasional "break" in his trailer when Van was in a scene without him. However, at the end of every day, it was Liam and Vanessa who left together to create another "couple alert" while I returned home to life as a pathetic high schooler.

I'd decided to wait until after filming to tell Vanessa about me and Liam, figuring it would lessen any potential awkwardness on set. After all, it was only a few more days, and I kind of liked having the time to adjust to having a boyfriend before I had to talk about it. He was like my fun little secret, and, to paraphrase him, getting to hide in his trailer with him for a while at the end of a long evening sure made my day not suck.

Still, I was almost relieved to be back in the hospital with my dad during spring break the next week, just for the sake of putting life into a little perspective.

Unfortunately, even on meds, my dad could tell something was up.

"What's the matter, honey?" he asked fuzzily, reaching out a hand to stroke my head while we watched some boring talk show on TV. We had to watch it on fairly low volume; private rooms weren't covered by insurance, and we could no longer afford for my dad to have one.

"Nothing important," I said dismissively. "How are you holding up? Do you want another blanket?"

"Nah, I'm okay." He smiled weakly, and I smiled back, but God, it was hard to watch him like that. His body was retaining water, and it was making him bloat in his button-down PJs. His hair, which had previously held just a sprinkling of salt and pepper, was starting to get seriously gray at the temples. His skin looked ashy, and he was constantly hiccupping. But, of course, he never complained for a minute. "Can we watch something else, though? This is incredibly boring."

I laughed and reached forward to squeeze his foot, the only body part sticking out of the blanket that wasn't hooked up to wires. "Hey, you know your feet are weirdly soft?"

"Yeah, that's because the stuff running through my system right now makes me shed all the skin there."

"Oh. Gross."

He smiled, clearly tired, and ruffled my hair again before turning over in an attempt to fall asleep.

I flipped through the channels, but nothing looked any more interesting, so I stopped flipping and settled back in the sleeper chair, hoping to catch a little nap myself. I was jolted out of my seat two minutes later, though, by the sound of Van's voice.

"Liam's so great. With the two of us, it was really just, like, instant chemistry, you know? He's such a gentleman, and he's so smart."

I rubbed my eyes and sat up while I tried to determine where her voice was coming from, and a shift in the bed next to me revealed that my dad was doing the same.

"Is that Van on TV?" Dad asked.

Sure enough, there she was, being interviewed by Madison Something-Something, going on and on about all of Liam's wonderful attributes. At least she was being accurate.

"Yup, that's her," I confirmed. "Cute dress, too." I wondered if that was a new purchase or if she'd been styled. It looked like she'd just been ambushed on the street, though. It took me a moment to realize that Liam was at her side, his eyes on the ground as he trailed a foot or two behind.

"She has a new boyfriend?"

I tipped my head. "Sort of."

"Do we like him?"

"We like him very much," I confirmed, afraid to say any more in case his roommate might have been listening. "He's a great guy."

"Good," Dad murmured, already starting to slip back to sleep. I waited until I heard the sound of his light snoring before padding out to the waiting area with cell phone in hand.

Liam picked up on the second ring. "Hey, Al." I could hear the smile in his voice, and even over the phone, it seemed to brighten up the dull hospital walls. "How's your dad?"

"He's okay. He had to move into a shared room because private ones aren't covered by insurance and they're, like, thousands of dollars more. It's making him pretty miserable, but right now he's asleep. We actually just saw you on TV, sort of."

He groaned. "That stupid ambush interview from last night?"

"That's the one. Did you at least get better food this time?"

"Sushi. It's a step up, but still not as good as pizza with my actual girlfriend," he replied, dropping his voice for the last bit.

I had to bite my lip to keep from smiling too broadly. "Sorry you're suffering so much," I teased. "Your actual girlfriend is *very* available for pizza tonight if you are. It's kind of awkward being in the room with that other guy so I think I'll probably leave soon anyway."

"I—" The rest of his response was lost in the sound of an argument going on behind him. "Sorry, one sec," he murmured into the phone. I heard some more arguing, and then Liam muttered, "You're fucking kidding me."

"Everything okay?"

"Zoe came in hung over and can't seem to remember any of her lines. We're gonna be here forever. I'm—"

The yelling that cut him off this time was *much* louder, and I realized that he was the target. I winced when I finally recognized Zoe's voice screaming, "Who the hell are you talking to, Liam? That had better not be the press! I will kill you!"

I quickly hung up the phone, suddenly terrified for both Liam's and my safety. Zoe had mostly limited herself to the occasional nasty comment about why I was on set so often and diatribes about why she deserved to be Bailey, but I'd hate to be on the receiving end of her genuine wrath.

I scrambled back into my dad's room to grab my stuff. If I wasn't going to stick around here and I wasn't going to see Liam, I had a practice AP to take.

★★★★★

I went to sleep on the later end that night, opting to take my mom's mind off my dad's absence with a chick flick and a pint of Cherry Garcia, but I'd been asleep for hours when I heard my cell phone ring. A quick glance at my alarm clock revealed that it was a little after 3:00 a.m., and I had no idea who would've been calling me that late, although I hoped it was Liam since we hadn't gotten another chance to talk that day.

Sure enough, his name and an adorable picture I'd taken of him in his apartment flashed onscreen. "Hey there," I greeted him sleepily.

There was no answer on his end.

"Liam?" I yawned. "Hey, babe, you called me, remember? How was the rest of your day? I hope it was worth missing out on pizza with me."

Silence, and then Zoe's voice, cold and triumphant: "I knew it."

Shit.

"Zoe, what the hell are you doing on Liam's phone at 3:00 a.m.?"

"What the hell are you doing *expecting* a call from Liam at 3:00 a.m.?" she returned smugly.

"It's not what you think," I said lamely, too sleepy and fuzzy-brained to think of anything less cliché to say.

"Oh, really?" she said mockingly, ignoring my question. "So you're not secretly dating Liam while he pretends to date Vanessa so the two of them can become even bigger stars while I get shoved into the background?"

Okay, maybe it was exactly what it sounded like.

"It must kill you to watch them, doesn't it?"

"Not as much as it apparently kills you," I replied, immediately realizing that it was pretty much the stupidest thing I could've said. *Way to confirm everything, Alexandra. Job well done. And while simultaneously antagonizing her! Do they let people that stupid go to Columbia?* "Listen, Zoe, I'm not going to call any gossip sites and tell them you were out partying or whatever. *Daylight Falls* secrets are just that—secrets. I get it. I promise."

"Do you, Vanessa's Little Friend? Because you are around an awful lot, and you don't seem to get that you don't belong there."

I will not let her bait me. I will not let her bait me. "Uh-huh," I responded through gritted teeth. "So is that what you want? Me to be around less? Consider it done. Isn't this your last week of filming anyway?"

"I don't want anything," Zoe said smoothly. "After all, you probably hate Vanessa just as much as I do for doing this to you, no? That's good enough for me—just having someone else acknowledge that she is a thieving bitch."

I barked a laugh. "Oh, please. That part was never yours, and it wasn't even her idea to audition for Bailey. If you're looking for a co-prez of the 'I Hate Vanessa Park' fan club, you're not gonna find it here."

"So you really don't mind that it was her idea to date Liam for publicity even though he's your boyfriend?"

"Nice try, Zoe," I snapped. "It was *not* Vanessa's idea. She doesn't even know—" I froze, realizing my mistake as the words came out of my mouth, but it was too late.

Zoe's laughter floated over the phone, and I winced against the harsh sound. "Goodnight, Vanessa's Little Friend," she cooed, and then she hung up.

Oh God, oh God, oh God. Despite the ridiculously late hour, I immediately called Van. It went straight to voicemail. I tried again. Same thing. I hoped the third time would be the charm, but when it wasn't, I left her a message telling her we had to talk first thing in the morning. With nothing else to do, I put my phone away and attempted to fall back asleep.

★★★★★

I don't know when I finally dozed off, but I woke up bright and early with a feeling of dread still sitting heavy on my shoulders. No missed calls from Van, probably because she wasn't even up yet, but I knew I had to try her again and get to her before Zoe did.

No chance I was going to be able to get through this phone call without a morning coffee, though. I swapped my nightshirt for my comfiest jeans and the worn-out *Viva la France!* T-shirt my mom had given me when I got my first A+ in French. Then I slipped on my flip-flops, grabbed my car keys, and I was good to go.

I shuffled down the stairs as quietly as I could so as not to wake my mom and made a mad dash for the front door. I could practically inhale the wonderful scent of Coffee Bean & Tea Leaf from here.

Unfortunately, I had a much ruder awakening waiting for me.

"There she is!"

"Alexandra Duncan, is it true *you're* the one who's dating Liam Holloway?"

"Ally, over here! What does your *best friend* Vanessa Park think of the fact that *you're* dating her onscreen boyfriend?"

"Ally! Are you and Vanessa still friends, despite the fact that you stole her boyfriend?"

"Miss Duncan! Miss Duncan! Who stole whose boyfriend? Were you dating Liam Holloway, or was she?"

Holy mother of God.

Panicked, I screamed the same thing I'd seen Vanessa say way more casually on a number of occasions: "No comment." Then I jumped back into the house and slammed the door behind me. My heart was pounding, and despite the fact that it was still pleasant out this early in the morning, I could feel myself sweating from head to toe.

Who would do this to me? The obvious answer was Zoe, but how would she have any clue where I lived? Plus, I'd already told her I wouldn't talk to the paparazzi about her drinking, so why would she send them straight to my door?

I wouldn't have thought it was possible, but my stomach dropped even further, and I started to shake so hard I needed to grab onto the kitchen counter for balance. Was it possible Van had done this? Had Zoe gotten to her first and made her so angry that she'd sicced the paparazzi on me? After all, she knew this sort of thing was my worst nightmare and one of the absolute biggest reasons I had no desire for her life. The revenge was almost too perfect for it to have been anyone else.

Still, it was hard to imagine Van wanting to hurt me this much just for keeping one measly secret from her. (Okay, so it wasn't so measly. Still.) After all, I wasn't the only one who came out bad in this scenario; it didn't really do any favors for her either. God, I hoped that meant it was Zoe, even if the idea that Little Miss Crazy had my home address chilled me to the bone.

Before I could contemplate any further, my cell phone rang. *Please, please tell me the paparazzi doesn't have my number now.* I checked the caller ID, praying it wouldn't be a restricted number. Instead, I saw Liam's name and the picture that used to make me smile and now made me want to throw up.

I was tempted to ignore it but knew that I couldn't. "Zoe?" I asked immediately. "What did you do?"

"Ally!" It was indeed Liam, and he sounded relieved to hear my voice. I couldn't decide yet how I felt about hearing his. "I heard what happened. Are you okay?"

I was still shaking, so no, I was probably not okay. I told him as much.

"Al, I'm so sorry—"

"How do you have your phone?" I interrupted him.

"What do you mean?"

"Zoe called me on your phone all of four hours ago. How is it possible that she had your phone at 3:00 a.m. and you have it now?"

Liam groaned. "That bitch. My doorman handed it to me this morning when I went out for a run, said someone turned it in. She must've stolen my phone and then come by my building to drop it off after she called you."

I inhaled sharply. What the hell was happening to my life? How had I become a walking, talking episode of *Daylight Falls*? I couldn't deal with this now. Not with my father in the hospital and me without my coffee and psychotic starlets out to ruin my life.

"Look, Liam, I have to go. Can we talk later?"

"Yeah," he said quietly, his voice still tinged with concern. "Sure."

All I wanted was to climb back into bed for the rest of the day. So I hung up with Liam, tossed my cell phone onto the kitchen counter, and did exactly that.

★★★★★

When I finally emerged from my room, it was nightfall, and I was relieved to see my mom downstairs, unharmed, and an empty front lawn. I could tell from the look on my mom's face that she had a zillion questions and no idea where to start, but she simply said, "I sent Lucy to sleep at a friend's."

"Definitely a good idea," I replied, walking to the fridge. I was starving after my day of self-imposed exile. "I'm really sorry about this whole mess, Mom."

"Would you mind explaining exactly what's going on?" she asked, and I could tell she was trying to keep her voice calm.

I sighed, pushing around various containers on the shelf until I found some leftover tuna casserole that had been brought by one of the neighbors. "I wish I knew exactly what was going on."

"Is it true that you're dating this boy?"

"I was," I said with a shrug, putting the casserole in the oven; I suspected my mom hadn't eaten much either. "Not sure if I still will be after today."

"And he was Vanessa's boyfriend?" she asked, sounding confused.

"Only for paparazzi purposes." I explained how the publicists had set it all up before I'd even gotten a chance to tell Vanessa there was something going on between me and Liam. "Anyway, now everything's a mess and there's a part of me that's afraid that Van's the one who did this to me."

"Sweetheart." My mom walked over and tucked a messy strand of my hair behind my ear. "You know Vanessa. She would never do this to you, to us. Especially not with your father like this." At the mention of my father, I felt a wrenching in my gut. None of us had visited him today, thanks to the monsters in the front yard. He was all alone. Well, not *all* alone—he had his grumpy stranger roommate. I only hoped my dad was too out of it on meds to notice that he'd had no company.

"That may be true," I said, "but I knew better than to let Van find out from someone else that I had a boyfriend, so who knows? Things have changed."

"I'm sure they haven't changed as much as that." She walked over and kissed me on the forehead. "I'm going to go visit your father. Your phone rang a few dozen times while you were in your room. You might want to see to that." She left me alone in the kitchen, my traitorous cell still on the counter where I'd left it and the smell of tuna casserole filling the air.

I picked up the phone and scrolled through the missed calls, grimacing at the number of them that had come from numbers that were either restricted or totally foreign to me. Peppered in with those were several from Dana, Leni, Liam, Van, and a text from Nate that just said, "Nice going, Duncan."

No chance I was dealing with Dana and Leni now, and I still wasn't quite sure what I wanted to do about Liam. I did know, however, that I needed to talk to Van ASAP. I immediately dialed her back, and she picked up on the first ring.

"A! Are you okay?"

"Still breathing," I assured her. I hesitated before saying anything else. On the one hand, I wanted to apologize for keeping Liam a secret. On the other hand, if she *was* behind this, I was a whole lot less sorry.

"Liam told me what Zoe did. I swear, that girl is crazy."

I breathed a sigh of relief. It *was* Zoe. Thank the Lord. "An absolute psycho," I agreed. "How did she even get my address?"

"No clue," said Van, "but she's a serious creep. It doesn't surprise me that she could track it down."

"Listen, Van, I'm so sorry I didn't tell you about Liam. I just wanted you to be able to do what was best for your career and I really didn't want to make things weird for you."

"I really wish you would've just told me the truth so I could've made an educated decision when Jade asked us to do this. I never would have agreed if I had known."

"I know. That's why I didn't tell you."

"That's not how things work, Ally. You're supposed to be the one person I can trust, and in return, I expect you to trust me to make decisions about my career based on all the facts. Okay? You might not have faith that my show will do fine without a stupid publicity stunt, but I do."

I winced. Van sounded more authoritative and, well, adult than I had ever heard her. She sounded hurt, too, which was something I never wanted to hear in her voice, especially not as a result of something I'd done. "Van, I'm really, really sorry. I promise I wasn't trying to suggest that I thought you *needed* it. I was just trying to do what I thought was best for you. You've done so much for me, especially lately, and it felt like the only way I could return the favor."

She paused before responding, and I was afraid that she was going to lecture me again. Instead, she said, "Actually, you can return the favor by giving me some deets on the BF like you've probably been dying to do for days anyway. So can I come over now or what?"

"Yes," I breathed, so incredibly relieved at the idea of having my best friend back and being able to talk to her about things like a normal human being. "Please God. And bring some ice cream with you. This tuna casserole is just not gonna cut it."

UNFORTUNATELY, THE PAPARAZZI continued to arrive at my house in droves the next day, in addition to calling my cell and—I discovered when I finally checked—bombarding my e-mail account. Fortunately, Lucy was still at her friend's, and my mom braved it to get into the car and away from the house so she could spend the day at the hospital with my dad.

Knowing I wouldn't be able to escape nearly as easily, I stayed locked in my house for yet another day. I tried calling Liam, to no avail, and Van wasn't picking up either, so my day was full of nothing but scholarship applications, random schoolwork, and forcing myself to return Dana's and Leni's calls. All in all, not my ideal day, but it picked up considerably when my mom got home in the early afternoon and informed me that my dad had miraculously been switched to a private room at no cost to us and was now much, much happier.

"At least one thing is going well," I murmured, flopping back down on the couch to return to my viewing of a *Simpsons* rerun.

"Is this really how you want to spend your time?" Mom asked, pouring herself a glass of juice. "This doesn't seem like much of a break for you, honey. Nor do you seem very 'springy.' Isn't there anything you could be doing that doesn't involve locking yourself in our house, the set, or the hospital?"

I was about to respond that no, in fact there wasn't, when I remembered my brief conversation with Nate in which he mentioned hanging out with him and his friends. Despite the fact that both hanging out with his friends and exposing myself to UV rays held zero appeal to me, getting out of the house to do something normal sounded kind of...awesome.

"Excellent suggestion, Mom," I replied, shutting off the TV and walking over to kiss her on the cheek. "I think I'll see about doing just that." I dug my cell phone out of my back pocket while I walked upstairs to my room and promptly called Nate.

"Yo, Duncan, what up?"

"How genuine was your offer to hang out?" I asked without preamble.

"Totally and completely," he responded. "I'm actually going to the beach in a bit with a bunch of guys from school. Any interest?"

"In hanging out with a bunch of guys?"

"I was using it in the...whatever sense includes both guys and girls in there."

"Gotcha. And yes, I have interest."

"Cool, I'll pick you up in, say, half an hour? You're on Highland, right?"

"Right. Awesome. Thanks, Donovan."

"No prob, Duncan. See you then."

And just like that, I had real-life, high school-senior plans.

★★★★★

An hour and one liberal coat of SPF 70 later, I was stretched out on a towel between Nate and Macy Easton, blocking out some late-afternoon sun while devouring a historical romance novel.

"I can't believe you're reading on the beach," said Macy in that high-pitched voice of hers, sweeping her long, blond hair back into a ponytail. "And isn't SPF 70 a little extreme?"

"Not when your dad has skin cancer," I replied without so much as a glance in her direction.

She winced, and I instantly felt bad. It's not like she knew, and before the melanoma, I would've probably thought anyone who wore above 30 was nuts too.

"I should probably acquaint myself with a spray tanner," I conceded, putting down the book. "I could definitely use some color."

She simply nodded, which made me feel even more awkward.

"So now what do you guys do?" I asked, eager to recapture the normalcy of the afternoon.

Macy just continued to look at me strangely for another moment, and then she lit up with a smile. "Hey, I know. You could tell us what's *really* going on with you and Liam Holloway."

I'm embarrassed to admit that I did not see that coming; I was so wrapped up in the idea of a normal afternoon that I'd forgotten that my now-abnormal life would still follow me absolutely everywhere.

Fortunately, Nate chose just that moment to come save me. "Hey, Duncan, let's go in the water."

I flashed my best apologetic smile at Macy and dashed off to join Nate, relishing the cool breeze against my skin and warm sand under my toes as we headed toward the ocean. "Sorry about that," he said as we waded in cautiously. "I forgot that Macy's an obsessive gossip fiend. The guys are cool, though."

As if on cue, two of said guys, Sam Washington and Chase Marino, joined us in the water. "Hey, Bro," Chase greeted Nate. "Hey, Ally."

Hellos were said all around, just in time for a big wave to throw me down on my butt.

The guys all laughed, and Sam immediately reached a hand down to help me up. "Careful, the waves are really rough out there," he teased.

"Yeah, that's exactly why I had to give up my competitive surfing career," I joked, rubbing my bruised backside in what I hoped was a subtle attempt to get the sand out of my bikini bottom.

The guys laughed again, and just like that, my stupid slip was forgotten as the conversation changed to imagined hobbies and water sports. We stayed in the water for a while, joking about nothing and jumping over waves, and when it got chilly, we got a volleyball game going and I got to show off my negligible athletic prowess.

The afternoon was fun, but even as I joked with Sam, spiked sets by Macy, and talked classic rock with Chase, I couldn't help wishing that Van was the one offering me terrible sangria from a Thermos. I certainly wished that Liam, and not Nate, was the one rubbing a new coat of sunscreen on my back. Most of all, I wondered what my dad would think of the fact that I was lying in the sun, exposing myself to the very same elements that had him lying in a hospital bed that day.

But of course Van and Liam weren't there, because they were actors, and they were too busy with their soul-sucking, all-consuming jobs to do the things normal teenagers did, the things I should've been doing every day instead of running lines, researching belly-dancing classes to find out which one would best improve Vanessa's abs for her bikini scenes, and dodging cameras. And in my heart, I knew nothing would've made my dad happier than seeing me out and having a good time. Which I was. Mostly.

"You okay there, Duncan?" Nate asked, wiping his hands on his thighs and reaching into a small cooler to offer me a can of beer, which I politely declined.

I shrugged. "Just thinking."

"You do way too much thinking. There's no way I'm the first person who's ever told you that."

I smiled weakly and wrapped my arms tighter around my knees. The sun was starting to dip below the horizon, and though it was beautiful, there was a slight chill in the air that made me think it might be time to pack it in and head home. "How'd you guess?"

"I'd say you're predictable, but I think you've proven otherwise in the last couple of weeks," he said with a grin, popping open the can. "So, did you have a decent time today?"

"Yeah, I really did, thank you. Nice of you to let me tag along."

He pulled his knees up to his chest and took a long sip from the can. "I wouldn't call it 'tagging along,' but I'm glad you had fun. You should come hang out more often."

"Sure, maybe." I wasn't sure when I'd have the time now that spring break was ending and I was going to have to kick the studying into high gear. Plus the last day of shooting on the pilot was next week, and then Van would need actual assistance handling her auditions for summer projects. But it was nice to think it was possible, to know the option was out there. Besides, barring what would basically be a scientific miracle, I'd need a *lot* of distractions come August, when my dad's projected six-month lifespan hit its end.

He shook his head. "Why is it that you'll do just about anything for Vanessa but you can't commit to anything when it comes to your own life?"

"You say that like the two are disconnected," I pointed out. "Working for Vanessa *is* committing to something for my life. She's helping me go to college. You realize that, right?"

"Yes, but—"

"And it's not like she's my *raison d'etre*," I reminded him. "For your information, I haven't been on set all week. The only place I've gone besides the beach today is the hospital."

"Because you were trapped in your house by paparazzi," he responded with a grin, bringing the can back up to his mouth for another swig.

"What's your point, Walter?" I deadpanned, quoting *The Big Lebowski*, which I knew was one of Nate's favorite movies.

"My point is that this isn't you. Don't you ever just stop and think that you're living the wrong life?"

"And what life should I be living, exactly?"

I expected a quick response but there was none, and I realized from the look on his face that he'd expected neither to say the words that had come out of his mouth nor to hear the ones that had come out of mine. He suddenly seemed...dazed. I wondered if he was drunk, but I was pretty sure he was on his first beer.

Oh. God. He was going to kiss me.

I froze, completely panicked. The idea of bringing up Liam after that conversation seemed ridiculous, and yet, he *was* my boyfriend, wasn't he? At least, for all intents and don't-kiss-other-people purposes.

But then, he was probably out with Van at that very moment, locked at the lips for all of Hollywood to see and all of America to read about. I knew he didn't have feelings for her, but kissing someone else was kissing someone else, wasn't it? I didn't feel a damn thing for Nate, but the thought of him touching his lips to mine made me want to hurl.

So why didn't the thought of kissing Vanessa seem to do the same for Liam?

"Surf's up!" Nate declared suddenly, jumping to his feet so quickly that he sloshed beer on his board shorts. Without another word to me, he ran off to the ocean, leaving me alone without so much as his half-empty can.

★★★★★

I'd made a concerted effort not to check my phone all day—an easy task since the glare from the sun made it impossible to read the screen anyway—so I felt bad when I returned home only to find that I had a couple of missed calls from both Van and Liam. Compelled by the BFF code (and my lingering guilt), I called Van back first and ended up killing two birds with one stone.

"Hey, A! Where have you been?" I started to explain that I'd been at the beach, but she cut me off. "I'm in the car with Liam, and I'm putting you on speaker."

No, that funny feeling in the pit of my stomach wasn't jealousy that they had spent the day together. Not. At. All.

"Hey, Al," Liam said in that low, sexy voice that always made me feel all melty, and suddenly I felt bad that I'd been caught calling Van first.

I didn't have much time to dwell on the petty politics of return phone calls, though, because Van immediately jumped in again. "We're just coming from a meeting with Jade, and we talked about how to fix this whole thing. We're gonna give an interview together to say that it's all a stupid misunderstanding, someone for some reason leaked bad info to the press—"

"Someone?" I said wryly. "You sure you don't want to call out Zoe? Because I sure do."

"Trust me," said Van, "I wish we could. Anyway, we'll confirm that we're dating, explain that you're my assistant and obviously have to deal with Liam sometimes, et cetera, et cetera. Everything should blow over in no time."

Yeah, maybe. But something about the way they'd once again made a whole plan without asking my input until the end didn't sit quite right. After all, this was my life too, and I might not have been a star but I *should* have had a say in my own relationship. Besides, if I was going to stay on board with this stupid publicity plan, I needed to know that my opinions would matter.

"I have an even better idea," I said slowly as a plan that was either incredibly brilliant or incredibly stupid formed in my mind.

"Do you?" Liam sounded amused but curious, and I hated that I couldn't see his face.

"I do," I said firmly. "How about we go on a double date? I'll bring Nate. You can announce that we're obviously not together, seeing as I have my own boyfriend; Nate gets a date with his dream girl; and you and I finally get to go 'out' out on a date. Everybody wins." *Plus, it'll remind Nate that I'm* not *available to be maybe-kissed*, I mentally added, though I clearly wasn't going to say that out loud.

"Yeah, everyone but me," said Vanessa, but from the teasing note of her voice, it was obvious she would do it. "Call Nate. Tell him he's got a date."

"What do you think, Liam?" I prodded.

"I think...that I'd do pretty much any stupid thing if it meant seeing you tonight. Oh, stop making that gagging face, Vanessa."

"You guys are gross."

I laughed. "Just you wait, Van," I said cheerfully, glowing from Liam's sweet words. "Maybe you and Nate are meant to be."

THEY WEREN'T.

It wasn't hard to get Nate on board—he *loved* the idea of witnessing the whole spectacle, not to mention getting to see Van in the miniskirt I promised she'd be wearing. Once the date—a late dinner at some Mexican restaurant I'd never even heard of but which Jade had apparently put a lot of thought into—actually got underway, however, it quickly became clear they had nothing in common.

"Get it?" he tried explaining to Vanessa for the third time. "The dog is a *robot*."

"Right, right. A robot." She took another sip of the sparkling water in front of her and shot me a sideways glance.

At least, I'm pretty sure she did; I was otherwise occupied, playing a voracious game of footsie with Liam under the table. Suddenly, I heard my cell phone beep with a text, and I glanced at it.

You look seriously gorgeous in that dress. Just thought you should know.

Heat rose to my cheeks but I forced myself not to outwardly acknowledge the compliment. I was about to text him back when I heard a minor commotion near our table. I looked up and saw that it was just a couple of teen girls coming to ask Van and Liam for their autographs.

"Hmm, how come they don't want ours?" I joked to Nate, but he didn't even smile. I couldn't really blame him; he and Van weren't clicking in the slightest.

"Guess peons aren't so exciting," he muttered back.

I punched him in the knee. "Can't you at least pretend to have a decent time? Like, literally just freaking pretend? You're on a date with a hot girl in a good restaurant. Seriously, how miserable can you actually be?"

"I'll be a lot less when my food actually gets here," he grumbled.

"We just ordered five minutes ago," I reminded him. "Just eat some chips and shut up."

"Shouldn't your superstar friends be getting us some special treatment or something?"

I rolled my eyes and pointedly plucked a chip from the basket in the middle of the table. "Being on TV can't magically cook your nachos any faster, Donovan." I dipped it in guacamole and popped it in my mouth.

He grumbled something unintelligible, and I didn't even bother asking him to repeat it. Instead, I figured I'd try to see if I could get a conversation going that would actually interest both Van and Nate so that he'd have a better time. I racked my brain for something they had in common, but came up empty. Van loved TV, clothes, detective novels, and pretty much everything British. The only thing I knew Nate watched on TV was soccer, he'd once told me he wished school had uniforms so he wouldn't need to waste five seconds of thought on what to wear in the morning, I'd never seen him read a book for fun, and I had no idea where he stood on the UK except that I'd once heard him humming Oasis.

Vanessa ended up speaking first, only it was to me, not Nate. "You look tan," she observed. "I think you got some more freckles, too. Does this mean you actually left the house since last we spoke?"

"We went to the beach today," said Nate as I lifted my hand self-consciously to my nose. I'd never been crazy about my freckles. "It was a lot of fun. Ally actually hung out with some people besides you guys and those two wastes of space she calls friends."

"Nate!"

"What?" He shot me an innocent look. "Don't pretend you like them."

"Dana and Leni?" asked Van. "They're nice. What's wrong with them?" She turned to me. "You don't like them?"

I shifted uncomfortably in my seat. Why was Nate doing this? He seemed almost mad at me, but I had no idea what I'd done to earn that. Wasn't this pretty much what he'd been begging me to do for him for months?

"They're fine," I said, shooting Nate a quick look of death. I was relieved to see a waiter approaching as I did so. "Hey, food's here!"

Thank God. Plus, I was pretty damn hungry by then. I had to sit on my hands to stop myself from reaching out to pluck a nacho from the huge platter we'd ordered before the waiter could even place it on the table.

"Mmm, that looks awesome," said Van. "We've barely had anything to eat all day."

There was that "we" again. Not that I noticed.

Liam took a chip loaded with absolutely everything imaginable and devoured it in one bite. "Ohhh, that's good," he moaned as he swallowed it down with a sip of water. "Nachos are seriously up there on my list of things I could eat every damn day for the rest of my life."

"I love that all your favorite foods are the kinds of things that could be sold at roadside stands," I teased. "I remember when we went out to dinner at some French place to celebrate Van's first successful audition—"

"Aaah, for that totally stupid doll commercial!" Van giggled. "So mortifying to think about it now."

"Aw, it was a cute commercial," I assured her. "Anyway, remember when your parents fed you escargot without telling you what it was and you absolutely *loved* it until they mentioned after dinner that it was snails?"

She moaned. "I remember throwing up all over the parking lot, that's what I remember."

I laughed. "I remember that too, especially since I was so freaked out by the fact that you actually *liked* them until that. That's how I knew you were meant to be a star—you obviously had expensive, fancy taste."

"Oh, really? It wasn't my stunning, natural charisma?"

"Is that the same stunning, natural charisma that convinced me to cut all the hair off my Barbie dolls when we were four?"

Liam laughed. "You don't even let me pick movie snacks and you let her dictate the hairstyles of your favorite toys?"

I shrugged innocently and snatched a cheesy chip from the bottom of the pile. "I eventually got her back by giving her a terrible haircut during a sleepover when we were eight. Is that the sort of revenge you would like, Mr. Holloway?"

"I remember that!" Van shrieked. "I had an audition two days later, too! I think that was the maddest I've ever been at you."

As we joked around and stuffed our faces, Nate eventually warmed up and joined the conversation, and for a minute, I thought we might actually end up having a good night.

Of course, that's exactly when the flashbulbs swooped in.

"Vanessa! Liam! Over here!"

"Here! Over here!"

A microphone was thrust in my face. "Is it true that you're really just friends and they're the ones who are dating?"

I was tempted to say "no comment," but this was exactly why we were here tonight. "Yes," I said, pasting a smile on my face and recalling the lines we'd practiced. "As you can see, I have my own boyfriend." I wrapped a possessive arm around Nate's shoulders. "I guess people just can't wait until *Daylight Falls* starts to get their fill of teen drama!"

The reporter laughed, and several others crowded around, firing questions in our direction, but after we'd established the general party line, they switched over to focusing solely on Van and Liam, leaving me and Nate with nothing to do but watch.

"This is gross," Nate muttered as he dragged a chip through the guac, drawing angry lines in the chunky green dip.

"Then don't eat it," I said sweetly through the fake smile plastered on my face.

He snorted. "Yeah, because I'm talking about the food, Duncan."

I took a sip from my water glass, peering at Van and Liam's intertwined hands over the rim. It really *was* gross. *They're just playing pretend*, I reminded myself as I let a piece of ice fall into my mouth and bit down on it. *They're actors. It's what they do.*

Obviously Nate wasn't going to help distract me from the train wreck in front of me, so I decided that the best way to face it was head on. If I saw how clearly fake they were being, it would remind me just how staged and stupid this whole thing was, right?

"So, lovebirds, tell us, what do you do in your free time?" asked a balding reporter wearing a pair of way-too-tight pinstriped pants.

Van flashed her perfect "no question is too stupid" smile. "Same things as every other couple. We have dinner out with our friends, we see movies, we go shopping, we go to the gym..."

My eyes were threatening to roll out of their skull. Liam would never go shopping voluntarily, and he absolutely hated going to the gym. If I needed to be convinced this was all fake, that certainly–

"You guys are so cute," said another photographer, this one a woman with bleached-blond hair and a crooked front tooth. "I mean, look at you two! You can't keep your hands off each other!"

Huh? I interrupted my mental pep talk to take a better look at Van and Liam. Sure enough, she'd settled into the crook of his arm with an ease and comfort that made it look like she practically lived there, and her perfectly manicured hand curved around his denim-clad kneecap without a hint of self-consciousness. Their words might've rung falser to me than a Real Housewife's boobs, but their gestures...

"Excuse me," I said to absolutely nobody as I slipped out of my seat and walked to the *chicas'* room in the back of the restaurant. I wasn't sure whether

I was about to cry or throw up my nachos, but both were seriously bad choices for public viewing.

A minute later, the door pushed open, and I scrambled into a stall to hide, but not fast enough.

"Duncan?"

"Nate! What the hell are you doing in the ladies' room?"

"Uh, coming to find you, obviously? Now can we please get out of here?"

I examined my face in the mirror. Now-streaky eyeliner? Check. Mascara everywhere? Yup. Red and blotchy mess? Of course.

"Just give me a minute." I attacked my face with a damp paper towel, but though the black streaks disappeared, the blotchiness did not. I blew out a breath and exited the bathroom with Nate anyway.

"Are you really going to deny that this is killing you?" Nate challenged.

"Just shut up, Donovan." I pressed my fingertips to my temples. My head was pounding, I couldn't think, and he really wasn't making things better.

"You need to stop this," he continued, ignoring me completely. "You obviously can't handle it."

"Just shut up!" I repeated, whispering fiercely. "Stop pretending you give a shit. You're just pissed because you have no idea how to talk to the girl you've been fantasizing about going on a date with for God knows how long. I'm sorry you haven't enjoyed your evening, but stop trying to make it about me. She's the one you need to be working on."

"I know that," he spat. "But..." The venom seemed to drain out of him as quickly as it entered, and suddenly he looked strange and young and helpless.

"But what?" I pushed. We'd been gone from the table long enough, and I really didn't want this argument to drag on any longer than it had to. Not that I could imagine returning to my seat. I felt overheated and tightly wound and in no mood to chow down on copious amounts of beef and cheese.

"But she's *not* the one I care about, Ally."

"Wha– Oh. *Oh*."

He looked down at the floor. "Yeah."

"Nate, you can't... I mean, I can't..."

"I know," he snapped. "Trust me, I'm not any happier about it than you are."

"Hey, don't get mad at me! I *told* you I was with–" I looked around to make sure no one was listening. "–Liam," I finished, dropping my voice just in case.

Nate snorted. "Yeah, I see how much you're 'with' him," he said, obnoxious air quotes and all. "He's in there right now making out with your best friend for everyone to see, and you're hiding in the bathroom with a fake boyfriend who *actually* likes you. How is it possible that you operate in a world where all of this makes sense to you?"

"How is it possible that you like me when you have the world's lowest opinion of me?" I countered. "God, it's like everything out of your mouth is about how stupid I am–"

"Not stupid," Nate corrected, "just naïve. Incredibly, incredibly naïve. Why do you even bother with this shit? They're not real people, Duncan! She's not your best friend, and he's not your boyfriend. They're two people who get paid to be fake. Isn't that how you've always described Hollywood?"

"They're different," I insisted, though it felt ridiculous that I even had to state it. It sounded so weak, and yet I knew it was true. At least for me.

"Sure. Okay. If he's your boyfriend, he'll be taking you to prom, right? He'll come to whatever graduation party inevitably gets thrown at someone's house, and he'll go to the beach with us over the summer, and make sure you're wearing your sunscreen, and hold your hand when you guys walk down the street, and–"

"Enough, Nate. I get it."

"Do you?"

I didn't bother to dignify him with a response. After a minute, he reached into his pocket, dug out his wallet, and pulled out a few bills. "Here," he said, pressing them into my hand. "I'm leaving. Say goodbye to the golden couple for me, will you?"

He started to walk off but stopped when I called his name. "Nate, come on! You can't leave."

He turned slowly. "You're kidding me, right? *Why* the fuck would I stay? I hate watching you watching him. You hate watching him with her. And if he likes you as much as you think he does, then he probably hates this too. I'm not you, Duncan. I don't thrive on misery."

Ouch. Not that I could really argue with him about the success of this evening. But I couldn't let him leave–it would ruin everything.

"You're fucking kidding me," he said slowly. "You actually want to stay."

"Apparently you're aware of just how infrequently I get to go *out* with my boyfriend," I whispered fiercely, "so yeah, I'd like to stay. This was my idea, you know."

"So stay." He turned to walk out again, but I clamped a hand on his shoulder.

"I can't stay without you. Just go, okay? I'll meet you at your car and you can drive me home. I need to go say goodbye and pretend you weren't feeling well so this doesn't turn into a giant mess."

He rolled his eyes. "Whatever." He walked out the back, and I went up to the paparazzi-besieged table and said my dishonest goodbyes, ignoring both Van and Liam's silent questions.

Two minutes later, I was in Nate's passenger seat, buckling myself in for the world's most awkward ride home.

★★★★★

The house was dark when I entered, but as soon as I flipped on the light in the kitchen, I saw my mom had left me a note on the counter. Apparently, my dad had been having a particularly rough night—she didn't include any further details—so she'd dropped Lucy off at a friend's and gone to stay at the hospital.

Huh. A house all to myself and absolutely no way to take advantage of that fact. Hopefully I could at least make up for the fact that I hadn't actually gotten to eat my dinner. I changed into a pajama top and shorts, grabbed some baby carrots and hummus from the fridge, and flopped down onto the couch.

No sooner had I settled in and switched on an old episode of *Sex and the City* than my stupid phone rang. So much for getting my lousy night off my mind. I trudged to the kitchen counter where I'd left my clutch and unsnapped it to grab my phone.

Liam.

I was almost afraid to answer. I didn't even know how I felt, really. Should I have felt guilty about everything with Nate? Angry for being put into the stupid position of watching him pretend to date my best friend? Angry at *myself* for the fact that I hadn't asked him not to do it when I had the chance, and for coming up with tonight's stupid idea?

I decided to answer with an expressionless "hey" and see where he took it from there.

"Can I come over?" he asked, skipping over any pleasantries.

I was considerably more surprised than I probably should've been. Then again, we were dating–sort of–and he'd never even been to my house. Just one more thing to add to Nate's list of reasons our relationship was weird and possibly all in my head.

"Yeah, okay." I gave him my address to put into his GPS and hung up.

I knew I probably should've made myself look cute and straightened up the house or whatever, but I just didn't have the energy. I simply took my cell phone back to the couch with me and resumed eating carrots while I watched Carrie buy shoes that even I knew no one could possibly afford on a writer's salary.

After about fifteen minutes, Liam called again, and I peeled myself off the couch and padded over to the front door to let him in. He looked gorgeous, as always, but he also looked nervous, and I couldn't help wondering if he'd come to tell me that we were over already.

He didn't kiss me hello, which I took as a bad sign, and I stepped aside to let him in without a word. It was strange, having him in my house. Stranger than having any old boyfriend in your house should be, I imagined. Liam had his own apartment, his own career, his own real life, and here he was, standing in the house I still shared with my parents and Lucy. The house in which I did chores and homework and danced around to Queen when no one was watching. Because while his average nights were spent at clubs or on set, mine were spent doing problem sets and essays and letting my little sister paint my nails.

I started to walk to the couch, but after a few steps, I realized he wasn't following. Whatever he'd come to say, it seemed he'd come to say it quickly and then bolt. Fine. If that was how he wanted to handle it, that was okay with me. Another episode was coming on in five minutes anyway, and there was still plenty of hummus.

The silence was killing me. "Just say it, Liam."

He shifted uncomfortably, digging his hands even further into the pockets of his Diesel jeans, the ones that made his butt look extra cute. Way to add insult to injury. "I'm sorry."

I shrugged, hoping to express an apathy I didn't remotely feel. "It's cool. We were obviously a ridiculous idea to begin with. No hard feelings." I turned around again, hoping he'd let himself out before the tears pricking at my eyelids actually gained some movement.

"Wait, what?" He reached out and turned me around. "You're breaking up with me?"

Huh? "I thought you were breaking up with *me*," I replied, utterly confused now.

"Jesus, no, I just meant I was sorry that tonight ended up being such a train wreck. It was a stupid idea, and I'm sorry I let Van and Jade talk me into all of this. Real or fake, I don't want to be with anyone but you. Unless..." He scratched his head and gave me a look like he expected me to finish his sentence.

"So we're in agreement then," I said, fingering a button on his navy-blue shirt, another one of my favorites.

He let out a sigh of relief, and in response, so did I. We both laughed lightly, and then he grazed my cheek with his fingertips and our mouths found better things to do.

I pulled away after a minute. "Wanna come up to my room?" I asked, then paused. "I swear that wasn't the line it sounded like."

"That's a shame," he teased, looking me up and down appreciatively before following me upstairs.

Once there, though, he seemed more interested in checking out his surroundings than in making another move. "You weren't kidding about being a classic rock fan," he observed, taking in the posters on my walls along with my unfortunately modest vinyl collection.

"I find there's little that's not made better with the Rolling Stones playing in the background." I watched him examine the framed pictures of me and my family that lined the top of my bookcase, the collection of classics on the shelf beneath them, and the photo strips of me and Van tucked into the mirror.

"Your room looks exactly as it should," he said, making it sound like a compliment. "I like it. It's like being in Allyworld."

"Like Disney World, only Ally-er?"

He grinned. "Exactly." He walked over to my desk and glanced at the piles of books and papers that littered it. "Please tell me you haven't been spending your break doing work."

"Just a little bit," I conceded, wondering what he'd look at next.

"Right, right. I forgot you went to the beach today." He walked over and curled one hand around my waist, then used the index finger of his other hand to tap the tip of my nose. "The source of the *very* cute freckles."

I blushed and ducked away. "Stop that. I hate them."

"Well, I like them," he replied, "and I hope to spend a lot more time looking at them." Despite his flirty words and the way his darkening eyes slowly traveled down my body before meeting my gaze, he made no move to touch me again. "Something tells me I'm not the only one who feels that way."

I froze. "What are you talking about?" He couldn't possibly know—

"Nate likes you, doesn't he?"

Well, he might've been pretty but my boy wasn't stupid. I bit my lip. "He thinks he does, yeah," I said slowly.

"And you don't?"

"I think he's just confused," I said dismissively, hoping I was correct.

"Or maybe you're just irresistible," Liam returned, taking a step toward me. He lifted up my chin and stroked my bottom lip with the tip of his thumb. "Seriously, Ally, I know you don't realize how gorgeous you are, but don't let your shortsighted vision of yourself get you caught off guard, okay? I know he's your friend, but there's something about that guy that's just weird. He gets a little too angry on your behalf."

"Maybe I don't get angry enough on my own behalf," I said lightly, nipping on his fingertip.

Liam's lips curled up in a one-sided smile. "Maybe. Why don't you tell me right now what you actually think when you see me and Vanessa together."

"I think I hate you both and hope the set explodes."

He threw back his head and laughed. "Maybe dial back the anger just a little bit."

I smiled sheepishly. "Sorry, I can't help it. I hate it."

"I know," he said, kissing the top of my head. "I promise, I'll make it go away. I just haven't figured out how yet."

"Liam, there's no way to—"

"Shh." He put a finger over my lips. "I said I'll figure it out, and I will. You know I hate this stupid shit just as much as you do."

"Yeah," I said grimly, "but I also know firsthand how important it is to shut up when that 'stupid shit' is paying the bills."

He exhaled sharply and raked a hand through his hair. "Fuck. I hate this. I just want to be with you like a normal person. Why is that so much to ask?"

I was about to respond, but I realized I didn't want to get into this now. We were alone in my bedroom. No cameras, no costars, no Nate, and now, no secrets. Why the hell were we spending the time we had together talking about how miserable we were when we *couldn't* be together?

"Hey, Liam?"

"Yeah?"

"Stop talking." I pressed my lips to his and reached up to undo his top button, and then the next one, and then the next, revealing the soft white undershirt he wore underneath. "God, you smell good."

He smiled against my lips. "Funny, I was just thinking the same thing about you."

"Is that so?"

"Well, that, and one other thing."

I quirked an eyebrow. "That this would be a lot better with the Rolling Stones on?"

He slid his hands up the back of my pajama shirt and pulled me close for another kiss. "Exactly."

★★★★★

An hour later, we lay comfortably on my bed, *Sticky Fingers* playing softly in the background. Liam lightly traced a line on my skin between my belly button and the spot just below the little lavender bow that marked the center of my bra, which was currently bared by the pajama shirt he'd slowly opened while we kissed.

"It's amazing the way being with you calms me down," he murmured.

Funny–being with him had the opposite effect on me. Despite the laziness of his trailing finger, it felt like he was blazing a path of fire everywhere he touched, and had he attempted to go any higher or lower, I was sure I would've let him do whatever he damn well pleased. It was so different from the feeling I'd had on the beach with Nate, the "whatevs, I've known you forever" comfort.

"Aren't I supposed to get your heart racing or something?" I asked lightly, wondering if implicit in Liam's words was the fact that he found me boring.

He laughed, low and sexy, and took my hand, slipping it under his T-shirt so that it pressed right over his heart, which was indeed thumping at a healthy pace. "Trust me," he said, kissing me where neck met collarbone. "You have the exact right effect on my heart."

Emboldened by the hand he'd already placed on his skin, I used the other to lift up his undershirt, which he agreeably pulled over his head, revealing his magazine-cover-ready abs. There were so many lines to trace, I didn't even know where to begin. "What's this like?" I asked, pressing a finger lightly to his sternum.

"A little ticklish, but worth it."

I smiled. "No, I mean...looking like...that. What's it like?"

"Getting forcibly chest-waxed is a bitch that I don't like to talk about." He leaned in for another kiss, but I pulled away.

"Come on, Liam. I'm asking you a question. Be honest with me."

He sighed, falling back on the bed. "You really love asking the awkward stuff, don't you?"

"I like understanding what goes on inside your head," I corrected him. "So sue me. It's almost like I have a crush on you or something."

At that, he smiled. "Well, since you have such excellent taste, I suppose you deserve a response." He gave me another quick kiss, and then the smile slowly faded. "As long as you won't think I'm being an ungrateful asshole again."

I raised my eyebrows as if to say, "I promise nothing," but curved the corners of my lips so he'd know I was kidding.

"It's weird. I mean, obviously it's nice not to be ugly, but it feels ridiculous to have things handed to you because you look good, especially since I have absolutely nothing to do with my appearance. I look like a less bloated version of my dad, minus the eyes which are one hundred percent my mom's."

"You get points for being less bloated," I pointed out. "You *do* run every morning."

"Yeah, but that's more to burn off steam than anything else. The rest is just genetics. Who wants to be liked for the random outcome of the genetic lottery?"

"We're all random outcomes of the genetic lottery," I pointed out. "My facility with languages totally comes from my dad, and we both know how much you love my French."

Liam made a face. "Al, I'm sure your dad is great, but please do not ever mention him and French in the same sentence."

I laughed. "It wouldn't be gross if you didn't have the brain of an eight-year-old boy."

"But I do," he pointed out with a grin. "And yes, I am very grateful to your parents for creating you exactly as you are. I'll be sure to send them a thank-you card with a lovely bottle of Dom."

"They will be elated to know that you can procure alcohol with ease, let me tell you."

He smiled and leaned in to kiss me, long and slow this time. When he finally pulled away, he said, "The worst part is never knowing why people like you, if it's just because of how you look. There's a reason I didn't do much dating before you."

"I have the same problem with never knowing if guys are going for me just to get closer to Van," I admitted. "My first real kiss in the seventh grade was with a complete creep who suggested immediately after that we invite her over and play Spin the Bottle."

"Gross. I hope that guy remains a virgin forever."

"I heard he already lost it to Gail Thurber in the parking lot at Disneyland, but I choose to believe that's a lie for a whole plethora of reasons." I traced the lines of his abs with my index finger, marveling at how smooth the skin was there. "So how'd you know I was a safe bet?"

"I didn't *know*," he admitted, shivering slightly as I grazed what must've been a ticklish spot, "but the fact that you've been best friends with my costar basically since diapers seemed like a decent sign you weren't after my D-list fame and fortune."

"Oh, come on," I teased. "You're a solid C-minus."

"Maybe once *Daylight Falls* gets picked up," he conceded with a smile. "Anyway, usually the first sign that someone just wants to hook up with a celebrity is that they're, ya know, actually nice to said celebrity, as opposed to getting into an argument with them every chance they get." He tapped the tip of my nose, and I scowled, which made him laugh.

"Maybe it was all part of my master plan."

"Was it?" he asked, his fingers returning back to the bow, this time to trace the curves above it.

"No," I replied softly, tingles spreading through my entire body at his touch. "I was pretty prepared to find you an irritating and stupid Ken doll."

"Sorry if I disappointed." He bent over my neck, leaving a light trail of kisses down my throat and along my collarbone as his lips slowly met up with his fingers. "I guess that's the other side of it—you never know who *dislikes* you for the way you look either."

My breath was coming in shorter waves now, and my eyelids fluttered as he slid one bra strap down with his teeth. "I judged; I admit it." Forcing myself to regain some semblance of control, I took his face in my hands and looked him in the same blue-green eyes that had soothed me from my bedroom's tiny television screen back before we'd ever met. "I'm sorry for that. It was hard to imagine that someone so pretty—"

"Devilishly handsome?"

"Sure, that. Anyway, that you could also be so... sweet. And smart, and funny, and supportive." I sat up slightly to touch my lips to his. "I felt so stupid when I realized I was into you. I was so sure it was a waste of my time. That's why I blew up at you in your trailer."

"Ah, that makes sense. I just figured you had your period."

I whacked him on the arm. "Jackass."

He smiled slowly before leaning in to kiss the hollow of my throat. "What about now? Am I a waste of your time?"

"Never," I whispered, sliding back to the mattress as he slowly slipped my other bra strap off my shoulder and pressed his lips to the newly revealed skin.

"Damn straight," he murmured in agreement, and then there were no more words at all.

14

IT WAS A RELIEF THAT MY PARENTS were at the hospital that night, because they would've killed me if they (or Lucy) had seen Liam sneak out somewhere around 5:00 a.m., just in time to evade the paparazzi who usually showed up an hour or two later, although their numbers had thinned. I'd allowed myself to banish Nate's words from my mind the entire time I'd been with Liam, but planning his morning escape around the arrival of the paparazzi had brought all the confusing feelings back.

Nevertheless, I managed to get a few hours of sleep, and when I woke, Lucy was back and my mom had returned from the hospital, which allowed me to go visit. I was grateful for the distraction from my thoughts, though I suppose it's a bad sign when thinking about your dad's cancer is somehow more soothing than thinking about your own romantic life. I took that as a sign that I was maintaining the level of optimism he had requested from us and slathered on some sunscreen before heading out.

According to my mom, he'd been sleeping when she left, but when I arrived at his room, he was wide awake. "How's it goin', kid?" he asked as I strolled in and sat down on the sleeper chair next to his bed. "Lots of excitement, I hear."

I smiled sheepishly. "Yeah, not sure why I suddenly can't seem to keep myself out of trouble. You heard about last night?"

"Only that you went on some sort of double date. I know your mother gave me more details, but I swear, these drugs give me amnesia every damn day. I'm like Guy Pierce in goddamn *Memento* over here."

I laughed. "Trust me, it's not even worth remembering. Just another publicity stunt." I looked around appreciatively and commented how glad I was to see him back in a private room.

"You and me both, AlGal. I don't know what angel made it happen, but I'm just relieved it did. It's uncomfortable enough without having strangers around." He hiccupped. "Plus, it used to drive him crazy when I hiccupped. Like I can control that on these meds." He hiccupped again, and I started to search for a cup of water when he told me not to bother. "Nothing makes it go away except for drugs," he told me, "and even those work maybe half the time. Drives me crazy. I just got a dose this morning so they won't give it to me again until later. Keep me distracted in the meantime."

I nodded. "Detailed drama it is, then."

He smiled.

"So, obviously you know the whole thing with Van and Liam's costar outing me and Liam to the paparazzi, right?"

"I can't believe those words are–*hic*–coming out of your mouth right now."

"Tell me about it. So, Van tried to fix things by telling the paparazzi that it was all a lie, she and I were still best friends, and she and Liam really *were* together.

That way, they'd back off me." I paused for my dad's hiccups as I explained the background information. "I, in all my Ivy League-accepted wisdom, decided the best way to prove it was to have them announce that they were going on a double date with me and my *actual* boyfriend, who's really this friend of mine from school—Nate—who also happens to have a huge crush on Vanessa."

"Everybody wins. *Hic.*"

"Exactly. Except that we all go out for dinner, and watching them is pretty much killing me, and Nate totally calls me out on it. Only to make things even worse, he ends up telling me that *he* likes me."

My dad laughed weakly. "Jesus. I mean, don't get—*hic*—me wrong, you know *I've* always thought you were wonderful and wondered why you didn't have more boyfriends, but when it rains, it pours, huh?"

"I'm guessing that either being taken made me magically more attractive to Nate or he just wants to like me because it's better than wanting Vanessa, who was so not into him."

"And how do you feel?"

I swirled the plastic spoon around in his Jell-O. "Being with Nate would be easier, logistically. There's no question about that." I snorted. "God, listen to me. Being with a cute guy from school would be easier than dating the TV-star-slash-model I'm already seeing."

My dad laughed. "Sounds like plenty of girls' dream scenario."

I sighed. "Not mine. I never wanted any of this. I wasn't even looking for a boyfriend. The only reason Nate kept talking to me after I was done tutoring him is because of Van. The only reason I know Liam is because of Van. Sometimes I wonder if the two of us staying friends was just a ridiculous idea to start with. I just don't belong in her world."

"Come on, now, Al–*hic*–Gal. You and Vanessa probably couldn't have stopped being friends even if you'd wanted to. You'll probably still be friends when you're old and gray and she's been the matriarch on a soap opera for forty-seven years."

I laughed at the image. "Maybe. But what about the boys?"

"Doesn't really sound like there's a question there. I'm sure Nate is a nice–*hic*–boy, but do you like him the way you like Liam?"

"Not even close."

"Well then. You and Vanessa have stayed friends against the odds; maybe you and Liam can work out despite them too."

I reached out and squeezed his smooth-as-a-baby's-bottom foot. "You're a wise old man, Papa Duncan. You know that?"

He smiled. "I've got the new gray hairs to prove it."

★★★★★

Neither of us had gotten much sleep the night before, so it was no surprise that we both dozed off shortly after, he in his bed and me in the trusty sleeper chair. What *was* pretty shocking, though, was waking up to the sound of familiar voices talking quietly in the doorway and my eyelids fluttering open to see Liam and Vanessa standing there and watching me sleep.

I rubbed my eyes. "What are you guys doing here?" I whispered as I eased myself out of the chair and padded over to the door, careful not to wake my dad.

"Volunteering," explained Van as Liam gave my hand a hello squeeze and stepped into the privacy of the room to give me a peck on the cheek. "*Quel* coincidence, eh?"

"Is it?" I asked, raising an eyebrow.

"Oh, hush," Van responded, exchanging a glance with Liam that I couldn't read. Apparently, they were on secret-glance level now. "People of all ages and ailments are instantly cheered by my beautiful face. It'd be wrong not to share that with the world."

"I could've done without that one old lady asking me to lift up my shirt," said Liam, "but otherwise, it's been a nice day." He nodded in the direction of my dad's bed. "How's he doing?"

"Depends on the hour," I replied. "His energy level's pretty low and he can't bring himself to eat anything, but he's sleeping now, which is a good sign. He's been getting hiccups that drive him nuts and usually make it impossible for him to get more than ten minutes of rest at a time."

"Hey, who's that?" my dad's voice suddenly asked hazily.

I smiled sheepishly at Van and Liam. "Spoke too soon." I turned around and walked back to the bed. "Hey, Dad. Vanessa came to visit." I glanced back to see if Liam was taking the opportunity I was giving him to slip out—my dad was clearly still too sleepy and drugged up to recognize him from the couple of times he might've seen him onscreen—but he stood still right inside the doorway, waiting for an introduction. "And she brought Liam."

"Hey, Sweetie," Dad greeted Vanessa, mustering up as much energy as possible. "So—*hic*—nice of you to stop by." Then he turned to Liam. "And you brought...Liam?" Dad asked fuzzily, and then a flash of recognition crossed his face. "The boy."

Liam laughed good-naturedly. "That's me," he said, taking a step forward. He started to reach out his hand, then thought better of it and waved instead. "Nice to meet you, sir."

Dad laughed weakly, ending on a hiccup. "Sir. The kid from those cell phone commercials is calling me 'sir' while I'm holed up in a hospital bed wearing pajamas. I love it."

Liam blushed, the first time I'd ever seen him do so. It was incredibly cute. "God, please don't judge me by those. They're incredibly stupid, I know, but I got such a kick-ass—um, really great—cell phone from them, and I needed the cash for an awesome backpacking trip."

"Where'd you go?" Dad asked, and I groaned. Liam had totally just hit on one of my dad's favorite topics. He could talk for *hours* about this one time he backpacked through Central America. I know; I'd heard him do it. Many, many times.

"The Australian Outback." Liam started to edge closer, then stopped himself again.

"It's fine," I assured him. "Just put some of that antibacterial stuff on your hands and don't step on any tubes."

"Right." He still had a funny look on his face, and I wondered if seeing my dad in the hospital brought back any memories of his mother. He was only eight when she died, even younger than Lucy was now, but Liam was so guarded there was no telling what kinds of dark thoughts he harbored. He squeezed some of the gel onto his hands, rubbed them together, and walked farther into the room so he could converse more easily with my dad, who was only too eager to ask more questions about his trip and share his own stories.

"Maybe *they* should date," Van joked as she put some gel on her own hands. "They're certainly a better fit than me and your little friend Nate. What happened to him last night, anyway?"

I grimaced. "What, was my story about him not feeling well not convincing?"

Van rolled her eyes. "Leave the acting to me and your boyfriend, 'kay?"

I forced a laugh, but I couldn't help thinking about just how much I hated all the acting they were doing. And now today they were volunteering together? I mean, it was incredibly sweet of them to come visit my dad—and obviously to visit the sick at the hospital at all—but did they have to look so...perfect-couple-y doing it?

"Everything okay?" asked Van.

I forced myself to clear my head and smiled. "Everything's great. Thank you guys so much for coming."

"Of course!" she replied cheerfully. "Now, if you'll excuse me, I need to pry Liam away so I can get some time with the patient!"

★★★★★

Van and Liam had been brought to the hospital by limo, so when the time came to leave my dad to his sleepy solitude, I insisted on driving them both home. Liam had never actually been in my old Nissan, but Van slipped right into the passenger seat without even thinking about it, the same way she'd done a million times before. When it became clear she wasn't going to offer him to switch, he slid into the backseat and closed the door behind him.

"So, your dad seems pretty good," Van said as I pulled out of the hospital's parking lot.

"Totally," Liam echoed, though his optimism was less convincing.

"Well, it doesn't really matter how he seems, unfortunately," I said as I pulled up to a red light. "Either the stuff's working or it isn't, and it's too early to really tell."

"He's still got his hair," said Vanessa. "That's a good sign, right?"

"It's not chemo," I reminded her. "Hair loss isn't a side effect of immunotherapy."

"Oh." The car grew quiet for a minute until Vanessa again tried to lift the mood. "So, what are your plans for the rest of break? You have to do something fun!"

I snorted. "Yeah, I've tried that a couple of times this week. So far, not that fun. I think I'd rather chill at the hospital."

"Well, we're not doing anything now," said Liam. "Why don't we all go out?"

I glanced up into the rearview mirror and caught his eye, then raised a brow. "Seriously? After last night, I think I'm done going out in public with you guys. No offense."

"None taken," Van said wryly.

"Okay, so we can just go to my apartment and chill," Liam suggested.

"Lame," said Van. "We've spent the whole day at the hospital. Let's go out! Do something fun!"

Liam and I exchanged another glance in the mirror. He shrugged helplessly, and I felt so frustrated I was surprised Van couldn't feel it rolling off me in waves. "You guys go," I said flatly, unwilling to concede. There was no chance I was sitting through a replay of last night's date. "I have to work on this project for school.

I totally fell behind when my dad was first diagnosed and I promised I'd have it in when I came back from break." It was a small lie—I had a whole extra week to do it, since my art teacher, Mr. Kim, was about my dad's age and therefore extra freaked out and sympathetic about the whole situation—but a necessary one.

"Oh, come on," Van pleaded. "You already got into college. Who cares about one stupid project?"

"I do," I reminded her. "And so do those lovely people who hand out scholarships. If you wanna go out, just tell me where to drop you off." Only after I said it did I realize that if she got out of the car alone, Liam and I were free to do whatever we wanted. We could go back to his place, and Van would have no idea. I got so excited by the prospect, I actually felt guilty for how much I was looking forward to dropping her off.

Then Van's cell phone beeped with a text. "It's Jade," she announced. "She says she can get us into the afterparty of the screening of Ryan Gosling's new movie and we *must* go."

A party to celebrate watching a movie. How freaking Hollywood.

Liam groaned. "Can't we just skip it?"

"Stop being such a hater," Van chastised him. "It's bad enough you won't get a Twitter account."

I snorted. "You're one to talk, Van. You make me do all your tweeting for you."

"Yeah, but at least I tell you what to tweet most of the time. Liam refuses to put any effort into anything."

"We just went out last night," he reminded her. "We answered like four hundred thousand questions and smiled for about a zillion cameras. Then we did it again today at the hospital for—" His mouth snapped shut, but before I could ask why he cut himself off, he repeated, "We just did it today. Aren't you tired?"

"The sun's not even down yet! Besides, we agreed to Jade's publicity plan, and this is exactly the kind of thing we talked about."

Obviously, Van had gotten a lot more sleep than Liam and I had, because I could see with one glance into his baby blues that he was just as ready to collapse as I was after our late night together. I waited for him to tell her no, that he was just going to crash tonight, leaving us free to chill on his couch while Van went out, but when he finally opened his mouth, it was to exhale and say, "Yeah, whatever, let's go."

I could feel him trying to meet my eyes in the mirror—whether it was to beseech me to join them or to apologize for having to go, I didn't know or care. (Much.) A few minutes later, I pulled up in front of Van's house and let her out so she could change for the party.

As soon as she was safely inside, Liam slid into the front seat next to me. "Listen—"

"Don't," I grunted, pulling out of Van's driveway, all excitement at potentially having the evening together disappearing. Tears pricked my eyes at the realization of just how quickly he would ditch me at someone else's say-so, especially after last night. It was like I was a freaking understudy in my own relationship, to be brought out only when lead actress Vanessa had other obligations for the night. "I just can't, okay? It's been a long day. You've got stuff to do, I've got stuff to do, let's leave it at that."

He opened his mouth and promptly closed it. We drove in silence the rest of the way to his apartment, and when I dropped him off, our goodbye consisted of him pecking me on the cheek before letting himself out of the car.

I finally let go of the tears as I watched him disappear, aware for the millionth time that I was in over my head with their world. I loved Van, but I couldn't and wouldn't compete with her. I didn't look like she or Shannah or Zoe did, and I couldn't party like them either. I couldn't make Liam do what I wanted with a snap of my fingers and a "Jade says." I was basically a way for him to kill time in between doing his famous-person things, whether he saw it that way or not.

Obviously, Nate was right about one thing: Life as it was didn't seem to be making me happy. But what the hell was I supposed to do about it?

THE NEXT DAY, I DIDN'T EVEN bother connecting with either of them; the last thing I wanted to talk about was some stupid Hollywood party I hadn't been invited to. I rolled out of bed around eleven, thinking how nice it would be if I had the kind of boyfriend I could actually go to a lazy brunch with right now. Since I obviously didn't, I called Nate. He agreed, if a bit hesitantly, and we met up at the Lunchbox at noon. Normalcy FTW.

"So is this a date?" he asked as soon as we sat down. He didn't sound hopeful or flirty, just curious.

"I'm not a bitch if I say no, am I?"

"Is this where I'm supposed to say 'you couldn't be a bitch if you tried'?"

I smirked. "I wouldn't even believe you if you said it."

"Then what made you call?"

The waiter brought us a couple of menus, and I immediately opened mine to study it as if I didn't know the Lunchbox's brunch offerings by heart. Menus are a totally underrated way to avoid eye contact.

"We're friends," I said awkwardly, wondering how true that even was. "I wanted to make sure we were okay."

It was the truth, but not the whole truth; somehow, I didn't think Nate would respond well to "I was sad and lonely and wanted waffles with my boyfriend." Though now he wasn't responding at all, and after a minute, I was forced to look up to make sure he hadn't vacated the table.

He hadn't, but his raised eyebrows and pursed lips made me wish that I could.

"Is that a no?"

"No, it's not a no. I just don't understand why you even give a shit. You don't want to date me, you don't want to hang out with me and my friends–"

"Yes, I do," I interrupted quickly. Then I blushed, realizing what I'd just said. "Want to hang out with you and your friends, I mean," I amended.

He snorted. "So you finally admit that you actually had a good time and didn't just spend a few hours wishing America's Sweethearts were there instead?"

"I told you I had a good time," I replied, though I couldn't remember if that was actually true. "And I'm not incapable of having fun without Liam and Vanessa, you know."

"Glad to hear it," he said dryly.

I was about to respond but the arrival of our waiter cut me off. I ordered my usual brunch selection–banana chocolate-chip pancakes–and Nate got an egg and sausage platter, which was something of a relief since it meant he certainly wouldn't be trying to kiss me later.

I decided to curtail all talk of Liam and Van; it hurt to think of being ditched by them last night, and I certainly didn't need Nate to know that. "So," I began, handing my menu back to the waiter, "what are we doing today?"

Nate took a sip of his water, shooting me an amused look over the rim of his glass. "We?" he asked as soon as he'd swallowed.

I shrugged. "We're friends, right? We hang out. I wanna hang out."

He laughed. "No, you don't. At least not with me."

"I said that I do," I reminded him. "Will you stop acting like I'm obsessed with them? They're my friends—my best friend and my boyfriend. I'm allowed to like them."

He rolled his eyes, and I knew he was about to go off on yet another rant, so I quickly steered the conversation back to the day at hand.

"Well," he said, raking a hand through his shaggy hair, "I don't know about today, but Chase is having a party at his place tomorrow night to celebrate the end of break."

"Perfect!" I took a long sip of my Arnold Palmer and smiled. "I love parties."

"No, you don't."

"Okay, maybe not, but I will. I am going to love parties. I am going to love *Chase*'s party."

Nate laughed. "What's in that drink of yours?"

I stuck my tongue out at him and tossed my hair back in what I hoped was a firm, defiant gesture. "I am going to learn to appreciate high school and real life," I informed him.

"So you acknowledge that life among the actors isn't real?"

I narrowed my eyes. "You know what I mean. Normal, average, daily life."

He smirked. "You're not improving your case."

"Oh, just shut up." I took another quick sip. "I have a little over four months until my life will never be normal again. I just want to enjoy what there is. I don't like reporting drama to my dad in the hospital room every day." I wished I had the menu back so I could avert my eyes again. This was a whole lot more honest than I'd planned to be with Nate. "I just want him to know that I'm going to be okay."

Nate simply nodded. "You are, you know."

I fiddled with the scratched-up flatware. "I doubt it. But I'm not ready to think about that yet."

"Fair enough. So what do you want to do today?"

I thought about how I would've answered if Liam had asked, and a flood of options came to mind. I would've loved to drive up Pacific Coast Highway to the Getty Villa, which Liam mentioned he'd never done. Or taken him to the La Brea Tar Pits, which he'd loved going to with his mom as a kid but hadn't returned to since she'd passed away. Or have dinner at the Mongolian barbecue place Liam had gone to the year before and told me I'd love. Or simply walk around the Grove or the Third Street promenade, shopping and holding hands.

But none of that was going to happen with Liam today. And I didn't want to do any of those things with Nate. The only thing I really wanted Nate for was to escape.

So maybe we would do just that.

"Let's drive to Mexico," I blurted.

His eyebrows shot so far up they were practically part of his messy hairline. "You want to go to Mexico? With me?"

"Just for the day," I clarified quickly. "It's not so far, and I've never been to Tijuana. It'd be fun!"

"Of course it'd be fun," Nate said, "if you ignore the incredibly long drive and the ridiculous amount of time we'd spend at the border crossing. Anyway, aren't you forgetting a few things?"

"I don't think so," I said sunnily, willing him to shut up.

"Uh, your dad's in the hospital, you have a boyfriend–"

"Okay, you know what?" I broke in. "Never mind. Forget I said anything. I actually forgot that I have to, um"–*think*–"take my little sister to the dentist." *Nice. Totally believable.* "You're totally welcome to my pancakes."

"Ally–"

"Sorry to not eat and run!" I chirped, already up and out of my seat. I dug into my tote and pulled out my wallet, tossing a few bills on the table so quickly I had no idea what they were. It was entirely possible I'd just tipped my entire week's salary.

"Ally! You can't just leave–"

"Whoops!" I pretended to look at a watch I wasn't even wearing. "I'm already late! I'll see you around, Nate." I hurried out to my car, turning deaf, humiliated ears to the sound of him calling my name.

★★★★★

When I pulled into my driveway, I was surprised to see another car had beaten me to it. My father was still at the hospital, my mother was at work, and though my mom had been hiring a housekeeper lately to help out a bit, she should've been gone by then. Not that any of them drove anything like the black Range Rover I'd just blocked in with my silver Sentra.

I knew only one person with a black Range Rover, but I hadn't spoken to Liam all day and I couldn't imagine what he would've been doing at my house. And yet, when I let myself through the front door, there he was, sitting on the couch, reading from what looked like sides. I racked my brain to recall if we'd made plans, and though I felt fairly certain we hadn't, I still braced myself for having to respond to the inevitable "Where were you?" by responding that I'd been at lunch with That Guy You Don't Like Who Likes Me.

But I needn't have worried. All Liam did when I walked in was smile like he'd just noticed the sun was out and then get up and walk over to kiss me hello.

"Hey, Al," he said after the briefest of touches. "Sorry, I didn't realize you'd be out for a while. Your housekeeper let me in and said she thought you'd just run out for coffee. I guess I lost track of time memorizing lines." He smiled. "You look cute. I like that shirt."

Objectively, they were nice words, but they weren't the ones I needed. "Cute" didn't make you say "Fuck off" to a publicist and ride off with a girl into the sunset. A shirt I'd had since the eighth grade couldn't compete with whatever Van and the other actresses present had (or hadn't) worn the night before. No wonder I always got relegated into the background; I practically faded into it. On what planet did a girl like me belong in a world like theirs?

And how long would I be able to stay in his—their—orbit?

Not to mention that after all my stressing about last night—what he'd been doing with Vanessa, how much fun they were having—he didn't seem to give a shit about where I'd been when he arrived. He didn't even care that there was another guy out there who wanted me. Or did Nate even want me? He hadn't exactly jumped at the chance to spend more time with me. Maybe I was just unwantable. Either way, my usual butterflies at seeing Liam weren't the happy-go-lucky type this time around.

"Thanks," I mumbled, glancing anywhere but at him. "So, what brings you by?"

"I got an audition for the new James Gallagher movie," he said, oblivious to my less-than-sunny demeanor, "but it's not for another few hours, so I thought maybe we could hang out."

The prodigal understudy role returns. "Thanks for squeezing me into your schedule." I walked past him into the kitchen to pour myself a glass of water.

If he wasn't oblivious, he was an even better actor than I thought. "Anything special you want to do?"

I whirled around. "Actually, yes. I'd really like to go to the Getty Villa, or the Tar Pits, or that Mongolian barbecue place. Which of those extremely public things would you like to do with me, your non-celebrity girlfriend?" I asked sweetly.

"Ally..."

I let him trail off, but it was obvious he wasn't going anywhere. He and I both knew all there was to say about that.

"Fine," I declared, putting my glass down on the counter. There was more than one way to recover from the fact that we'd both spent the past twenty-four hours with people we shouldn't have. "New plan." I walked over to him determinedly and put my hands on either side of his face, pulling it down for a not-so-gentle kiss.

I'd obviously caught him off guard, but it didn't take long for him to warm up to the kiss and return it with equal fervor.

Until he felt my fingers undoing his belt.

He pulled away, short of breath. "Ally, what are you doing?"

"Nobody's home," I reminded him, pulling him back by one of his belt loops. "It's just you and me and a few hours until your audition."

"Ally, stop." But he made no move to actually pull my hands away as they successfully worked at the buckle.

"Why?" I stood on my toes to kiss his neck in a spot that had worked wonders the other night in my room, but he remained frozen and silent. Finally, I reached to undo the button of his jeans, and this time he pushed me away, gently but firmly.

"Ally, we're not doing this."

"What's the matter? Aren't you attracted to me?" I challenged, shame at his rejection burning my cheeks. "Or am I just some 'cute' friend of your hot costar girlfriend's. You certainly don't seem to have trouble getting it up for Van."

"Jesus Christ, where is this coming from?" he demanded, raking a hand through his hair. "First of all, I've never *had* to get it up for Vanessa because I've never had sex with her, or done anything else with her that hasn't been documented on camera. Second of all, You're. The only. One. I want. How can you not know that?"

"Maybe if–"

"And I thought it was pretty damn obvious I find you obscenely hot," Liam continued, refusing to let me interrupt. "Frankly, I spend a ridiculous amount of time thinking about it. Imagining that you're the one I'm with is the only way I get through any of that stupid publicity shit, and if you don't think I'm dying to sleep with you—when the time is right, and not when you're standing here fuming at me with something to prove—you're crazy."

Well, there wasn't really any good response to that, now was there? So I went with the worst one possible. "I was at lunch with Nate. I asked him to go."

"Why?"

"I don't know." And I really didn't. Yes, a part of me had wanted to make sure things were okay, but a bigger part of me had known that things weren't going to magically normalize themselves over pancakes. And I did want to escape, but it was Liam I wanted to do that with, not Nate. I knew this morning was a mistake, but it was like the rational part of my brain had wanted to sleep a little longer before waking up in a world where it had to watch my boyfriend kiss someone else on TV. "Maybe I just wanted to feel what it was like to go out with a guy in public."

"And how was it?" he asked, an edge creeping into his voice.

I didn't answer. I wanted to tell him that I'd had a great time—see how *he* felt about me going on a "date" with someone else—but the lie wouldn't emerge from my mouth.

He sighed. "I don't know what you want from me. You *told* me to do this. You told *us* to do this. If we stop now, the backlash will be awful, and they might be forced to replace one, if not both, of us on the show."

"They wouldn't do that."

"Pilots are recast all the time, for worse reasons than the general public thinking there's bad blood between costars," he pointed out. "Besides, the 'rumor' about you is still recent enough that you'd probably be blamed for it. Do you really want paparazzi swarming your house again?"

"I *want* to have a normal relationship," I said quietly, self-loathing at my childish outburst already settling in. "I just want to be with you without worrying when you're going to be ripped away from me."

"Don't you think I want that too? Do you think I like this any better than you do?" I started to respond, but he jerked his hand up to silence me. "Never mind—obviously you *do* think that. And I don't really know how to get that idea out of your head short of fucking you on demand."

"Well, that was crude." And sort of hot.

He raised an eyebrow. "And taking off my pants five minutes after you took another guy for a boyfriend test run isn't?"

"Touché," I muttered, looking away.

He stepped in front of me and tilted up my chin so I had no choice but to make eye contact. "Look, I don't want to fight with you about things we can't change right now. Can we just start this day over or something? I'd like to spend the afternoon with you. I can't go somewhere public, and I'm sorry for that. Apparently, you've already eaten, and I think we've established that our first time together is not going to be today. So, can I stay or would you rather be alone?"

I was still upset, but about what exactly, or even at whom, I was no longer sure. I grumbled my assent and started to walk toward the couch for yet another "date" spent watching a movie when his gentle hand on my abdomen stopped me in my tracks. He pulled me into his arms and planted a long, soft kiss on my lips.

"Hey," he said softly, sweeping a strand of hair behind my ear. "There are still plenty of fun things to do behind closed doors."

I could only nod before he kissed me again. It was seriously hard to stay angry when you were being kissed like that.

"I'm sorry," I offered when we parted. "Going out with Nate was stupid. I just...after last night..."

"I get it." He stroked my lower lip gently with his thumb. "I mean, I don't *like* it, but I get it. I'm sorry about last night too. For what it's worth, the whole thing sucked. I missed you like crazy, and we got into a fight with an asshole reporter about whether making Bailey Korean-American was Hollywood 'bowing to the demands of the PC police.'"

"Seriously? What a prick."

"Exactly." His lips brushed my forehead. "I can think of much better ways to spend my time."

"Is that so?" I clasped my arms around his waist to pull him close and looked up into his eyes, the sparkling blue-green of the Pacific at sunset. "Anything I can help with, maybe?"

"Maybe." That dimple was probably going to be the death of me. Totally worth it. "Let's see what we can do about turning this into a date with your *actual* boyfriend."

★★★★★

In the end, we semi-compromised by ordering takeout from the Mongolian barbecue place and eating it picnic-style in the backyard. I offered to help Liam with his audition, but he insisted that he'd gone over it plenty of times and didn't want to take any time away from our date. I forced him to run his lines with me for twenty minutes anyway, just in case, and before I knew it, four o'clock had come and he was kissing me goodbye.

"Text me and let me know how it went?"

"Of course." He squeezed my hand as I walked him to the door. "I've got to pack after my audition, and then my flight to Berlin is really early in the morning, so I probably won't see you until we're back on set on Monday." Cupping my face in his warm palms, he planted a slow, sweet kiss on my lips that spread through my body like fire. Good thing, since apparently it had to keep me warm for almost a week. "I'll call you when I land."

I just nodded; I didn't trust myself to do anything else, given all the stupid things I'd already said that day. And then he was gone, and I was alone with the queasy feeling in the pit of my stomach.

Then I remembered what Liam had said about the night before with Vanessa, and I pulled out my phone to call her. She answered on the fourth ring. "Hey," she whispered. "I'm at yoga. What's up?"

"Answering your phone during yoga isn't very zen, but I appreciate it. You wanna hang out afterward?"

"Oh God, yes. I will pay you a billion dollars to get me Pinkberry and bring it back to your house for a movie night. Bonus points if you let me sleep over so I can avoid the billionth 'Perils of Life Without a College Degree' conversation with my parents this week."

I laughed. "I'm your assistant, Van. I already get paid to get you Pinkberry. But I'm on it; just do me a favor and shower before you get here."

"Deal. Eep, gotta go! Namasté!"

She hung up, and I shoved my phone in my back pocket, then grabbed my keys. The thought of going on a fro-yo run was oddly rejuvenating.

Van was at my house before I even returned from Pinkberry, standing on the front porch, furiously typing something on her phone. "I left yoga a minute after we hung up," she explained without looking up. "Fro-yo just sounds so much better than downward-facing dog."

She hit send on whatever she was typing and shoved her bedazzled phone back into her purse. "Just warning you now, Jade will probably text me four hundred thousand times." We air-kissed hello, and I passed her her usual kiwi strawberry yogurt before pulling out my keys and letting us both inside. "Did Liam tell you about the psycho last night?"

"Barely." We dropped our bags on the living room floor and took up our usual spots on the couch with yogurt in hand. "Just that the reporter was a racist asshole."

Vanessa rolled her thickly lined eyes and took a long, slow lick of the glob of yogurt on her spoon. "Beyond. The jerk had the nerve to ask if he could interview me for an article on 'Affirmative Action in Hollywood.' Because everyone's just *throwing* parts at Asian-American actresses, you know? Those poor, poor skinny blondes."

"As if they didn't get to audition for the same part, either," I added, rolling my eyes. This type of garbage was so typical and exactly why I wanted to get out of this place ASAP. "Like it's your fault Zoe can't emote through that nose job."

"I thought Liam was gonna punch him in the face when he asked about our relationship." She took another lick of the spoon. Van was the slowest eater on the planet. "He tried to get him to admit he had some sort of Asian fetish. Because of course, what white guy would want a Korean girl unless he had some sort of obsession with my daintiness and slanty eyes, right?" She shook her head. "Anyway, I had to hold Liam back and make us walk away, but I might've uttered a few choice words first. Jade is...not pleased."

"With you?" My jaw dropped open. "The guy was a racist prick! You should've let Liam punch him. Though, honestly, I can't even really imagine what Liam punching someone looks like."

Vanessa laughed. "It's true. It was actually interesting seeing him go a little nuts to defend my honor. He's usually so chill."

A tiny twinge of jealousy that Liam had broken said chill exterior for Vanessa squeezed my gut, but I instantly tamped it down, recognizing it for the stupid pettiness it was. Of course he should've defended her; Lord knew if I'd been the one at her side last night, the way I used to be, I probably would've let my fists fly.

"Yeah, I'm glad he was there," I managed. A half-truth, but better than nothing.

"I'm actually surprised you wanted to hang out with me tonight. Isn't Liam going to Germany in the morning?"

"I *always* want to hang out with you," I teased, "but he has an audition. That James Gallagher movie. He actually left here just before I called you."

"Ohhh, no wonder you had time for little ol' me," she said with another lick. Her voice was teasing, but I suspected she wasn't; it took all the self-control I possessed not to point out how much more time she spent with my boyfriend than I did. "You know, you haven't said a word about...things." She waggled her perfectly threaded eyebrows. "Are you really gonna leave a girl hangin' on that front? I need details, obviously. Especially since living under 'Park house rules' means I have absolutely nothing of my own to report."

I laughed. "I thought you didn't want to know anything because it'd be impossible to look him in the eye on set."

"I changed my mind. I need to know things. I assume I'd know if you'd given him your ladyflower...?"

"Not if you insist on calling it a ladyflower, à la Mama Park." I tossed a throw pillow at her head, taking care to avoid the yogurt spoon she was still holding up like a lollipop. "And yes, you'd know, and no, I haven't." I thought about earlier that afternoon, when I almost had, and I could feel a blush creeping up my cheeks in response. I jammed a spoon of yogurt into my mouth, hoping it'd cool down my skin before Van noticed.

No such luck. "Alexandra Mabel Duncan, you are keeping something from me! What did you do?"

"I didn't do anything," I assured her. "I just may have...come on a little strong today. Possibly thrown myself at him a little bit."

Van's eyes widened and her spoon froze halfway to her mouth. "And he wasn't into it?"

"They were unusual circumstances," I admitted wryly, wishing I hadn't said a word. I took another bite of yogurt. "Anyway, things are fine, and I can tell you he's a great kisser and fabulous with his hands, but that's all I can tell you right now."

"You don't sound very happy about that, young lady."

I couldn't even meet her eyes, and I dug into my cup instead. The truth was, I hadn't really been thinking when I'd come on to Liam earlier; I'd just acted on impulse. But now that it was over, I was left wondering what it would've been like if we'd gone through with it. Considering how he kissed and touched me, I suspected I would've been floating around on a cloud of bliss right about now.

Vanessa burst out laughing. "You wanna bang him so hard. God, I wish you could see yourself blushing right now."

I reached for a throw pillow, but I'd already thrown the only one within reach. "Oh, shut up."

"You guys are super-gross."

"Thanks so much for your thoughts on my sex life," I replied dryly, as if her approval didn't mean the world to me, even though it actually did. Both Vanessa and I happened to be virgins, but of the two of us, she was definitely the "Save it all for The One" type. If she thought he was my One... The thought admittedly made me a little mushy.

"Ugh, stop it. I'm sorry I said anything." Vanessa threw the pillow back at me, and it landed smack in my cup of yogurt. We both stared it for a few seconds and then lost it completely.

After we cleaned up, Vanessa picked out a movie—indie, she insisted, since she didn't feel like watching anything where she knew any of the actors personally—and we popped some popcorn and settled back in for the night. We even let Lucy join us when she got back from her ballet lessons.

It was exactly what I needed to forget that stupid brunch, forget that Liam was leaving for a week, and even forget about everything with my dad for a bit, though the latter was made much easier by the fact that my mom was visiting him for the night. Van had promised to make my spring break better, and truly, she had never broken a promise.

THE NEXT DAY, THOUGH, was entirely about my dad. I showed up at the hospital bright and early—well, relatively bright, considering I was still pre-coffee, and relatively early, given that Van and I had both passed out on the couch and overslept—and parked myself in the chair right next to his hospital bed with a bag full of textbooks.

"You're looking cheerful," he observed as he watched me settle in, his own eyes tired. Then he hiccupped.

"Still doing that, huh?"

"Unfor-*hic*-tunately. Not as frequent. How's your break going?"

"Not bad. Van actually came over last night to watch a movie. Well, sort of watch a movie. Lucy kept asking her questions every five seconds, including a zillion about Liam."

He laughed weakly, which brought on another round of hiccups. It was his fifth day of that stretch in the hospital, which meant he'd had a crap-ton of drugs pumped into his system. His body was always shot by this point, and it was harder to pretend everything was normal. "How is your sister?"

"She's good. She misses you a lot." I felt a twinge in my gut when I thought of my last real one-on-one conversation with her; I'd never actually answered her question, and I still didn't know how. But I did know that keeping her fully in the dark while he was in the hospital didn't help. "I wish you and Mom would let her visit."

There was a rasping sound in response, and I quickly brought him some water. "I'll probably be home tomorrow," he said after taking a sip. "My creatinine levels are high. I'm not sure I'll get another dose today."

The defeat in his voice broke my heart, the way it always did when he was nearing the end of a course of treatment. It was for his own good that the stopping point in each cycle was dependent on his kidney function, and I knew from reading up on statistics that he tolerated more than most, but he still seemed to take it as a personal failing every time his levels hit the magic number that had him packing up his hospital pajamas.

"You did great," I assured him, even though I knew it was falling on deaf ears, on top of the fact that he was drifting off to sleep.

He waved a hand dismissively, just as I knew he would.

I sighed. There was no point in fighting that battle, but I still wanted to fight Lucy's. "You need to let her visit during your next round. It drives her crazy, sitting at home and wondering what you look like in here. I'll bring her and stay with her the whole time, I promise."

"I'll talk it—*hic*—over with your mother," he mumbled, but he was already half-asleep. I settled back into the reclining chair my mother had slept in the night before and pulled out my Calculus textbook.

I got no more than a few pages in when I drifted off right along with him; apparently my night on the couch with Van hadn't been all that restful, and Calculus wasn't exactly mind-whirling. At least not in a good way. When I awoke, it was to the sound of my phone ringing, and I immediately grabbed it and answered before it could wake up my dad too, even though the number didn't look familiar.

"Hello?" I whispered as I quickly dashed out of the room and into the waiting area.

"Al? You okay?"

Liam's concerned voice washed over me. "I'm fine," I replied at normal volume. "I'm in the hospital. I mean, with my dad. He was sleeping. I'm fine."

He laughed. "So, you're fine, is what you're saying."

"More than fine, now," I said with a smile as I curled up in a chair, rubbing the sleep from my eyes with my free hand. "Glad you landed safely."

"Me too. How's your dad?"

"Same old. I'm trying to talk him into letting Lucy come visit next time. I'm...sort of making headway."

"How sort of?"

"The 'I'll talk about it with your mother' kind of sort of. Which I hate, because I *know* this is the right thing for Lucy. She feels so left out, and if these really are his last couple of months–" I broke off to take a deep breath. "I just want to do what's right for her."

"I know. I'm sorry. I wish I could help."

"I wish you could too," I said with a little laugh. "Oh well. I'll figure it out. How's Berlin?"

"Couldn't tell you; I've barely seen any of it. I'm in a car on my way to the hotel now, but I'm pretty much just dropping my stuff and changing for a meet 'n greet thing. Then tomorrow I film the commercial, and then I have to meet some director, and the next day I'm doing a photo op at some...something. I don't even know." He yawned and I laughed.

"You sound very excited by it all," I teased.

"I would fucking run home to you on the autobahn right now if I could."

I started to respond, but then Liam said, "one second," and I heard him talking to someone for a minute before he returned. "I'm here," he said apologetically, "and I really gotta go. I'm sorry, Al. I'll call you tomorrow if I can."

The thought of letting him go so soon made me ache, especially in the stark loneliness of the hospital, but I knew I didn't have a choice. "Okay," I said softly. "Thanks for checking in."

"Of course. I miss you."

"I miss you too. And hey, Liam?"

"Yeah?"

"Make sure someone teaches you how to say 'please' and 'thank you' in German. You don't want to sound like a d-bag."

His laughter flowed rich and warm into my ear, closing the 10,000-mile gap between us, if only for a moment. "I *really* miss you, Al. No, wait. *Tu me manques vraiment.*"

Good thing I was already in the hospital; I was in serious danger of my heart melting right out of my body. "*Tu me manques vraiment aussi. Je ne peux pas attendre de te voir lundi.*"

"Too much, Al."

I grinned. "I can't wait to see you on Monday."

"Same here. *Auf Wiedersehen.*"

"*Auf Wiedersehen.*" I hung up, but instead of putting my phone away, I kept staring at it, tracing the screen with a green-polished fingertip. That had been our first taste of a long-distance relationship, and although it had been a sweet phone call, I couldn't help wondering if that would be enough when I no longer had my dad to go back to afterward.

★★★★★

I'd thought the rest of break would drag, but between my dad coming home, Van putting me through the wringer with errands, and studying like a machine, Monday arrived in a flash. The good news was, that meant seeing Liam. The bad news—I had to sit through everyone talking about their awesome spring break trips first.

"I can't believe you missed it," Dana gushed as we set our trays down at their usual table in the cafeteria. "It was soooo fun."

"Soooo fun," Leni echoed, picking slices of tomato off her veggie burger.

"We got drunk and hooked up with hot guys, like, every night. Oh my gosh, Len, remember Barry?"

"Barry!" Leni cracked up and Dana joined in, and I sat there, sipping at my Coke and waiting for an explanation that never came. Barry must've been a real riot.

"Barry was so funny," said Dana, as if reading my mind. "Like, we had this waiter, and we thought he didn't speak English, but then it turned out he just had an accent and he was speaking English the whole time, and then Barry was all, 'Oh my God, that was *English*! Whaaat?' It was hilarious."

"Mmhmm," I murmured around my straw.

"Maybe you had to be there," Leni said generously.

"Sounds like it." *I definitely had to spend thousands of dollars to go to Jamaica to do exactly what we could've done at one of Macy Easton's parties any weekend. Definitely*. "Glad you guys had a great time."

"How was here?" Dana asked with a sniff.

I shrugged. "Good. Hung out with Vanessa. Spent time with my dad."

"Fun," Leni offered, and I could tell she wanted to mean it.

"Not with Nate?" Dana asked coolly.

I froze. Had she seen me with him at the Lunchbox? She couldn't have. "Why would I hang out with Nate?"

"I saw you on CelebriTeens.com with Liam and Vanessa, at some restaurant. Apparently he's your boyfriend now?"

Oh God. "It is so not what you think," I assured Dana, racking my brain for how I *could* explain it. "He was just...helping me deal with that whole paparazzi mess, to make it clear there's nothing going on between me and Liam." There—that was close enough to the truth, if a little pathetic-sounding.

"If you say so."

"I say so. There is definitely nothing going on between me and Nate, I assure you." *At least not from my end.*

"Well, he's right over there," said Leni. "I'm sure he can settle this." She always had a way of developing thoughts at the worst times. "Hey, Nate!"

Nate had been heading toward his usual table, but he stopped in his tracks at the sound of Leni's voice and turned to us. His expression quickly flitted from surprised at being summoned by Leni to something considerably less readable when he saw I was sitting with her. "Hi, ladies."

"Come sit with us," Dana offered, her voice syrupy sweet as she indicated the empty chair next to me.

His eyebrows rose, but after a quick look at his friends, he slid his tray onto the table and sat. "How was your break?" he asked Dana and Leni, avoiding eye contact with me completely.

"Good." Dana drew out the word, in full flirtation mode now. "Lots of sun, tequila, and bikini time. What more could a girl ask for?"

"Male company?" Nate suggested with a slow smile. If I wasn't mistaken, he was flirting right back. "Sorry I missed it. The bikini time, at least."

Dana's cheeks flushed a little at Nate's response, and I mentally threw up in my mouth. "Maybe next time. What'd you do over break?"

He didn't so much as glance at me, not that I wanted him to. "Just hung out," he said dismissively. "Nothing special."

I could feel Dana's smirk, even with my eyes still on my salad. "What about your 'date' with Ally? I saw it online."

Nate laughed. "First rule of Hollywood—never believe anything you see. Or hear. Right, Duncan?" He elbowed me in the ribs.

I was tempted to elbow him back elsewhere, harder, but I refrained.

"Needless to say, I missed having real girls around," said Nate, playing with the stupid black, yellow, and green bracelet Dana must've picked up in Negril. "Glad to have you ladies back."

This was pathetic. Nate had no interest in Dana, and I knew it. Did he think he was making me jealous? Why was he even trying?

"I always wondered when you'd drop that fantasy," said Dana, watching his fingers, Leni and I obviously fading into the background.

Nate laughed. "Vanessa's hot, that's it. Being famous doesn't automatically make you fun. If anything, it seems to make you pretty weird."

"Hey, fuck you," I broke in without even thinking.

All three of them turned to stare at me, and Nate's mouth twisted into an amused smile. "Come on, Ally. You have to admit that 'date' was lame." He turned back to Dana. "Celebrities are lame. And trust me, anyone who even tries to date one should be committed."

I knew if I sat there for a second longer, I was going to call Nate out on all his stupid bullshit, so I jumped up and started gathering my things. There was no way I was subjecting myself to this absurd conversation.

"Where are you going?" asked Leni, all stupid innocence again.

"Quiz next period," I lied apologetically.

"Shopping after school?" Dana asked, though her eyes were still on Nate.

"Can't. Work."

"Oh, good," I heard Nate say to Dana as I threw the last of my trash on my tray. "Then you're free tonight."

If I rolled my eyes any harder, they were going to fall out of my skull. I never thought I'd say this, but if I didn't get out of my real life and onto a TV set soon, I was going to lose my mind.

★★★★★

I skipped French that afternoon, partly because I really didn't feel like seeing Nate again and partly because sometime during Calc I'd started imagining giving Liam a very warm welcome back to the U.S. and now I couldn't stop. Even with my car radio blasting on the way over to the lot, the ride seemed to take forever. And of course I misplaced my pass, and of course I chipped my nail polish on the steering wheel, and of course I tripped and nearly fell on my butt on my way in.

But when I saw Liam across the room, wearing a tight blue T-shirt I knew probably did great things for his eyes and I could see did great things for the rest of him, I melted into a huge pile of no-other-crap-matters. He hadn't seen me yet—he was in the middle of a scene with Jamal—so I just stood patiently on the side and looked my fill.

At least until a hand gripped my arm and yanked me away. "Hey!" Vanessa said, her voice strangely loud. "You're finally here." She shoved her cell phone in my hand. "I need you to pull off my messages and then call that guy at the radio station and see if you can bump my interview an hour. Then cancel my morning krav maga; I'm having brunch with Liam at the Beverly Wilshire. I have Bikram Yoga in the afternoon anyway. And then Liam and I have that party tomorrow night. Bryn has some dress on hold for me; ask her about it, and then I need you to pick it up."

I was still trying to process the "brunch with Liam" part when she started tapping her foot. "Would you mind? I really need this stuff done."

"Yes, ma'am," I bit out, wondering why Vanessa was suddenly being so bossy. Then I activated her screen and immediately saw a note she'd obviously intended for me to see ASAP: *Reporter is here.*

Great. So much for even talking to Liam. If a reporter was watching, that meant Liam and Vanessa would have to be in full couple mode, and all of us would be trying extra-hard to prove I was nothing but hired help.

I got to work making the calls, then dealt with all the interview requests and texts from Jade's assistant,

Bryn, coming through to *my* phone. It was a good half hour before I got to look up from all the screens, and that was only to confirm to Vanessa that she could pull off the hot-pink top they'd decided to put her in to reshoot a scene.

I was just responding to a text from Bryn informing me exactly which bag by which designer I needed to pick up ASAP in order for Van to get photographed with it when another text popped up on Vanessa's screen. From Liam. *Hi, beautiful.*

My stomach clenched at the sight of his message to Vanessa. Holy shit. They really *were* fooling around behind my back. I looked up to shoot daggers at Liam and saw him grinning at me and waggling his own cell. *Oh. Whoops. Overreact much, Ally?* This was actually sort of brilliant. I finished my response to Bryn and switched over to Vanessa's phone. *Hi yourself, handsome. Missed you while you were gone.*

I missed you too. Never thought I'd be so happy to come to work.

I let the butterflies happily flit around for a few seconds before refocusing on the rest of the messages, then moved closer to set with the phone to try to get some good action shots to tweet. I snuck in a couple of shots of Liam, then boldly tweeted one: *Check out the cutie on set w/me today!!* <3

The responses flew in immediately, and I couldn't help the little swell of pride at how many admirers my boyfriend had. Sure, it usually freaked me out more than anything, but today, sneaking glances at him across the set, the feeling that I was just really, really lucky kicked everything else's butt.

At least until I heard, rather than saw, someone take the seat next to me, followed by an unfamiliar voice saying, "Ally, right?"

The reporter. Crap. Thankfully, Vanessa's phone was already in my hand, and I could easily tuck it under my thigh. "Right," I said in the best "I'm too busy for you" tone I could muster. Because Bryn's texts on what brand of flip-flops Van should be wearing for her beach photo-op that weekend were obviously of the utmost importance.

"I'm Gavin. Nice to meet you." He extended a hand, and I reluctantly shook it. It took no time at all to see he was the kind of guy who was used to getting his way with a charming smile, and admittedly, he was pretty hot. But Liam was hotter, and if this asshole thought his dimples were going to get him anywhere, he had no idea who he was dealing with.

And then I realized that was the point. Just like with the reporters on our disastrous double date, the story was whichever one we decided to tell.

"*Really* nice to meet you," I replied, feigning disappointment at the loss of contact when I took my hand back. "So, you're here to do a story on Vanessa and Liam?"

"I'm here to write about the show," he lied through his teeth as he put his recorder down on the table between us. Reporters never came to pilot shoots to write about the show. Until *Daylight Falls* got picked up, Vanessa and Liam were the only story that mattered, and we both knew it. "It's certainly getting a lot of interest for a pilot."

"It's a great show with great actors. I'm glad it's getting the recognition it deserves."

"Really great actors," Gavin said with a nod, though I was sure he was exactly the type who thought all teen actors were bullshit. "So were you surprised when Vanessa got the part of Bailey?"

"Not really," I lied, knowing exactly where this was going. "I mean, I know it had been written for a white girl, as pretty much everything in Hollywood seems to be, but Van's perfect for the part, as I'm glad you're getting to see today. Anyone who thinks she got the part for any reason other than her skill is going to feel like an idiot when they see the pilot. And I *know* her performances are going to encourage other writers and casting directors to write parts for actors of color, or at least be open to blind casting."

If Gavin was surprised by my vehemence, he didn't let on. I could feel him scrutinizing my face, though, and I hoped it meant he was intrigued enough by the topic to focus on what the real story should be. Instead, without missing a beat, he said, "And she's obviously got great chemistry with Liam Holloway, both on and off the set."

"That she does," I said automatically, waggling my eyebrows like we were both in on the joke that the two of them couldn't keep their hands off each other. Because of course he couldn't want to talk about anything important for five seconds. How could racism in Hollywood possibly trump two pretty stars kissing for the cameras? "They're so supportive of each other's careers. It's really nice to see. So refreshing."

"Has Vanessa had past boyfriends who weren't?"

Ugh, crapweasel. "Of course not, but it's a vibe I get being around a lot of celebrities. There's always a feeling of competition. And for good reason—it's a competitive industry, and there's a lot of talent out there."

"There is, there is," Gavin said in a tone I'd come to think of as "Hollywood thoughtful." My phone was lighting up with a barrage of texts and e-mails, but I forced myself to ignore it, even though Gavin could plainly see I didn't have time for this stupid crap right now. I knew full well the second I turned him away, the story would turn into something ugly. "Anyone in particular come to mind?"

Zoe. "Nope. I mean, when I think of talent, sure." I laughed, the false sound unsettling to both of us, I was sure. "But at least on the *Daylight Falls* set, everyone has been awesome. Both to one another and to me."

"Even Zoe Knight?" Gavin asked conspiratorially, as if my answer would be a secret just between us. Because, sure, I'm probably just that stupid. Once, maybe. Not again. "I've heard a *lot* of rumors..."

"People get jealous," I said with a shrug, my nails digging into my thigh to force out the words I knew were necessary. "Zoe's really sweet, and she was thrilled for Vanessa when she got the part. Plus, she's so great as Grace. Like, right here, watch this scene where the two of them are talking about seducing Mr. Vasquez."

"But—"

"No, watch it. You'll see what I mean." My phone lit up again, and I took that as my perfect cue, even though it was probably just another text from Bryn. "I gotta take this. Thanks so much for talking with me!"

I hopped off my chair and headed toward craft services for a little peace and decaf. It wasn't a text from Bryn at all, though; it was a call from my mom. My blood turned to ice. "Is everything okay?" I asked as soon as I picked up.

"Everything's fine," she assured me. "I was just hoping you might come home for dinner tonight. Your father and I wanted to talk to you about something."

"I'm at work," I said, keeping my voice low. Immediately, I felt like a bitch. Vanessa would've let me go; it was me who didn't want to. I wanted to wait around until the stupid reporter and everyone else left, and then spend some time with Liam. But apparently I should've paid more attention to the universe's sign that that wasn't going to happen today.

"Can we eat at, like, seven?" I added quickly. "I have to pick up a bunch of stuff for Vanessa on my way home, then bring it by her place later."

"Sure, honey. I'll see you then."

"Everything's okay, right?" I couldn't help asking again.

She laughed. "Yes, I promise."

"Okay. I'm trusting you. And I'll see you at seven."

"Bye, honey."

I said goodbye and hung up, slipped my phone in my pocket, and pulled out Vanessa's so I could look at Liam's last text. Then I wrote out my own, to give him a heads-up I'd be ducking out but allow us to at least say goodbye. *Ally has to leave on the early side, so if you need her to pick anything up for you from Kitson, let her know.* Then I went back to set. Vanessa was finally on a break.

"I have to leave at six," I told her, glancing around to make sure Gavin was otherwise occupied before slipping her phone back to her. "Thanks for that," I murmured before going back to my regular tone to say, "I'll pick up your dress and everything else and drop them off at your house tonight."

"Perfect," Vanessa said with a smile. "I'll see you back here Wednesday? I need to put in some more SAT time so my parents can stop moaning about how I'd better keep my looks or I'm going to end up working at a gas station."

"Ah, I do miss your parents, so much."

"Trust me," she said wryly. "They miss you even more." Then her phone rang, and she checked the screen and sighed. "It's Jade. It is *always* Jade. Sorry, I gotta take this."

I nodded and eavesdropped as she got set up on yet another date with Liam. Of course, to add insult to injury, I was then stuck making the dinner reservation and dropping hints on Twitter. I'd just hit Send when Gavin came up to me again, slipped me a card, and then walked away.

I glanced at the back, knowing exactly what I'd see there. I wasn't disappointed. *Let me know if you ever realize you've got more to say on...anything.* –G. It was by no means the first time I'd received a card like that from a reporter, and I knew it wouldn't be the last.

But as I watched Liam from across the room and knew I wouldn't even be able to kiss him goodbye, it was the first time I didn't immediately crumple it up.

"SO, WHAT'S UP?" I ASKED as soon as I got in the door. I dropped my massive amounts of "Vanessa purchases" on the living room couch and walked back into the kitchen, where my parents were sitting at the island.

"Good evening to you too, my dear." My dad rolled his eyes and kissed me on the forehead. "Your mother already told you it wasn't anything bad. Stop worrying."

I rolled my eyes. "You guys can't be trusted. Smells good, though. More peanut noodles, huh?"

"Of course." We took our seats at the dining room table just as my mom brought out a steaming bowl of said noodles. My dad's treatment wasn't without its side effects, and whatever it did to the inside of his mouth meant he could barely tolerate any food textures in his first few days out of the hospital. Apparently, the peanut noodles from Golden Wok around the corner were the perfect amount of slimy.

"Where's Lucy?" I asked as my mother returned to the kitchen to grab whatever she and I were eating for dinner in addition to the salad that was already on the table; the rest of us had gotten sick of peanut noodles after week two.

My father coughed, and I knew Lucy was the topic at hand. I sighed. This was not going anywhere good.

"She's at Angie's," said my mother, returning to the table with a lasagna. "Listen, Ally, I know Lucy's a big girl, but she's still so young. I don't think it's a good idea for you to be talking her into coming to the hospital."

My hand froze midway to the lasagna. "Seriously? You think I talked Lucy into wanting to go visit?" I looked at my dad. "Is this because of what we talked about in the hospital?"

"We talked about this in the hospital?" His brows furrowed, and I sighed. Of course he wouldn't remember. His short-term memory when he was getting treatment was horrible.

"Lucy told me she talked about it with you and Vanessa the other night," Mom explained. "She said you were going to talk us into letting her visit."

"I said I would *talk to you* about letting her visit, and I *did* try to talk to Dad about it."

"What'd I say?"

"You said you'd talk to Mom," I admitted with a grumble. "But I think you're both wrong."

"Ally–"

"No," I said firmly, dropping my fork on my plate. About this, I was confident, and Lucy was my little sister–I'd promised we would all get through this together, and there was no reason that had to wait until *after* my dad died. "You *are* both wrong. This is ridiculous. You might be...this might be it. And poor Lucy's just going to think about all the time she missed with you. I know you don't remember our visits in the hospital, Dad, but I do. I remember you chatting with Vanessa. I remember you meeting Liam. Those aren't *bad* memories to me; they're important ones. And I want Lucy to have them too. They're part of our lives now."

My mother opened her mouth to respond, then instantly shut it. I was gaining ground for once, and I knew it. I hated fighting with them, hated that I was yelling, but couldn't they see how important this was? Couldn't *anyone* understand that time with loved ones wasn't something you could make up for after it had already passed?

Finally, they both sighed, and my mother said, "I don't know."

Of course she didn't. Because only half-acknowledging reality in this situation was her specialty. If only Liam were here, I swear he could've convinced them. Partly because he was just that charismatic, but partly because he'd *been* Lucy. I didn't know for sure that he had no regrets about seeing his mother in the hospital, but given how much he'd loved her, I couldn't imagine it. Suddenly, I was dying to talk to him, to ask, and I jumped up from the table and grabbed my cell phone from my bag.

"Ally!"

"I have to make a phone call," I said firmly to my mother. "I can't do this right now." Without another glance back at the table, I marched upstairs and dialed his number.

Four rings, then voicemail. I hung up and tried again. Same thing.

I was about to try a third time when the memory of making him and Vanessa a dinner reservation that night floated into my brain. Of course he was out with Vanessa when I needed him. *Of fucking course.*

I hurled my phone at the carpet, tears burning at my eyes. We had so little time left before I went to school, so little time left before my dad's...expiration date. How was *this* how we were spending it? A continent apart for a week and not even allowed to hug upon his return? Me needing him and him being on a date with my best friend? We still had another six weeks until upfronts, when we'd learn the fate of *Daylight Falls.* There was no way I could survive like this.

But what were my alternatives, really? Break up with him? I couldn't imagine that hurting any less. Just the thought of never hearing his soft "*Bon nuit*" in my ear again as I drifted off to sleep, my cell phone pressing into my pillow at a far-too-late hour, made me ache. Would I really be any less lonely if I ended things?

You would if you got with Nate, the devil on my shoulder informed me, and I immediately shook it off. I wasn't interested in Nate, and certainly not after his gross display with Dana earlier that day. Clearly he was still bitter about the double date, and if he really did like me, he had an awful way of showing it.

The only other option was burning a hole in the back pocket of my jeans. Telling Gavin that this was all a hoax would bust apart Liam and Vanessa for sure. But what else would it screw up? Nothing I was willing to take a chance on, no matter how mad I was. I finally did what I knew I should've done earlier and ripped the card in two before tossing it in the trash.

Then I curled up into a ball on top of my covers and stared at where my phone lay on the carpet until it blurred from my tears. By the time a soft knock sounded on my door a few minutes later, I was already half-asleep.

★★★★★

I woke up extra early to do all the homework I hadn't done the night before and saw that I had four missed calls from Liam and a text that said, *Are you OK??*

It was too early to call him back—if he *was* awake, he'd be out running without his phone anyway—so I just texted, *Fine, I just really needed to talk. I'll see you on set tomorrow.*

I might've forgotten for a few minutes last night that he was out with Vanessa, but I certainly couldn't forget that they'd be at brunch this morning or at a party tonight. Already I knew if I looked at CelebriTeens.com, I'd see pictures of them from last night, holding hands, maybe feeding each other. I wondered which were worse—the images in my brain or the images out there on the Internet for everyone to see.

He tried me again while I was in class, presumably when he woke up. I tried him again during lunch, but it went straight to voicemail. By the time he tried again, this time during French, I just shut off my phone. The frustration of our schedules forcing us off track was only mounting in my brain to the point where I couldn't concentrate.

"Doing okay there, Duncan?" Nate whispered.

"Great," I replied tightly. "Heard you had a good date last night."

"*Très bien*, actually."

"Really?"

He snorted softly. "What do you think?"

I still had no idea what to think, honestly, but I certainly wasn't going to tell Nate that. I went back to focusing on Madame Boulanger and debating whether or not I was going to bother trying to call Liam after school. I was afraid if I got his voicemail one more time, I would throw my phone again, and this time there'd be no carpet to cushion its fall.

I was still trying to decide when I turned my phone back on during my walk to my car and saw a text that said, *This is ridiculous. Can you please come over when you get out?*

I wanted to, with every bone in my body, but I couldn't help thinking how painful it would be to spend time with him, only to watch him leave to spend the evening with Vanessa yet again.

Don't you need to get dressed for the party?

His response was immediate. *I need to get undressed first.*

So sue me, a girl could only think so rationally after a text like that.

★★★★★

It took all my self-control to stay within the speed limit on the way over to his apartment. I debated slipping on sunglasses to head upstairs, but there was no point; his doorman knew full well who I was, and I never bumped into anyone else. I spent the short elevator ride reminding myself that I wanted to have a real conversation, but then he opened the door in nothing but a pair of low-slung pajama pants and words flew out of my brain.

"Hey," he said warmly, tapping the door shut behind me since I was too frozen to do it myself.

"You play really dirty," I said with a groan, dropping my bag and letting him pull me into a kiss.

"Pretty's all I got," he murmured against my lips. "I gotta take advantage."

"It is not, and you know it." I raked my fingertips through his newly cut hair, grazing his scalp, and relished the way it made him lightly shiver against my body. "But I'm definitely not complaining about you taking advantage of anything right now." I continued the trail of my fingertips down his smooth, well-muscled back. "I missed you."

"I missed you too. So much you have no idea." He ducked low to kiss the spot where throat met collarbone, sucking at my skin just enough to make me purr. "Seeing you and not being able to touch you is torture. I thought I was going to physically throw that reporter asshole outside."

"Next time, feel free." My skin tingled as he kissed his way down to the edge of my T-shirt. "You can feel free to do away with this shirt, too. I wouldn't want us to be uneven or anything."

"Alexandra Duncan—always out for justice," he said, smiling against one of the curves peeking out of the neckline, then sliding the shirt up and over my head. "Remind me to ask you later what he said to you."

"You can ask me now," I pointed out breathlessly as hands and lips caressed my skin.

"I don't give a shit now," he rumbled in my ear, pulling me firmly against his chest. "I care about my incredibly hot girlfriend now."

Key word being now, I thought for only an instant before he went back to the tried-and-true spot on my throat and thinking—among other things—got much, much harder.

"You really did miss me," I murmured as he rose up to kiss me again, pressing closer, the thin pajama pants leaving nothing to the imagination and no question as to how badly he wanted me.

"That's what I've been saying." He held me in place with a strong arm wrapped around my waist and rocked his hips against mine. "I thought about you nonstop."

"How nonstop?" I teased, sliding my hands down his chest, over those impeccable abs, and down to the drawstring of the pants.

"Very." He sucked my lower lip into his mouth, then nipped it. "At very inappropriate moments."

"Were the moments inappropriate?" I asked, drawing the string lightly across his six-pack. "Or were you?"

"Both. Definitely both." His tongue caressed mine, and he stroked my rib cage with his big, warm palms again. "You definitely got me through some lonely German nights."

My heart raced at the admission. For some reason, it was the sexiest thing of all knowing that when left to take matters into his own hands, I was still the one he thought about. That even with physical distance between us, I was the one who turned him on.

I stopped teasing with the drawstring of his pants and started working the knot instead. I wanted more of him, wanted him to know I felt the same way. Wanted to give him more to think about the next time we were apart.

"Ally," he breathed. "Jesus." He dropped his hands to loosely cover mine. "You might not want to do that."

"Why's that?"

"Because I'm going commando underneath."

My heart pounded at his words, and I didn't resist as he gently pulled my hands away and put them on his broad shoulders instead. "Didn't think we were quite there yet." His voice was warm and teasing in my ear, making my pulse pound.

Maybe we were there. Maybe I was an idiot to keep waiting when I had a boyfriend who had to disappear to Europe one day and kiss a gorgeous actress the next. Maybe it was time I gave him something else to remember on a lonely German night. I stepped back and drank in the sight of his shirtless body, all smooth golden skin and muscles like marble. He was, quite literally, perfect. It was unnerving. Feelings of inadequacy fought their way to the surface as I skated my fingertips over every bare inch.

"Am I passing inspection?" he asked hoarsely.

I swept over his shoulders, walked around to look at his smooth, hard back, the long legs I knew were toned from daily runs beneath the gray cotton. "A little too well, maybe," I joked, but it didn't feel funny.

He reached around and pulled me back, folding me into his arms. "Ally, listen to me." He tipped my chin up until I was staring directly into his ocean-colored eyes. "You are beautiful. So beautiful it hurts." He took my hand and placed it on the warm skin of his chest. "*Tu as mon...* How do you say 'heart' again?"

"*Coeur*," I answered, feeling my own squeeze.

"*Tu as mon coeur*," he repeated with a smile, stroking my cheek with his index finger. "I don't want to do something you're not ready for, ever, but please don't let it be because you see me as anything other than a guy who is completely crazy about you."

I closed my eyes, letting the words wash over me, but I already knew he had my heart too. Slowly, tentatively, he kissed me again, and this time, I let my fingertips wander back down to the drawstring.

"Ally." He tried to pull away, but I held fast, taking control. Nothing else in my life was on my terms, but this was, and somehow I didn't think Liam would have any complaints about that. His hands sliding into my hair a moment later cemented that theory. He kissed me deeply as my fingers worked the knot, and then a harsh, loud melody broke into the quiet, startling us both.

"What the hell is that?" I blurted, jumping back. "Is that your phone? What's that ringtone?"

"Shit. I didn't realize how late it was."

I looked at my own watch, which allowed Liam to grab his phone. "It's not even five. I thought the party was at eight."

"I have to look over the shots from Germany first. They came in while I was at brunch, and Jade wants approval before the party. She wasn't supposed to call until five, but..." He held up his cell so I could see her name flashing on the screen.

"Jade? What does Jade have to do with your photo shoot?"

He nibbled on his thumbnail, the closest thing I knew he had to a nervous gesture. "Well, since she was involved in so much of my life with this whole Vanessa thing anyway–"

No. *No no no.* "You *signed* with her? You signed with *Jade*? Now you're fully under her thumb too?" I got up and grabbed my shirt from the floor, dodging Liam's hand when he reached for me. "What the hell, Liam? Since when do you of all people want a publicist?"

"I don't *want*–I just...ugh, shit." He scrubbed his hands over his face. "I knew I should've talked to you. I'm sorry, Al. Please don't go."

My eyebrows shot up. "You think I'm staying for your call and your interview and your 'assignment' from Jade before you get dressed to go to a party with Vanessa, which is *also* Jade's doing?" I threw on my shirt, not even bothering to make sure I had it on the right way. "No, Liam. Just...no."

He watched quietly while I walked to the door to pick up my bag. "I'm so sorry," he rasped when I turned back around. "I just wanted to see you. I wasn't thinking about all this shit."

"'All this shit' is your life, all day, every day," I reminded him. "And being with you and working for Vanessa–it makes it mine too. It means you're not there when I call you. It means my 'reunion' with my boyfriend was a night of being ignored, followed the next day by what was basically a booty call. I just...I can't–"

The same unfamiliar ringtone started up again; Jade was nothing if not relentless. But this time, it was five o'clock on the dot. My slot in his schedule had come to an end.

"Ally–"

"Just get it, Liam. I'll see you tomorrow."

He glanced at the phone, then back at me, but we both knew which one was gonna win. Even when he dashed over to give me a warm kiss goodbye before answering it.

GAVIN'S ARTICLE WAS PUBLISHED on Friday, and I was relegated to a brief mention as "Ms. Park's dutiful assistant," with my only quote being about how fabulous Vanessa and Liam were together. I snorted and clicked out of the stupid story without reading the rest.

At least I'd tried. Not that I'd ever have a voice in Hollywood—not when it came to my personal thoughts and not when it came to my personal life either, apparently. Sure, Liam had called and apologized at some point later that night, and I knew he meant it, but for some reason, the ache in my heart from that argument still wasn't going away.

"What's the matter, honey?"

I turned in my desk chair to see my mother standing in the doorway, a basket of laundry in arm. "Nothing. Just more Hollywood stupidity. Need help?"

"Nah, I'm just tossing these into the machine." She set down the basket and came in to sit down on my bed. "Is this about Vanessa? Or about Liam?"

I sighed. "Both. Always both, seeing as those two are officially inseparable."

"I have to admit, I'm still not certain I understand this situation. You're dating him, and Vanessa's also dating him?"

"No. Well, sort of. I'm *really* dating him, and Vanessa's *pretend* dating him."

If I didn't think it sounded stupid before, the look on my mother's face confirmed it. "I see. I think. What does it mean that you're *really* dating him if she's the one actually...going on dates with him?"

I opened my mouth to answer her and snapped it shut. What could I say? That our "dates" so far had consisted of hanging out in either my house or his apartment, but I was verboten out in public unless it was as part of yet another publicity stunt for Van? That we sure liked each other a whole lot and made each other laugh, and talked for hours, and had touched nearly every inch of each other's bodies, but the idea of grabbing a slice of pizza around the corner was totally laughable?

"Never mind," she said with a wave of her hand. "I never understand teenage things. I think I'd just rather not."

"Then we're in agreement, because I'd definitely rather you didn't," I admitted, grateful to be given the out.

"Still, I'd like to meet this boy. When is that going to happen?"

My eyebrows shot up. "Excuse me?"

"He's *really* dating my daughter, isn't he? And has been for a few months? I think that entitles a mother to some sort of meeting." She crossed her arms. "Surely this could be arranged, especially if my daughter wants to continue to be able to operate with no curfew."

"Mom! I'm eighteen–"

"And yet you still live in this house and drive a car that I handed down to you, so I'm pretty sure that means you have to do what I say." She smiled, and it was so nice to see her joking around again that I couldn't help smiling back.

"You know I barely get to see him outside of the set."

"I'm sure you'll find a way. Your father's met him, after all."

The proverbial light bulb pretty much exploded over my head just then. "Tell you what—let Lucy go visit Dad when he goes back in."

"Ally—"

"Hear me out. I'll get Liam to come too—it always looks good for him when he visits sick patients, so Jade can't exactly object." Not that I had run this by Liam, of course, but he *had* said he wished he could help in some way. "We'll have a little family gathering, and she'll be so starstruck it'll be exactly the kind of fun, distracted, instant-good-memory visit she needs. She gets to see Daddy, you both get to meet Liam... Pretty win-win, right?"

She sighed and shook her head wearily. "You're not going to give up, are you?"

"Definitely not. Is that a yes?"

"If you can get your movie star boyfriend to sit down with your family in your father's hospital room... you've got yourself a deal," she said, bracing her hands on her thighs and standing up.

Hmm. Once she put it that way, maybe it wasn't such a gimme after all. No matter—it was worth a shot. And if I had faith in our relationship at all, I had to believe he'd give me this.

★★★★★

He did, though it wasn't entirely without a little teeth pulling. "Are you sure I'm not underdressed?"

"It's a hospital room," I reminded him. We both kept our voices low as we exited Liam's Range Rover and headed through the front doors. His head was down and sporting a Lakers cap, while mirrored aviators covered his very recognizable blue-green eyes. "My dad will be in pajamas. Jeans and a polo is fine."

"And you don't think it's stupid that I brought a DVD instead of flowers?"

"You're not allowed to bring flowers. A DVD is cute. My mom will love seeing you in a movie."

"I feel like an egotistical jackass."

I sighed. "You're ridiculous, you know that? You've already met my dad, and he loved you."

"I thought you said he doesn't remember me."

"He doesn't, but I remember he loved you, and so do you. You have your ID on you?"

"Jared McElroy, at your service."

"Perfect." We flashed them at the front desk, got my dad's room number, and made our way to the elevator.

"Thank you for doing this," I said to Liam as soon as the elevator doors closed, leaving us alone in the enclosed space. We still couldn't touch—not with the security cameras rolling—but I hoped my voice conveyed just how grateful I really was. "It means a lot to me and to my mom, and I know it will to Lucy."

"It means a lot to *me*," he replied quietly, and I hated that I couldn't see his eyes through the mirrored lenses right then. "Thank you for asking."

I pursed my lips, because if I didn't, I knew I would lean across the elevator and kiss him right then. Fortunately, if you could call it that, the elevator doors opened, and we walked out and through the little maze of hallways until we reached my dad's room.

"Let me go in first," I instructed, placing my palm lightly on his chest to stop him in his tracks. He didn't argue, and I slipped inside.

"Honey, there you are." My mother stood up from the chair next to my father's bed and came over to kiss me on the cheek. "Where's–"

"Mom said you have a surprise for me!" Lucy blurted, bouncing over. "What is it what is it what is it?"

I laughed, covering her mouth loosely with my hand. "Chill, Luce. For this surprise, you're going to have to be very, very quiet, okay? No screaming."

"I don't *scream*," said Lucy. "I'm ten years old, you know."

"If you say so." I stuck my head out into the hallway. "Sorry, Liam. I guess she's not that excited to see you after all."

"Ouch," said Liam, coming inside and pulling off his hat and sunglasses. "That kinda hurts, Lucy."

She screamed.

I rushed to shut the door behind him. "I said no screaming, Luce!"

"It's–it's–"

"Liam," he said, crouching down and lifting her hand to his lips. He was certainly no stranger to charming the tween set. "Nice to meet you, Lucy."

I rolled my eyes at my mom, and she smiled. "He's so handsome!" she mouthed.

"Duh," I mouthed back.

While Lucy continued to babble incoherently, Liam straightened up and extended a hand. "So nice to meet you, Mrs. Duncan."

"Nice to finally meet *you*, Liam. You two got here okay? No more paparazzi mishaps?"

For only the second time I'd ever seen, Liam blushed. "So sorry about all that, ma'am. Completely my fault, but it won't happen again."

Mom burst out laughing. "Ma'am. Wow. Haven't heard that one in a while. Let's just stick with Pam, shall we? And it's fine, Liam. My daughter's always brought a little drama with her everywhere."

"I do not!"

My parents rolled their eyes at each other, and Liam grinned. "I knew it."

"You knew nothing," I grumbled at him.

"So Liam, you're Vanessa's boyfriend, right?" Lucy asked. "Do you love her?"

The rest of us exchanged amused glances. We'd decided not to tell Lucy the truth about me and Liam, since her secret-keeping skills were revealed to be utterly nonexistent the day after she found out the truth about Santa Claus in kindergarten and my parents got a *lot* of angry calls from parents.

"Lucy, that's not polite to ask," I said firmly, trying to keep the smile off my lips.

"No, it's okay," said Liam. He crouched down until he was nose to nose with my sister. "Can I tell you a secret, Lucy? But you have to promise not to tell *anybody*."

Her eyes widened. "I promise."

"I actually like your sister. A *lot*," he whispered. "Don't tell anyone, okay?"

I smothered a laugh behind my hand as I watched Lucy's eyes widen even further, until I was pretty sure they were going to pop out of her skull. "But—"

"Our little secret, right?" He ruffled the top of her blond head. "You can keep a secret."

She nodded emphatically.

"Cool, I thought so." He looked up. "Ally, she can keep a secret, right?"

"I'm pretty sure you're playing with fire, Holloway."

He broke into a wide smile. "Nah, I can trust Lucy. We're buds now." He turned back to her. "So, is it true this is your first time here?"

"Uh-huh. I wasn't allowed to come before."

"And how's it going now?"

"Good. My dad gave me his pudding."

"Well, *you* are a very lucky girl! Your sister told me he hiccups a lot. Is that true?"

Lucy giggled. "*Yes*. Oh my God, before, he was trying to ask me about school, and he couldn't even say it, he just kept hiccupping. The nurse had to bring him medicine to stop. I didn't even know you could take medicine for hiccups! I always just hold my breath."

As Liam continued to chat with Lucy, I joined my mother in sitting back on the chair by Dad's bed. "He's wonderful with her," Mom murmured.

"He's wonderful with almost everything," I said ruefully. "The whole 'fake-dating my best friend' thing...not so much."

"I can see why they'd pair them up, though. He's really good-looking, isn't he?"

"He is."

"Good job," Mom whispered, and I smothered my laughter in response.

"Okay, my mom thinking my boyfriend is hot is way too weird."

"Sweetheart, your boyfriend is going to be on every TV set in America. I promise, many moms are going to find him attractive."

"If I vomit on the floor right now, can I blame it on Dad?"

She laughed, and we turned back to watching Liam and Lucy, my heart both swelling and aching at the sight of the beautiful normalcy between them and the recognition that it was only my father's illness, nearing its end one way or the other, that allowed for it.

WHETHER IT WAS THE WHOLE family's finally being together in that hospital room or Liam's visiting or my dad's vitamin supplements or just pure luck, my father's next scans revealed that the treatment was indeed working, putting him in a tiny, miraculous percentage of stage IV melanoma patients who actually got to see improvement.

My mother called me during my lunch period to tell me the news, and I was only too glad to have the excuse to leave the table—and our third scintillating conversation that week about the prom I wasn't going to—so I could answer in the relative quiet of the hallway. As soon as we hung up, I dialed Liam.

I tapped my foot frantically while I waited for him to pick up, my heart pounding. Just the idea of saying the words "the treatment is working" made my pulse pick up. I knew my dad was by no means out of the woods, but it was the best we could've hoped for at that point—the *only* thing we really could've hoped for, honestly.

The call went to voicemail, and I hung right up and tried again. This was not a voicemail message. This was a squeal-with-someone-you-knew-would-squeal-with-you kind of message. As the third ring sounded, I was hit with a burst of inspiration—after I told Liam my news, I would ask him to prom.

Yes, I knew that standing around in a tux with a bunch of high schoolers who'd probably just be gawking at him all night was probably the very last thing on earth he'd wanna do, and yes, of course there was the tricky little issue of the fact that he couldn't really be seen with me. But suddenly, with my father's health miraculously improving, anything seemed possible. I was going to use the same mantra my father had been using for the last three months: Focus on the goal and you'll find a way to get there. Well, my goal was to get to go to my senior prom with my boyfriend. I'd figure out the logistics later.

Voicemail again. So much for that. A call to Vanessa yielded similar results.

"Goddammit," I muttered, shoving my phone back in my bag.

"Everything okay?"

I whirled around. Nate stood in the doorway, looking at me curiously. "Everything's good," I answered. "Really good, actually." I was dying to tell someone, and even though I'd been working to establish a distance between Nate and me, and even though he'd been sort of a jerk lately, I knew he'd care, and I was desperate to share the news with someone who would. "The treatment's working. It looks like my dad's actually getting better." As the words came out of my mouth, I could feel a huge, goofy smile blossoming on my face.

"Duncan!" Nate leaped forward and wrapped me up in a huge hug, and he whirled me around in a circle as I laughed. "That's fantastic!"

"Isn't it?"

"Man, when I saw the look on your face, I thought it was bad news for sure. Glad to hear it was the total opposite."

"Just a little communication frustration," I said lightly. It took me a moment to realize he was still hugging me, and I gently disentangled myself. "I'm supposed to go to Calc from here, but I really just want to skip the rest of the day and go home to hang out with my family."

"So go," Nate suggested.

I laughed. "I wish it was that easy. My parents are both at work and Lucy's at school. I expect that tonight will be a night of celebration at the Duncan house, though."

"Sounds like fun."

I was tempted to invite him—I was so grateful for his having been there to hear and appreciate the news when no one else was—but I knew that made no sense. This was a family thing, and my family didn't even know Nate existed. Once again, I was just trying to use him to make up for the people I *wanted* to be available to celebrate, but *those* people weren't answering their phones.

"Hope so," I responded. "Listen, I gotta go look over my problem sets for class, but I'll see you in French?"

"*Bien sûr.*"

I hadn't actually planned to go over my problem sets; what I *really* wanted was a celebratory slice of chocolate cake from the caf. But being near Nate always forced me to fight the urge to thank him just for being there when I needed him, and Lord knew he didn't need any more ammunition in that department.

I tried Van and Liam each one more time, to no avail, and then I trudged off to the library.

★★★★★

Liam called that night anyway, just to say hi, but by the time we were done talking about how he'd gotten a callback for the James Gallagher movie *and* was asked to cohost some party in New York during upfronts week—the week pilot pickups were announced by the networks, during which he and the rest of the world would learn the future of *Daylight Falls*—I no longer felt like sharing my news or discussing prom. Instead, I told him I needed to get off the phone to have dinner with my family, which was actually true.

"Cool," he said. "Say hi to your dad for me. I'd come by myself, but the stupid paparazzi are out in full force since I'm apparently a frontrunner for this role. I'll miss you while I'm locked in my apartment, memorizing lines."

"Mmhmm." Whatever.

"Oh, but hey, Josh is having another party on Friday night, and you should come."

"Didn't you not only have a lousy time at Josh's last party but tell Van that I probably would've hated it too?"

"Yeah, but this one's different."

"And why's that?"

"Um, because we'll be there together?" He actually sounded hurt that I hadn't thought of that first.

"But not *together*-together," I pointed out. "Vanessa will be the one who's there as your date. I'll just be her friend who you let tag along."

"Except that A) Josh knows to only invite people who are discreet to his parties, considering all the shit that goes down at them, and B) as my best friend, he knows who my actual girlfriend is and he'll make sure we get some time alone together. So now will you come with?"

Hmm, a date where we could actually be out as a couple? Granted, I wasn't exactly dying to hit up one of Josh Chester's parties, but could I really pass up such a rare opportunity? No, I could not, I decided, especially not when he'd let it slip that he'd told Josh about me, which somehow felt like a Very Big Deal.

"Of course," I replied, feeling bad now that I hadn't been more enthusiastic about the invitation. "That sounds like fun. Just make sure I don't end up drunk and naked on YouTube, okay?"

He laughed. "Deal. *Bon nuit, ma chère.*"

★★★★★

Part of me was dying to tell Nate that Liam had come through as a "real" boyfriend after all by inviting me to the party, but I was so nervous about the actual event that I decided to reserve any and all bragging until I had proof that I'd gotten through the night without ensuring it wasn't otherwise a disaster of epic Hollywood proportions.

Of course, I had no idea what to wear, but that's what Van was for. She was still Liam's official date, but she promised that once we got inside the house (or mansion, really), he was all mine, especially since she was interested in some private time of her own with the host himself. (I didn't have the heart to tell her that Liam thought she and Josh would be an absolute disaster.) In the meantime, I was going to take serious advantage of both the styling skills Van had picked up on the set of *Daylight Falls* and her designer-heavy wardrobe.

I ended up going casual—or as casual as one can possibly look in clothing that costs more than a semester of dorm fees—in a pair of my own skinny jeans (Van's were so tight I needed to take periodic "breathing breaks" by opening the button); super-high, black patent leather Louboutins; a Chloé tank; and a Marc Jacobs blazer I was relieved to see fit nicely even though I had a good fifteen pounds on Van. She even did my makeup, using what seemed like every Dior product known to man, and when she was done, I looked like a considerably hotter version of myself—exactly what I was going for.

Of course, we then needed another hour to get Van ready, and by the time I texted Liam to pick us up, we were firmly in the "fashionably late" category. Once again, Vanessa got into the passenger seat like she basically co-owned the car, but on the chance the paps *were* tailing Liam's SUV, I could hardly argue. I climbed into the backseat as gracefully as I could considering the height of the heels and squeezed the hand Liam reached behind him to say hello.

I don't know what I'd pictured Josh's place looking like, but nothing could've prepared me for the fact that he lived in what appeared to be the Playboy mansion, only with far more brightly colored lights and crazy-expensive cars in the driveway. Liam left the car in one of the heavily monitored reserved parking spots and circumvented the front entrance with the comfort of a guy who'd been there a couple thousand times.

Van and I followed him around to the back of the house, which turned out to be a tremendous pool area complete with a waterslide, a massive wet bar, and even a grotto a la Chez Hef. Hip-hop blared from the speakers, and even from a distance I could see the bartenders performing some impressive tricks with bottles of liquor in the light of the tiki torches that dotted the yard. Behind it all, the beach was plainly visible, the last traces of the sun still peeking out over the glittering water of the Pacific.

"Ridiculous, right?" Liam murmured in my ear, taking advantage of the thick crowd and dim lighting to snake an arm around my waist and pull me close. "He loves to give me shit for living in a one-bedroom apartment instead of creating my own little amusement park like he did."

"He does seem to have a whole lot more fun with his money than you do," I acknowledged. "You're eighteen. How do you *not* spend your money like this?" I swept my arm around the area, indicating the outdoor pool table (on top of which some couple was currently making out), the massive grill/fire pit area from which delicious smells were emanating, and the row of cabanas that lined one side of the property.

Liam shrugged. "Let's just say Josh and I have different ideas of fun." He leaned in and kissed my neck, brazenly confident in the shadow of a palm tree. "Except for one very, very similar idea."

I swatted him away teasingly. "I'm not *that* easy," I informed him. "At least, not until you get some of whatever is creating that awesome smell from the grill into me. And maybe a piña colada."

"Fair enough!" We glanced back to make sure Van was still with us and then took off for the bar. I could see Van's dark eyes darting around as she searched for Josh, and admittedly, I was curious to see him myself.

"Hey! Holloway!"

All three of us turned around to see the devil–er, host–himself heading in our direction, holding a noxious-looking drink. He wore only a lei and board shorts, revealing a toned and well-muscled body that had Van visibly drooling.

"Hey, man." Liam held up his hand for a high five that turned into some complicated handshake of the secret-society variety. "You remember Van."

"I do," said Josh, taking her hand and lifting it to his lips. He turned to me. "And you must be the lovely Alexandra I've heard so much about."

I hoped my blush was well-hidden by the dark. I knew he was hot from his movie posters, but up close he was heartbreakingly good-looking. I could only imagine what kind of havoc he and Liam could wreak as two single-boy BFFs on the prowl. Not that I *wanted* to imagine Liam as a single guy.

"Just Ally," I replied, letting him kiss my hand as well.

"Well, Just Ally, welcome to Casa Chester. Now please, eat, drink, and be merry!" He lifted his drink in the air in a toast and waltzed off to talk to a couple of blondes in bikinis.

"I'll drink to that," said Van, continuing on to the bar. We waited patiently behind a heavily tattooed chick I was pretty sure I recognized from a later season of *The Real World* and the kid from one of those Disney shows my sister was always watching. I couldn't even imagine Lucy's reaction to seeing him drink absinthe with The Girl with the Dragon Tattoo.

Then we were up, and I got myself a piña colada while Liam got a Red Stripe and Van a vodka with cranberry juice.

"I'm getting my teeth whitened on Tuesday anyway," she said dismissively as she took a long sip.

We continued on through the yard, stopping periodically for Van and Liam to say hi to various familiar faces and to pluck grilled shrimp or chipotle sliders from the trays being walked around by models in French maid costumes. More than one of the servers shot Liam a hungry look that had nothing to do with the contents of their plates, and resisting the urge to possessively grab his hand got harder and harder.

The urge grew even stronger when we happened upon none other than Shannah Barrett.

"Liam!" she cooed, bouncing over to air-kiss him on both cheeks. "I was wondering when you'd show up! We were just about to hit the hot tub. Care to join?" She grinned wickedly. "Bathing suits are optional, obviously."

I didn't know her, but God, I hated her. I literally had to bite my tongue to keep from pointing out that Liam wasn't there alone. Even if she didn't know I was Liam's girlfriend, she still should've felt shame talking that way in front of Vanessa, shouldn't she?

Hey, wait. Where *was* Vanessa?

"Maybe later," Liam replied with an annoyingly genuine-looking smile. "Ally's never been here before, and I promised her a tour of the house."

Shannah's gaze flicked over to me, clearly having just noticed my presence, and then flicked back to Liam as if I wasn't even worth a once-over. "Suit yourself," she sang, turning to head toward the hot tub, but not before lifting her crocheted white halter top over her head to give Liam a thorough glimpse of her tiny string bikini top.

At least he had the grace to blush. "Sorry," he murmured. "Shannah has a tendency to come on a little strong."

I raised an eyebrow. "If I had that body, I probably would too," I admitted. "And I'm guessing you've seen a whole lot more of it than that."

He glanced away and took a sip of his beer, and I knew I was right. Ugh. Not that I'd expected Liam to be a virgin—we'd never had the official "talk" but I wasn't naïve enough to assume any almost-nineteen-year-old guy was one, let alone a brutally hot model/actor—but knowing whom I'd be compared to in the event we *did* sleep together made me want to strap on a chastity belt.

"So!" he said brightly, obviously intent on changing the subject. "How about that tour I pretended I promised?"

I laughed. "Sounds good. Oh, but wait—where's Van?"

Liam gestured with his beer to where Van was blatantly flirting with Josh, cracking up at something he'd just said while her fingers gently massaged his knee, a move I recognized from many a successful usage. Clearly, Van was doing just fine and having a good time, which meant it was my turn to do the same. I followed Liam through the crowds, around the pool, and through the French doors at the back of the house, and found myself standing in the biggest personal media room I'd ever seen. Three walls were literally lined with DVDs, creating a 3-D wallpaper effect that made me dizzy. The fourth wall was entirely covered by a screen, onto which *Wild Things* was currently being projected.

Liam shook his head. "As far as Josh is concerned, this is the greatest classic of all time," he informed me, pointing up at the screen. "I cannot begin to tell you how many times he's forced me to sit through this movie."

"Forced, huh?" I said wryly as I watched Denise Richards emerge from a pool. "God, yeah, that must've been awful for you."

Liam laughed and tugged my hand. "Come on, I'll show you the game room."

The game room was equally incredible, packed with classic arcade games, a pool table, a small bank of slot machines, and an alcove with a poker table and seating for eight. We went through Josh's home gym—complete with sauna—a state-of-the-art kitchen my father would've killed for that I was sure Josh had never once touched, and a room devoted solely to Josh's guitar collection and a drum kit Liam confided to me Josh had no idea how to play.

"This place is absolutely ridiculous," I said to Liam as he led me upstairs. "How does he even have this kind of money? I think I've seen him in one movie, ever."

"Well, first off, his parents are completely loaded," said Liam as we walked past a bathroom that was done in marble from floor to ceiling. "His dad's a studio head and his mom's been on the same soap for like twenty years. I don't think they've even seen each other since Josh was conceived."

Well, that was pretty sad. I couldn't imagine life without my family's neat little nuclear unit. My stomach tightened as I realized that sometime in the near future, I might have to. Oh God, what if my dad's positive response to the drugs was a one-time thing? What if we really did end up becoming a family without a father? I used to be so good at forcing myself to internalize the negative possibilities, but things had been so relatively normal lately—positive, even—that I'd forgotten to stay prepared for the worst-case scenario. Hell, when was the last time I even did a mole check?

"Hey, you okay?" Liam snapped his fingers in front of my face. "Ally? Where'd you go?"

I blinked. Right. I was in public. With Liam. Not a great time to be lost in my own crazy head. "Sorry," I mumbled, taking a long sip of my piña colada. "Just got a little wrapped up in my own thoughts for a second there."

"Yeah, no kidding," he said softly, wrapping his fingers around mine. "Is everything all right?"

"Yeah, great," I replied. It was true at the moment, anyway. As of now, my dad was in a good place, and so were Liam and I. *Better than good*, I thought, looking down at our hands. We were standing at a party, with other people, and Liam was holding my hand. Granted, no one was actually around—the entire second floor was pretty quiet—but it was a real, public party nonetheless. For once, we actually felt like a legit boyfriend and girlfriend, and I liked it very much indeed. So much so that I pulled him close for a nice, long kiss that tasted like beer and coconuts.

"Mmm, what was that for?" he murmured when we parted.

"It's nice to be here with you," I replied softly, kissing him again. *Now*, I told myself. *You're finally alone, and he's in a good mood. Ask him about prom.* "And speaking of it being nice to be together—"

"Hold that thought." He took a long drink from his beer, draining it, and left it on a table in the hallway, freeing up both hands to circle my waist and pull me close. My eyes fluttered shut as I awaited the pressure of his lips on mine again, but instead I felt them press against my neck. My body shuddered slightly in response, nearly causing me to spill the remainder of my drink. I promptly set the glass on the table.

"Come on," he whispered into my ear, and the next thing I knew, I was being gently led to a pair of double doors at the end of the hallway that appeared to be locked by some sort of electronic combination.

"What the...?" I trailed off as I watched Liam punch in a series of numbers and then push open the doors to what was unquestionably Josh's master suite, complete with a set of totally cliché black silk sheets.

"It's ridiculous, I know, but it's the only place to get any privacy," he assured me, closing the doors behind us.

I'm not sure what expression was on my face—I was feeling such a swirl of emotions at that point—but obviously a hint of my anxiety was showing, because Liam instantly said, "I'm not trying to hint at anything by bringing you to a bedroom, just to be clear. It's just quiet. And comfortable."

I nodded dumbly. I didn't particularly feel any pressure from Liam, but I *did* feel like I wanted him to shut up and pull me into that bed immediately. For what, I wasn't sure, but that didn't seem to matter right now. I shrugged out of my borrowed blazer, tossed it on a ridiculous oversized chair shaped like a cupped palm, and kissed Liam with everything I had in me.

He responded instantly, pushing me back toward the bed so gently I didn't even realize what he was doing until my butt hit the plush mattress. I slipped off my shoes and lay back, watching with hooded eyes as he pulled off his shirt without so much as undoing a single button before climbing on top of me like a very gentle lion approaching its prey.

I might not have looked a damn thing like Shannah Barrett, or Van, or any of the other toned and tanned starlets milling around downstairs and outside, but the way Liam's sea-colored eyes raked over me before moving in for another kiss, you'd never have known I wasn't the hottest thing at that party. It was exactly what I'd wanted to feel the day I'd come onto him with the force of a cougar. Sexy. Wanted. And not "I want to be near you" wanted. More like "I want to be *in* you" wanted.

I sucked in a sharp breath as Liam kissed his way down the borrowed cami before slipping it up and over my head. The sheets were even softer than the shirt, and the combination of the silk of the fabric and the silk of his lips and tongue was making every inch of my skin prickle with heat. His fingers toyed with the button of my jeans and he looked up to meet my undoubtedly glassy gaze with one of his own. I nodded before I could even give it another thought.

I'd purposely worn the sexiest underwear I owned for just such an occasion, but watching the inch-by-inch revelation of my white lace boyshorts as he slowly pulled my jeans down my legs, it was as if they belonged to another person. What had I been thinking, wearing something so ridiculously virginal? I mean, I *was* a virgin, but I didn't really need to remind him of that with my little wedding-night ensemble, did I?

Judging from the row of butterfly kisses he placed along the entire length of the waistline, Liam had no complaints about my lingerie choice. He ran his hands lightly up my thighs, and I shivered.

"God, you're beautiful," he whispered, his breath tickling my skin through the lace in places it'd never before been tickled. It was all I could do not to beg him to hurry up as he slowly, painstakingly kissed and touched his way back up to my belly button before hooking an index finger into the waistband and giving it a gentle tug. I held my breath as I prepared to be exposed.

Until the door flew open, revealing none other than Josh Chester himself.

I shrieked and leapt away from Liam, grabbing a black-silk-covered king-size pillow to shield myself as I rolled off the bed on the other side.

"Fuck!" Liam yelled as he too jumped up, though he was dressed far more modestly than I was, still wearing his jeans. "What the hell are you doing here, Chester?"

"It's my room!" Josh pointed out, although he sounded far more amused than annoyed. "Besides, I'm guessing I'm here for the same reason you are. Were," he amended. "Ya ain't gotta go home but ya gotta get the hell outta here."

Liam must've finally realized that all of my clothes were on the other side of the bed, out of my reach, because he tossed me his soft blue button-down. "When's the last time you actually made it up to your own bedroom to fool around?" Liam asked sourly, motioning for Josh to move so he could grab my clothing from the floor.

I could see Josh's smug grin from across the room. "Shannah wanted to see it."

Two thoughts immediately flashed through my mind as I slipped on the shirt. The first was: *Ugh, Shannah.* The second was: *Crap. Van.* Not that she had any actual feelings for Josh, but it wasn't going to make her feel good to know she'd been passed over for yet another typical white Hollywood blonde. Once I was relatively covered up, I emerged from my hiding spot behind the bed and held out my hand to get my jeans and cami from Liam before whirling into Josh's en suite bathroom to get dressed.

"So you're really *not* banging Vanessa Park," I heard Shannah say, her voice muffled through the door. "Dammit. I owe Zoe a hundred bucks."

"You of all people should know not to believe everything you read in the tabloids," Liam chided her. "But feel free to refrain from sharing information with Zoe. She's already fucked things up as much as she possibly can."

"That's what you get for banging random little girls," Shannah replied. I inhaled sharply at her bitchy comment and almost missed her next statement, which she delivered in a considerably lower tone. "If you stay and play with us, maybe I'll forget that I saw you slumming it."

Slumming it! I could not get my jeans on fast enough to jump out there and slap her in the face as she so roundly deserved. Didn't she see my Louboutins out there on the carpet? Okay, granted, they were Van's, but Shannah didn't have to know that. Who the hell did she think she was? And ew, was she seriously propositioning Liam with me in the next room? For a threesome, no less?

Liam must've dropped his voice because I couldn't decipher his fierce whisper through the door. I finally yanked my jeans over my hips and zipped them closed, then tossed on the cami and threw the door open to face three seriously pissed-off-looking actors.

"Come on, Ally," Liam demanded, yanking my blazer off the chair and tossing me my shoes. "Let's go."

Apparently, I wasn't going to be able to stay long enough to put on my heels, not that I really wanted to linger in the presence of Shannah's smug face or Josh's disgusting smirk any longer. They mashed their mouths together before Liam and I were even out the door.

"What the hell just happened in there?" I asked when we were safely back down the hall. We stopped in front of the table that still bore my piña colada so I could use it to balance while I slipped the shoes back on my feet and gave Liam his shirt, which he jerked on over his head. I was still too overheated from the anger and embarrassment of our encounter with Josh and Shannah to put on the blazer, but I took it from Liam in one hand while I grabbed my drink and downed it with the other.

"Nothing," he muttered, raking a hand through his hair. "You okay?"

"Hmm." I tipped my head while I pretended to consider the question. "A movie star and a TV star who both happen to be tabloid regulars just saw me in my underwear about to..." I trailed off as a furious blush threatened to overtake my entire body. No way could I finish that sentence out loud. Had I seriously almost just gotten naked with Liam in some other guy's bedroom? What was wrong with me?

"Probably wasn't the best place to fool around," Liam conceded as if reading my thoughts. He wrapped an arm around my waist and pulled me close to whisper in my ear. "You are sexy as hell, though."

The heat already spreading throughout my body intensified by about a million degrees. *Oh, yeah,* that's *what's wrong with me. I turn into a crazy nympho whenever Liam's around.* I gently pulled out of his grasp; I'd already learned once tonight just how incapable I was of making decent decisions when he got too close.

"I need a drink," I said firmly, heading for the stairs without even checking to make sure Liam was following.

He was, though, and he frowned disapprovingly when we returned to the bar and I asked for a couple of tequila shots instead of my usual colorful mixed drink. I'd never actually taken a tequila shot before, but I'd seen other people do them at parties and they always seem to have the instant-drunkenness effect I was dying for right now. I grabbed a salt shaker from the bar, tipped it onto my wrist the way I'd seen tons of others do, and licked it off before tossing back a shot.

Oh my *God*, it was disgusting. I almost gagged from the taste, and I turned away from the bartender so he wouldn't see me.

Liam sighed and handed me a wedge of lime. "Here. This is kind of an important part of the whole tequila shot thing."

I narrowed my eyes at him as I snatched the lime from his hand and sank my teeth into the sour fruit. What the hell gave him the right to be frustrated with me? He was the one who'd dragged me to this party at his stupid friend's house. Sorry—*mansion*. He was the one who'd assured me we'd have privacy upstairs. He was the one who'd slept with stupid Shannah, who was probably going to ruin everything just because she could. I was so riled up that I grabbed another tequila shot and tossed it back, not bothering with the salt this time. The second one was a little better, so I called the bartender back and started to order a third when Liam yanked me away from the bar.

"Ally, that's enough. Tequila's not like a piña colada. You're gonna feel like shit if you keep drinking it."

"Thanks for the advice, professor," I said dryly, wrenching my arm out of his grasp. "I thought you said we were going to have fun at this party."

"We still can," he said, taking my arm again, more gently this time. "You don't have to get drunk to do that. Let's just go hang out in the game room or something. Or we can just go home if you'd rather."

"No, we can't," I reminded him, and we both turned at the same time, as if suddenly remembering Van's existence. There was no sign of her dark head anywhere in the crowd, and my stomach started to clench in fear. Why the hell had I left her alone in this crazy madhouse? I should've come down the second I realized she was no longer with Josh. Then again, I'd been kind of busy with my own drama.

"She's fine, Ally," said Liam, taking a sip from the beer he'd gotten at the bar. "It's just a party. We know a lot of these people. We may not *like* them, but we know them."

"Oh, that makes me feel so much better." I broke away from him to begin my search for her, and I heard him sigh behind me as he followed.

She wasn't in the hot tub or playing in the volleyball game, or floating in the pool. She wasn't eating barbecue or frolicking in Josh's little grotto of hoes. I called her cell for the third time as we walked into the house, but she didn't pick up. She wasn't in the media room or the game room or the kitchen.

Frantic now, I pulled Liam upstairs, and as we went from room to room, I had to force myself not to stop and stare at all the familiar faces locking lips or snorting coke in every nook and cranny of the house. When it became clear Van wasn't on the second floor, we went back down to search the front of the house, and sure enough, there she was, sitting on a leather couch, talking to a slightly older woman I didn't recognize.

Liam, however, appeared to know exactly who she was, because he muttered a curse as soon as we saw her and tried to duck away, only to have Van call out, "There he is! Liam, sweetie, come here!"

"Who is that?" I whispered to Liam from where I hid behind the living room wall.

"Holly Crenshaw, the fucking nosiest gossip blogger in the world who basically exists only because Shannah uses her to plant positive stories about her. Josh probably let Shannah call her just to fuck with me." He pressed his beer into my hand, pasted a smile on his face, and walked into the living room to join Holly and Van while I made sure to remain out of sight.

"Holly!" he greeted her cheerfully, and I glanced around the corner of the wall just in time to watch him air-kiss her before sitting down beside Vanessa and wrapping an arm around her shoulders.

"I've been looking for you everywhere," Van cooed in a voice that made me sick to my stomach.

"It's so hard not to get lost in this place," said Liam in a voice so fake it made me even sicker.

"The house really is amazing," Holly gushed. "I'd always heard Josh threw great parties, but I'd never been able to make it to one before."

More like you've never been invited before, I thought, knowing Liam and probably Vanessa had the exact same thought running through their heads.

"Glad you were able to this time," said Liam, bracing his hands on his thighs. "I hope Vanny here wasn't boring you too much."

Vanny? Gag me.

"Not at all," said Holly. "We were just talking about whether or not there was any truth to the rumor that you two were having problems. A little birdie told me your relationship is just a publicity stunt to drum up attention for the new show—which we're all super-excited about, by the way."

Van laughed easily. "That's ridiculous. *Daylight Falls* has gotten plenty of publicity on its own. We don't need to make anything up to get people to watch." To my horror, she covered Liam's hand with her own, her fingers perilously close to areas they definitely shouldn't have been. "Right, sweetie?"

"Exactly," Liam agreed.

"So then, your friend Ally, who was seen here with you tonight—"

"Just a friend," Liam assured her without so much as a flicker of a glance in my direction.

Ouch. Even though it was obviously the party line, the ease with which he said it was like a punch to the gut. Especially given that he knew I was standing there, watching and listening.

"My *best* friend," Van added, the loyalty in her voice an interesting contrast with her current body language. "Trust me, there would *never* be anything going on between her and Liam."

"I should hope not!" said Holly, and they all laughed. The effect of their combined laughter left my insides feeling twisted in knots. I knew I should've walked away then—that I probably should've walked away the second Liam put his beer in my hand and left me—but I kept watching with some sort of inexplicable fascination. I'd been so good at avoiding tabloid reports and gossip sites, but now that it was all happening in front of me, I couldn't look away.

"So what's up next for *Daylight Falls*' hottest couple—offscreen *and* on, if my TV sources are correct?"

"Man, our pilot hasn't even been picked up yet and you're already looking for spoilers?" joked Liam.

"We're just exploring our options for the summer right now," said Van, sounding every bit both the girlfriend and the professional. "Can't wait until upfronts to get moving, you know?"

"Speaking of upfronts, will you two be in New York for the announcements?"

I knew they were both planning on going, although I didn't know exactly when. Van answered in the affirmative, as I knew she would, and then tacked on, "And Liam will be co-hosting the LuxeLens party on the eighteenth with Ryan Kehoe, which is basically going to be the hottest event of the week—if you don't count the impromptu pajama party I'll totally be throwing in my hotel room once *Daylight Falls* officially gets picked up!"

The three of them laughed, but I felt numb. The eighteenth. Upfronts were in May; I knew that much. So Liam was going to be in New York on May 18.

May 18 was the date of my prom.

And just when I thought things couldn't get any worse, Van leaned over and laid a big wet one on Liam's lips. The lips that had just been all over my... everything.

It hit me then that I just couldn't do it anymore. The lying, the hiding, the pretending to be okay with it. I was done. Completely and totally done. Done with standing on the sidelines while they acted like the perfect couple, done with compromising on what I wanted in a boyfriend, and done with having a best friend who was even capable of kissing my boyfriend under any circumstances.

I was done with Liam. I was done with Van. And I was done with this party. Without a single word to the happy couple, I turned on my borrowed heel, walked outside, and called a cab to take me away from the world of absinthe-chugging role models and elitist sweethearts. I was going back to reality.

HALF AN HOUR LATER, I was feeling violently ill but had arrived safely home and changed into my favorite cupcake-print pajamas. "Who's Next" played as loudly as I could stand it with my pounding headache. I was sitting up in bed, chugging glasses of water while I waited for the aspirin I'd popped a few minutes earlier to kick in, when my phone rang for what must've been the hundredth time since I'd left the party. I should've known Liam would freak out at my absence, but I hadn't really thought that part through when I'd stormed out of Josh's house. As soon as I saw his face on my caller ID display, I knew I couldn't deal with him yet. I pressed Ignore and went back to groaning with my head up against the cool wall behind my bed.

A few minutes later, the aspirin had started to take effect and I grudgingly acknowledged to myself that it wasn't fair to keep ignoring his calls. I'd panicked when I couldn't find Vanessa, and she'd known plenty of people there. I could only imagine how worried he was when he couldn't find me...now that he remembered I existed.

"I'm fine," I informed him when I picked up. "You can stop calling."

"Where are you?"

"Home. I gotta go."

"Wait, Ally, is everything okay? Is your dad okay?"

Ugh, of course he'd be all nice and caring now. *Remember, Ally, he's not really yours. If he was, he'd be taking you to prom. If he was, he would not leave you at a party to converse with some trashy blogger while he pretends to be banging your best friend. He's Vanessa's, and Jade's, and Holly's, but he is definitely not yours.* "My dad's fine. I'm fine. I need to go. Enjoy the party."

"I don't understand. You're *home*? How'd you get home?"

"I took a cab."

"But *why*? I still don't understand—"

"No, you really don't," I bit out, rubbing my throbbing temple with my free hand. "I can't do this anymore. I can't pretend I'm okay with the fact that you make out with my best friend in public. I can't pretend I'm okay with the fact that I've been working up the nerve to try to convince you to come to my prom with me for weeks and you're going to be hosting some party on the other side of the country instead."

"Your...what? Ally, I didn't even—"

"Look," I cut him off, because I knew if I didn't get it out now, I'd just be back in the same place the next night and the next week and the next month. "I really like you when you're just Liam, my boyfriend, but when you're *Liam Holloway*, you're..." I stopped myself before I could say "kind of a tool." The truth was, Liam was a decent guy, but he was in an indecent profession, and I'd spent my entire friendship with Van trying to convince myself that the two were not inseparable. After watching her kiss Liam tonight for some stupid *gossip blogger*, I was officially un-convince-able. "It's just not working," I said finally.

"You're breaking up with me?"

He sounded both surprised and sad, and I steeled myself not to crumble. "You'll be fine," I said, trying to keep my voice light. "You have another girlfriend right there."

"That's not funny."

"Yeah, well, neither is being left at the party so you can make out with Vanessa for some stupid blogger. The woman's entire job is to write shit on the Internet, Liam. Who the fuck cares what she thinks?"

Huh. Even I hadn't realized quite how angry I was until the profanity came spewing forth, undoubtedly assisted by the two tequila shots. But there it was. All the backyard picnics and whispering French nothings in the world couldn't make up for the fact that Liam couldn't and wouldn't give me the normalcy I so desperately needed. Yes, I had agreed to the stupid publicity plan, but what did I know? He and Van were trained for this sort of thing; I was just a stupid eighteen-year-old girl who'd thought wanting the best for her boyfriend and best friend would be enough.

Spoiler alert: It wasn't.

"Ally, come on, don't do this. I'm sorry I left you at the party, but I had—"

"You will *always* have to," I pointed out, cutting him off. "It's your job. And maybe it's not fair that I'm doing this after I said I'd be okay with everything, but I didn't know how much it would suck. How much it would fucking *hurt*."

"I never wanted to hurt you," Liam said softly. "Just tell me what I can do."

I thought for a minute before coming up with a response, even though I knew I had no shot at getting what I wanted. "Cancel on the party and go to prom with me instead."

"Even if I canceled on the party, you know I wouldn't be able to—"

"Just forget it, okay?" I couldn't let him finish, let him say that he couldn't be seen in public with me. It was bad enough that I knew I wasn't worthy in the rest of the world's eyes; I couldn't listen to him say it, too. "I'm sorry. I know it's not your fault, and I never even told you about prom or that I wanted to go. I just couldn't handle hearing you say no, and I can't hear you say it now." I heard some laughing in the background, and then a girl's voice calling Liam's name. My stomach clenched, and I had to remind myself that he wasn't mine to be possessive over anymore. "You should go," I told him.

"Ally, you can't just—"

"Liam, you and I both know this isn't working, isn't *going* to work. Hollywood is your life, not mine. And the Jades and Hollys and even the Vanessas of it might run your life, but I'm done giving other people this much say in mine. This is your career and I get that, but it's just a different world and it's one I'm not prepared to live in. I thought I could, but I can't. Now please, just go, before this gets any harder." As if it could; I already had tears streaming down my face as I said the words.

He was quiet for a minute, and then he said, "Yeah, I guess I should. I really am sorry, Ally. I did the best I could."

I didn't know if that was true, but I needed to get off the phone before I started crying for real. "*Bon nuit*, Liam," I managed, and then I hung up.

★★★★★

I barely slept that night, and as I spent the next day powering through studying for my Calculus AP, I couldn't help wondering if I'd made a really stupid mistake. Normally I'd have called Van in such a situation, but I had no idea how to even begin talking to her about this. I knew it wasn't fair to blame her for anything, but I couldn't help it. How had I let her suck me into this world after years of making sure I never strayed from the fringes? How had I gotten so desperate for money that I'd forgotten how much I hated all things Hollywood?

Of course, I knew the answer to that last question, and the irony was that I let stupid Hollywood crap take over my life specifically so that I could move to the very city I'd been planning my escape to for years.

For what it was worth, between the assistant job, the cash for tutoring, and the stuff Van and Liam had been giving me for months to sell on eBay, I'd made enough money to cover a dorm and textbooks for the first year. If I got a decent-paying summer job, my loans for the first semester would be totally doable, and if I did as well on this round of APs as I had on last year's, I'd end up with enough credits to graduate in three years. The unspoken truth in the Duncan house was that once I got that far, my father's life insurance would help take care of the rest, but I hated to think about that, for obvious reasons. I would've gladly gone to community college if it meant keeping my father alive, but, of course, that wasn't exactly in my control.

I both looked and felt like crap when I returned to school on Monday, which did not escape Nate's attention.

"Hit a rave this weekend, Duncan?" he asked as soon as I walked into French.

"Shut up," I muttered, in no mood to deal with him. For someone who said he liked me, he sure seemed to take pleasure in my misery.

"No, seriously, is everything okay?" he asked. "Your dad's still doing well, right?"

"Nothing new to report on that front." I fished around in my bag for some lip balm.

"Anything to report on any other front?" he asked, raising his eyebrows as we walked over to our seats.

"Actually, yes." I dropped into my seat with a thump. "I'm in the market for a prom date."

He snorted. "I knew you wouldn't be able to get him to come."

Asshole. He was right, obviously, but suddenly I didn't feel like telling him just how much harder I'd made it by breaking up with him. "Shut up, Nate."

"Sorry, sorry. And yes, I'd be honored to go with you."

I glanced over at him. "You know I didn't actually ask you, right?"

"As the French say, *touché*. Fine, then—I'm asking you. Alexandra Duncan, will you go to prom with me?"

I knew I'd brought it up, but hearing myself be officially asked felt strange. And it wasn't just because I'd been counting on going with Liam. It was because it was prom, and although Nate didn't know it, I was single, just as he was. That meant the normal "prom" things that would've been off the table weren't necessarily so...*if* I chose to tell Nate that Liam and I were no longer together.

Granted, I didn't actually have feelings for Nate, nor was I remotely as attracted to him as I was to Liam, but Nate was real and he was going to be by my side, whereas Liam...

There is no more Liam, I reminded myself. *Our little romantic comedy is officially a tragedy. Time for a new costar.*

"Yes, Nathaniel Donovan," I replied, flashing as genuine a smile as I could muster. "Yes, I will."

★★★★★

With APs looming and my father going in for another round, it actually wasn't that hard to keep my mind off both prom and my breakup with Liam. Sure, I missed talking to him every night, and it was hard being in that hospital room and remembering how adorable it'd been to watch Liam bonding with my family. And it sucked to know that when I went shopping for a prom dress, there'd be no reason to factor in the fact that he'd once told me he loved me in green, and...

What was I saying again?

Oh, right. Totally easy to forget about what's-his-name.

Okay, so I missed him, but I really *was* keeping myself busy, so I was less than thrilled when Van texted me on Wednesday to inform me that they were required back on set for two days of reshoots. *Totes swamped*, she added in a follow-up text. *Desp need my asst!!!*

Crap. My Calc AP was in a week, and European History was only a couple of days after that. I didn't have time to deal with Vanessa, and I *really* didn't want to go back to set and see Liam. Then again, though I was still secretly and unfairly mad at her for the whole publicity debacle, I couldn't desert her now that she actually needed me.

Any chance I can help without coming to set? I wrote back, hoping for a response in the affirmative. I still hadn't straight-up told her Liam and I had broken up—I *really* didn't want to get into why with her—but she knew enough to know things weren't good.

Actually, yes! she wrote back. *Emailing u a list of stuff I need in a few.*

I sighed as I walked into the school library and toward the computers to get her e-mail instead of heading directly to a study carrel like I should have. I pulled out my textbook to get a couple of minutes of studying in before her list arrived, but my eyes had barely made it down half a page when it came.

All three pages of it.

I groaned and stuffed my book back into my bag before printing the e-mail. No chance I was getting any more studying done today. Not while dry cleaning needed to be picked up, twenty copies of that week's issue of *LA Spectator* needed to be purchased somewhere so that Vanessa's grandma could show a recent interview to all her friends, and a variety of appointments from spray tanning to teeth whitening needed to be scheduled.

It wasn't a big deal to skip out on the rest of the day; after my study period all I had were Art and French, the former of which didn't matter in the slightest a month before graduation and the latter of which I was in zero danger of falling behind. I printed out the e-mail and started making phone calls before I was even out of the building.

Five hours later, I was wiped out, and the credit card Vanessa had given me had taken a serious beating. I was tempted to charge some new luggage and a prom dress to it; she probably wouldn't even have noticed.

I hadn't yet mentioned prom to Vanessa either. Like Liam, it wasn't exactly on her radar, and I didn't know how to bring it up without admitting that he and I were, as she would say, "totes dunzo." On top of that, also like Liam, Van didn't appear to be too crazy about Nate. I wasn't sure I wanted to hear what she'd have to say about the fact that I was going to prom with him.

Still, I knew I had to mention it if I wanted her to come shopping with me. And despite the fact that she wouldn't be going to prom, and she worked with my very recently ex-boyfriend—whom she was pretending to date—and she didn't like *my* date, and going shopping with her would probably mean getting interrupted for autographs and pictures every thirty seconds, I really, really did want her to come shopping with me. She was, despite all of it, my best friend, and isn't half the fun of prom shopping for an awesome dress with your bestie?

I texted her to let her know all the errands were done and to ask if she had time to run one of my errands with me that weekend. Almost immediately, she sent back a sad-face emoticon and said she had events and photo ops all weekend. I couldn't bring myself to reply with any more than a reply sad face before I trudged up to my room to finally tackle my homework.

I'd only just unloaded the necessary books from my bag when my phone beeped with another text.

OK, u got me curious—whats the errand?!

I grinned. No matter how exciting Van's life was, she always needed to know if there was something more exciting she could've been doing. I texted back, *Oh nothing, just need to go shopping for a prom dress.*

It was barely two seconds before she wrote back, *OMG yes!! Will find s/t to cancel & call u tom.*

Perfect. Sure, I was going to have to dip into my new college fund just a bit, but a girl only had one senior prom, right?

Right.

★★★★★

Okay, so I'm a big talker. I ended up stressing so much about paying for a dress that I took a babysitting job on Friday night even though I definitely should've been studying, especially since the evening before had been spent running yet another series of errands for Van. It was worth it, though, because before we could even hit a dress shop, I found the perfect pair of fuchsia silk pumps—on sale, no less.

"Now those are some serious fuck-me shoes," Van said authoritatively, adjusting the sunglasses she was conspicuously wearing indoors beneath the same Lakers cap she'd worn to meet me at the Lunchbox. "Does this mean you and Liam have made up?"

I could tell she was trying to sound hopeful and supportive, but the anxiety in her undertone was glaringly obvious for someone who was supposed to be a decent actress. Not that I could really fault her for not wanting Liam to come to prom with me; it would mean the end of what had been quite a successful publicity stunt thus far, just as her movie auditions for summer filming were rolling in.

Still, it hurt to know that after almost sixteen years of friendship, we'd officially hit the point where we could no longer wholeheartedly want the best for the other.

I decided to take advantage of both the opening and the distraction of shopping to slip in the truth. "No, Liam and I are finished," I said, trying to keep my voice light, even with the scratchy feeling of impending tears clawing its way into my throat. Something about saying the words to Vanessa made them extra real, even as I tried to make it sound like I didn't give a damn. "Hey, let's try Nordstrom. They always have gorgeous stuff on sale." I started to walk in the direction of the store when I felt her hand yanking me back by the fabric of my tank top.

"Wait a minute there, lady," she said firmly. "You're what now?"

"We broke up." I pulled my hair back into a ponytail in order to avoid eye contact for a few more seconds while I blinked back tears. "I don't really want to talk about it."

"Oookay," she said, falling back in line with me to walk to Nordstrom. "So who *are* you going to prom with?"

"Just Nate," I replied. "Seeing as you weren't available and all."

I expected her to at least crack a smile, but she simply glanced at me in disbelief. "Seriously, A? Are you *trying* to hurt Liam?"

I snorted. "Liam doesn't give a damn what I do, V. He probably doesn't even remember who Nate is."

Vanessa stopped in her tracks. "Okay, Ally, seriously, you have got to stop thinking of Liam as this big celebrity who used you like a little plaything to pass the time in between takes. He *really* likes you, and I *know* you know that. Or at least you used to. I don't know what happened between you guys, but I can tell you he definitely cares. Why are you doing this?"

As if I wanted to hear any more from Vanessa about what *our* boyfriend thought or felt. As if I wanted to be reminded that she still saw him and spoke to him and probably kissed him every single day, while I stared at pictures of him on my cell phone and cried my freaking eyes out thinking about how I'd never do any of those things again.

"You don't know what you're talking about, Van. Just drop it."

"But–"

"Drop it," I repeated, injecting a note of steel into my voice. I usually liked how well Vanessa knew me, but she was taking it too far right now. Where did she get off talking about my insecurities when it came to dating someone hot and famous? *She* was hot and famous! She was allowed out with Liam in public, and allowed to hold his hand. She was with him every time I needed to talk to him and got his voicemail instead. "Just stop."

"Fine," she replied, her voice every bit as stiff, "but I still think it's cruel of you to go with Nate."

"Who cares if it's Nate or Attila the Hun?" I demanded. "Liam doesn't know the difference."

To my surprise, Van kept her mouth shut, but as she held the door open for me to enter Nordstrom, I noticed a weird look on her face. I narrowed my eyes. "He told you about our conversation after dinner, didn't he? When I told him Nate thinks he likes me. I can't even *believe* he told you that. He had no fucking right."

"Once upon a time *you* would've been the one to tell me that," she replied. "And give Liam a break already. He was *jealous*, Ally!"

"Is that so? Because he sure didn't seem jealous to me."

"Because he was trying not to seem like an insecure asshole. He only ranted to me because he didn't want to tell you who to be friends with. You know how they tell you to pick someone you really hate to think about when you need to fuel an angry scene?"

"No."

"Well, Nate's Liam's guy," said Van, ignoring my answer as she followed me inside. "It drove him crazy every single time Nate touched you that night, and finding out that you spent the day with him on the beach didn't help."

"Hello, he's been hooking up with my best friend in public for weeks! What a fucking hypocrite!"

"Shh," Vanessa hissed. "Keep your voice down. People are starting to stare."

"Fine, but you know that's ridiculously unfair. I've had to deal with that times a thousand."

"It's different," Van argued. "Nate's a random guy who wants to see you naked. I'm your best friend, and you *know* I'm not into Liam."

"You know what? It's *not* different, and that doesn't make it easier," I snapped. "Trust me."

"Oh, come on, Ally, don't put this on me. I asked you if it was okay and you said it was fine. First, you neglect to tell me that you're dating, then you lie to me about being all right with the plan—"

"I wasn't lying when I said it," I broke in. "I thought I would be. I *tried* to be, so freaking hard, because I thought it was the right thing for you. I can't help that I didn't know how much it would absolutely suck."

"Like the fact that you and Liam *both* kept it a secret from me that you broke up?"

"I'm sorry that for *once* Liam didn't see fit to tell you absolutely everything." I rifled angrily through a few dresses without really looking at any of them. "That must've hurt since you guys are so damn close."

"We did this to protect you, or don't you remember?" Van whispered fiercely. "The truth was out there, and you ended up with paparazzi swarming your house. You can't have everything you want."

"No, that's right, only you guys get that. We mere mortals just have to take whatever scraps you guys throw at us."

"Because it's so easy going on dates with Liam and knowing how badly he wishes he was with you instead," Vanessa retorted. "It's so fucking fantastic to be somebody's second choice like that."

I rolled my eyes. "Yeah, Van, you really seemed miserable when you were jumping him in front of that stupid blogger."

I could tell from the flash of surprise on her face that she hadn't known I was there, and I couldn't decide if that made it better or worse. Either way, it only lasted for an instant, and then her face hardened again. "The fact that you're jealous of me and Liam doesn't make what you're doing with Nate right."

My mouth dropped open. Never in all the years of our friendship had one of us accused the other of jealousy. I meant it when I told my dad the lack of it was what made our friendship work. Hearing that word was like a slap in the face, and the only way I knew to respond was to hit back harder.

"You're kidding me, right? You think I'm *jealous* of you? You think I wish I could spend my life playing pretend every day? You think I wish I could be the kind of person who wouldn't even consider taking my girlfriend to her prom, or who'd kiss her best friend's boyfriend in front of her face? I'm not jealous of you and Liam; I feel sorry for you."

"Good to know," she said icily. "I'm so glad we could both help you with your much more important, real-life dreams, like going to prom with a guy you don't even like and attending a college simply because it's as far away from us as you can get."

Even if I could've managed words past the lump in my throat, I wouldn't have spoken them. There was nothing left to say, and we both knew it.

"Enjoy picking out your super-important prom dress," said Van, turning on her heel, her voice dripping with sarcasm.

I refused to give her the satisfaction of watching her walk out, but I was shaking so hard I wasn't sure I could've held my head up long enough to do it anyway. I'd never had a fight like that with Van before; never said or heard her say anything remotely like the nastiness we'd just exchanged. How had things gotten so bad so quickly?

And was there even any point in trying to fix them?

WITHOUT VANESSA'S ERRANDS to run, the time between the horrendous shopping experience and prom itself flew by in a whirl of studying, test-taking, and hospital visits. My dad continued responding to the treatment, which was great, but he still had about a million tumors, which was not so great. Nevertheless, I forced myself to adopt a single-minded focus, knowing that doing well on the APs was pretty much the best thing I could do for my dad right now.

I ended up going dress shopping with my mother, who was so happy to go with me that I felt bad for not thinking of it in the first place. The dress we got was much funkier than my usual style, short and gold and sparkly and a perfect complement to the fuchsia pumps. I had no idea if Nate would like it or hate it, and if I was honest with myself, I didn't really care. Not that I really felt like being honest with myself about that night; if I did, I'd admit there was only one person I wanted on my arm, and that person was now three-thousand miles away and hadn't spoken to me in weeks.

I had no idea how to match a bag to my outfit, so I didn't bother; I simply tucked some cash into my bra and figured I'd borrow someone else's phone if I needed it. I didn't care much about taking pictures at the actual dance, and I knew my mother would take plenty beforehand, especially since my dad was in the hospital again and missing it all.

One bonus (or downside, depending on how you looked at it) of this whole hospital thing was that it made my mother exponentially better at using modern technology. The instant I reached low enough on the staircase that I was visible to Mom and Lucy, I heard the click of her camera phone and knew she was about to picture message my father.

I couldn't help but laugh. "Mom, at least wait until I can actually pose or something."

"No way!" She took another picture. "I don't want to miss any part of this, and I don't want your father to either. The walk down the staircase is an integral part of prom."

I rolled my eyes, but it was kind of nice to have her make such a big deal out of it. It was about time someone acknowledged that it was actually a worthwhile event. I knew I was going to regret this, but I said, "You know, you can record on that thing, too."

"You're kidding! Show me!" I did, and she had me walk down the stairs all over again so she could take a video of it and send it to my dad. Then she took about a zillion shots of me—alone by the fireplace, standing with Lucy, close-ups of my face...It was exhausting, and I was relieved when the doorbell rang, signifying that Nate had arrived to pick me up for the pre-party at Sam's, from which we and a few other couples would be sharing a limo to the dance.

Of course, my mom insisted on taking another hundred pictures or so, but fifteen hours later, we were finally on our way.

"You look really nice, by the way," said Nate as he held open the passenger-side door to his Corolla. "I felt weird saying that in front of your mom."

I grinned as I slid inside. "Probably for the best, since she would've made you say it again so she could get it on video and send it to my dad."

He closed the door after me and got into the driver's seat. "That's pretty impressive. My mom can barely turn on a computer."

"That's a blessing, trust me," I informed him, examining my lip gloss in the side mirror. "So who's going to be at Sam's?"

"Sam and Leila, obviously. Chase and that junior he's bringing. Ethan and Jack, and... Who am I forgetting? Oh, yeah, Oliver and Dana."

My eyebrows shot up. "Dana's coming in the limo with us?"

Nate shrugged. "Yeah, why? I thought we were pretending to like her these days."

Yeah, except she *actually* liked Nate, and had had a good time with him on their date, and she was none too thrilled with me when she'd found out he and I were going to prom together. God, this was going to be awkward.

"I'm just surprised I didn't know is all," I only half-lied. I really *was* surprised to realize I had no idea that Dana was going with Oliver Trask, a cute basketball player, but then again, I'd been living so far inside my own head lately I probably wouldn't have noticed if she'd started hooking up with the Dalai Lama. I would've been even more surprised that Dana was going to be in a limo without Leni if I hadn't recalled somewhere in the recesses of my mind that Leni was off in Arizona, visiting her sister who'd just had a baby.

I looked down at my toes as we drove to Sam's, trying to decide how I felt about the color. I'd gone for a light neutral; everything else just seemed impossible with the fuchsia shoes. Van and I still weren't speaking, so going for mani-pedis had turned into yet another Duncan-woman extravaganza. Lucy was currently sporting some sort of fluorescent orange shade on her fingers and a slime green on her toes. Very chic.

It was only a five-minute drive to Sam's, and before the commercials had even ended on the radio, we were pulling up in front of his Spanish-style house, where a bunch of other cars were already parked.

"Looks like we're the last ones here," Nate observed.

I nodded, unsure if I was supposed to apologize that my mother had held us up for an extra few minutes to take pictures. As if it was our fault that my father was in the hospital, missing it all. I could feel myself growing annoyed, but then I glanced over at Nate and knew I was overreacting. I let myself out of the car.

I saw Dana first; if she was still pissed at me, it didn't show. "Allllllly!" she squealed, running over as fast as her twenty-inch heels could carry her to envelop me in a hug. "I'm so excited you're here."

"You too," I replied, because it seemed like the right thing to say. "I love your dress." It *was* cute, in a very prom-y way, all pink and ruffled. Like maybe what I should've been wearing instead of my sparkly gold mini thing, which suddenly looked more appropriate for a night on one of Van's red carpets instead of Hayden High's.

Dana swept us inside, where the others were already laughing, taking pictures of one another, and drinking flutes of champagne under Sam's mother's watchful eye. Nate and I went over to say hello and accepted our own flutes before posing for pictures with the rest of them.

I smiled and lifted my champagne with the crowd; smiled and kissed Nate on the cheek with one foot lifted in the air; smiled with my arms around Dana, Sam's girlfriend Leila, and a pretty girl I was pretty sure I'd never even seen before whose name turned out to be Morgan.

"You're Vanessa Park's friend, right?" she asked as we lined up in front of the Washingtons' mantel, holding out our corsage wrists for the camera.

"Uh-huh." I plastered yet another smile on my face, hoping that the fact that we were posing would shut her up, which of course it didn't.

"Is it true that you and Nate went on a date with her and Liam Holloway?"

I rolled my eyes toward Nate, but he simply shrugged. Fortunately, Sam's mother chose that moment to tell us to smile for a picture.

"Liam's so hot," Morgan announced as soon as Mrs. Washington pressed the button. "I mean, not as hot as these guys," she said flirtatiously as she rejoined Chase.

"No, he's pretty damn hot," Jack Fuentes said with a grin as he affectionately straightened Ethan Reinhardt's bowtie. "He's on both of our lists."

"Your lists?" asked Dana.

Ethan elbowed Jack and gestured at Mrs. Washington, who was definitely within earshot. I rolled my eyes.

"Celebrities they're allowed to screw without it counting as cheating," I informed her, keeping my voice low.

As if Jack and Ethan would ever cheat on each other. The only "out" couple in the entire school at present, they'd been together since they were assigned to be lab partners in bio freshman year. I wouldn't be surprised if they ended up being the one couple from the senior class to actually make it. Sam and Leila had been going strong for a while as well, but it was pretty well known that her conservative Persian parents weren't thrilled about her dating someone who didn't share her roots.

"Liam would be thrilled," I informed Jack and Ethan without thinking, smiling as I imagined his reaction. Liam had once complained that he didn't get nearly enough gay fan mail for him to believe he was as attractive as people said.

"So you guys are close?" asked Ethan, a curious smile lighting up his handsome face.

"Not exactly," I muttered, shifting my eyes to the floor as I felt Nate's gaze on me. I guess the cat was out of the bag on the whole break-up thing.

"So," Leila said brightly, after she and Sam had posed for one last picture, "everyone ready to go? The limo's here."

We all said our goodbyes and thank-yous to Sam's mom and started outside, but I felt Nate's hand slip into mine, pulling me back slightly, and I knew exactly what was coming.

"Hey, Duncan," he said, his voice low in my ear, "something you're not telling me?"

"Sounds like I just told you," I responded in the same low voice. "Surprise—your prom date is actually single."

"He broke up with you?"

I snorted. "Appreciate the vote of confidence, Donovan, but yours truly did the breaking, thank you." Not that it made me feel any better.

"Why?"

"What do you mean, *why*? You're the one who's been telling me for weeks how it's all bullshit, how trying to date an actor is an idiot move. You want a medal for being right?"

Nate's expression was unreadable. "Duncan–"

"Hey, lovebirds, get in the limo!" Sam hollered from where he'd stuck his head out of the sunroof. "You guys wanna miss the whole dance or what?"

Actually, I kind of did, but that would certainly not fall under the criteria of "normal," so I flounced ahead of Nate and made my way into the limo. I squished in between Morgan and Dana, who were pouring from yet another bottle of champagne.

I wasn't feeling particularly celebratory since the mention of Liam's name. Or rather, I couldn't help thinking how nice it'd be to be celebrating with him instead. It was like that ill-fated day at the beach all over again, except instead of wishing Liam was the one rubbing sunscreen on my back and playfully kicking sand at my feet, I wished he were the one intertwining his arm with mine as we drank from our champagne flutes.

What the hell was I even doing, trying to have a romantic evening with anyone else?

Stop it, I ordered myself as I drained my champagne. *Liam is at a fucking party in New York City right now, where he's probably getting it on with Vanessa.* I held out my flute for a refill. *If he wanted to be here with you, he would be.* I felt Nate slip his arm around my shoulders then, and I let him, even snuggling into the comfort of his hold. From somewhere very far away, I heard Vanessa's words about how much Liam hated Nate floating around my brain, but my brain retorted with a sharp, *Screw you, and screw Liam.*

Screw Liam... I giggled as I thought about how I probably would've been doing that in just a few hours if he'd agreed to come with me.

"What's so funny?" Nate asked playfully.

Oops. "Too much champagne," I said, which struck me as so funny that I dissolved into giggles again, after which I took another long drink.

The chatter continued on around me, and I tried to participate as much as possible while still getting in plenty of champagne. By the time we arrived at the ballroom of the Hyatt where the prom was being held, I was pleasantly buzzed and in a considerably better mood.

The theme of the prom was "In the Jungle," and the ballroom actually looked pretty stunning covered in glossy leaves and tropical flowers. I could've done without the random jungle noises like hooting monkeys startling me every few minutes, but the overall effect was pretty and coordinated quite nicely with my outfit.

"I'd offer to get you some punch, but I'm sure it's been spiked by now and I think you had enough in the limo," Nate teased as we walked into the room. His arm had slipped from my shoulders down to my waist, but I wasn't complaining. So sue me—it was nice to feel somebody's touch, since I obviously wouldn't be feeling Liam's again. "Do you want to go get our picture taken?"

"Actually, punch sounds positively delightful," I said, steering us toward the refreshment table. "Look at that beautiful green color! Clearly meant to be imbibed."

Nate looked doubtful, but he poured us each a glass. "To prom!" I toasted as we clinked glasses. If someone had spiked the punch, I didn't taste it, but

Nate must have because he instantly grimaced. Oh, well, more for me!

Once I had my fill, we went off to take our delightful date-y picture before I let Nate whirl me onto the dance floor. I wasn't a particularly good dancer, but neither was he, so we did just fine. Until he opened his mouth.

"Do you want to talk about it?"

"Talk about what?"

"You know." He made a face. "The guy."

"Oh." I made my own face. "No. Thanks."

He nodded and kept moving. One song rolled into another, and after a while, Sam and Leila came to hang out with us, followed by Chase and a camera-bearing Morgan. I had to remind myself I wasn't actually a celebrity when Morgan snapped a candid of Nate and me laughing at some joke Chase had told. Apparently, I still had paparazzi-PTSD.

"Have you guys voted for Prom King and Queen yet?" asked Leila.

"I don't even know who's in the running," I admitted.

"Nobody but Macy Easton for queen, really," said Leila, rolling her eyes. "There isn't really any point in voting for anyone else."

"We should just cross out 'Queen' and do a write-in for Jack and Ethan," I suggested. I wasn't sure if I was kidding, but at least in my tipsy mind, it sounded like a wonderful idea. Everyone else agreed, and we promptly swarmed over to the voting booth to cast our ballots and recommend to everyone around us to do the same.

From there, we went back to the dance floor, where we were joined shortly by a laughing Jack and Ethan who demanded to know whose idea it was to have them nominated co-kings.

"I cannot tell a lie," I said dramatically, draping the back of my hand over my forehead. "It was I. Or me. Whatever the grammatically correct response to that question is."

Ethan laughed and swung me around. "I like the way you think, girl. Wish we'd hung out more often."

"So do I," I said, and I meant it. There actually *were* some fun, decent people walking the halls of Hayden High. I hated how long it had taken me to realize that. Sure, I'd had Dana and Leni and Nate, and I'd always been friendly with other people in my classes or on the debate team or newspaper, but I'd also had a lot more time with Van, and I'd let myself think that was good enough. Well, obviously it wasn't, because she was AWOL, off partying in New York with my ex, and I was having a pretty damn good time without her.

We continued to dance and drink, and drink and dance, and pose for pictures, and when Jack and Ethan won Prom King and King, no one whooped and cheered louder than our limo. They insisted on taking a picture with me in between them, and Jack even let me pose with his crown. Then it was time for the last dance of the night—a slow one—and Nate pulled me into his arms.

"Have fun tonight?" he asked, though the tinge of smugness in his tone told me he already knew the answer.

"I had a wonderful time, Nathaniel, thank you."

"Yeah?" He bit his lip, like he was actually nervous for my response.

"Yeah," I confirmed, looking up into his darker-than-dark brown eyes. Okay, so it wasn't quite the magical evening I might've had if I'd gone with Liam on my arm, but I'd actually managed to enjoy myself quite a bit. "I really did. You're right—I should've come out with you more often."

"Damn straight." He returned my look with an intense one of his own, and I realized he was going to kiss me. And I so badly wanted to want it—to want *him*—that I closed my eyes and let him.

After only a couple of seconds, though, I felt a hand pulling my arm. "Come on, the limo's here."

"We're going home?" I asked, confused.

Nate laughed. "Are you nuts? Afterparty! Corrinne Robertson's parents have a beach house in Malibu. I swear, sometimes it's like you go to a different school."

No *kidding*. But I simply shrugged and followed him out of the hotel and into the limo.

THE LIMO BROUGHT WITH IT yet another bottle of champagne, and by the time we reached Corrinne's beach house, I didn't care that my shoes were growing pinchy...or that my date was. Clearly that kiss had given Nate some ideas, and the more bubbly I tossed back, the less I minded entertaining them.

I wished I could pretend we weren't those cliché kids who spent the entire ride to the afterparty sticking our heads out of the sunroof and yelling things while we swilled champagne and silently dared everyone we passed *not* to wish they were us, but I'd be lying. Cliché or not, it was damn fun, and having the newly crowned Prom Kings in our car made it that much more awesome.

Also awesome? Corrinne's parents' ridiculous beach house, which was not only beautiful, but enormous, and in a very familiar area; it was located just down Broad Beach Road from Josh's mansion, which would've made it a whole lot harder to forget about Liam if I weren't so pleasantly trashed.

"I was just here a few weeks ago," I confided to Nate as we wove our way through the other post-prom partiers into the house.

"At Corrinne's house?"

For some reason, I found that utterly hilarious. "No, silly. Josh Chester's."

Nate's eyebrows shot way up. "You were at Josh Chester's house?" he asked as we walked inside.

"Yep," I confirmed, taking a look around the enormous entryway. "It was even bigger than this, and it was craaaazy." I leaned in and whispered, "That's where Liam and I broke up, basically."

"I don't think you're being as quiet as you think," Nate informed me as he pulled me out of the entrance and down a hall.

"Where are we going?" I asked, trying to dig my heels into the carpet. Oops—there was no carpet. Was that a scratch on the hardwood? "Hold on. My shoes are pinchy."

He sighed and waited for me to slip off my shoes, and I dangled them from my fingers as I followed him down the hall.

"Where are we going?" I asked again.

He didn't answer, but judging by the way he was ducking his head behind each door as we passed, I wasn't sure he knew either. Finally, he found a small, empty bedroom and pulled me inside.

"Ohhh," I observed, pointing at the bed. "I see what's going on here."

"Holy jungle juice, you're drunk," he muttered, pulling his bowtie loose and tossing his tux jacket onto the dresser. "I just wanted you to be able to talk quietly."

"I don't want to talk," I informed him, my tongue feeling thick in my mouth even as I said the words. "Come on, let's go party."

"Maybe we should chill out a little first," said Nate, leading me toward the bed. "You've had a lot to drink."

"That's true," I said, nodding my head. I dropped my shoes on the floor and crawled onto the bed. Mmm, it was soft. Good job, Corrinne's parents.

Nate was just standing there, watching me, so I patted the mattress next to me and he slowly walked over and sat down.

He was completely quiet for what felt like an hour, so finally I said, "You know, you're being kinda weird."

"I'm not sure what to do now," he admitted.

I couldn't help giggling at that. "Nathaniel Donovan, are you a virgin?"

"What? No! But I wasn't sure—wait, are you?"

I smiled widely and tapped him on the nose. "I'm not telling!"

"That's mature, Duncan," he said, but the teasing had gone out of his voice and it was really more of a murmur and then he was kissing me.

It wasn't bad, to be perfectly honest. He was a nice kisser, if a bit nervous. At least I thought it felt like nerves. Maybe he was just drunk too. I really had no idea.

I could handle kissing. Kissing wasn't new. I'd been kissing since Freddie Carlton laid one on me in second grade. Granted, I hadn't done a lot of this tongue-swirling-around-mouth stuff with anyone but Liam, but it was probably time for that to change. After all, I was eighteen, about to graduate high school, and going off to college in New York City. I would probably kiss a zillion men who weren't Liam in the next four years. A bajillion, maybe. So what was one Nate in the grand scheme of things?

I relaxed into it and lay back onto the pillows lining the headboard, pulling Nate on top of me by the ends of the bowtie that still hung untied around his neck. Apparently energized by the action, he kissed me even more deeply, bracing himself over me just long enough to get his bearings before one hand made its way down my body and edged up the hem of my dress.

The tiniest butterfly–and not the good kind–started to flit around in my stomach as I felt his hand plant itself firmly on my thigh. I didn't know why I'd gotten the ball rolling on the sex talk, since I didn't actually want to sleep with Nate, but I had, and now it was probably going to happen. I forced myself to calm down and remember that sex was no big deal.

After all, I'd been about to have sex with Liam just a couple of weeks earlier, right? Well, at least I thought I had. That had seemed to be where it was going before Josh and Shannah had interrupted us, and I certainly didn't recall wanting him to stop at any point.

I wanted to be horrified by the idea that I'd almost done that with someone I'd broken up with less than an hour later, but the truth was, I was madder that it hadn't actually happened. So sue me, I'd wanted it–badly. Even thinking about it now was getting me considerably more in the mood, and I wrapped a leg around Nate's waist to pull him closer, aching to recreate the feeling of Liam's hard body pressed against mine.

God, he'd felt so good–confident but gentle, patient but always ready and able to take a cue to press on. Things just...clicked when I was with Liam, and it hit me then that I knew exactly what he meant when he said I relaxed him. He was comfortable and safe, despite there being nothing comfortable or safe about my feelings for him. I just knew he would never want to hurt me.

Which made it so much worse that he had, and so badly.

"Ally?"

Oh, Jesus. Had I seriously just spaced out thinking about my ex-boyfriend while making out with my prom date? Judging by the look on Nate's face, yes, I had.

"Sorry," I murmured, forcing myself to banish all thoughts of Liam as I pulled Nate back in for another kiss. Whether it was because I was drunk or because my head was three-thousand miles away, I didn't know, but it took me about a minute to realize that Nate wasn't kissing me back.

I pulled away and sighed, but I didn't want to be the first one to speak. What was I supposed to say, anyway?

Turns out, it didn't matter what I had to say; Nate had plenty. "You were thinking about *him*, weren't you?" he demanded, his jaw set.

"Him who?" I shot back, mostly because I needed to buy some time to figure out how to make myself sound less pathetic for pining after my ex who'd probably forgotten my name by now.

"You know who," Nate said coldly. "I'm so sick of trying to compete with that stupid pretty piece of crap."

"He's not a piece of crap, and you don't even know him. Besides, I broke up with him and I'm here with you; what more do you want?"

He looked at me pointedly.

I snorted. "You want to have sex? Let's have sex." Without waiting for a response, I rose up on my knees and pulled my dress over my head, leaving me in nothing but the same lace underwear set I'd worn to Josh's party. What was the point of holding on to it—to any of it—anyway? Prom and its fancy dresses were stupid. Waiting, only to lose the person you wanted to sleep with instead of losing your actual virginity, was stupid. Dwelling on long-gone Liam was stupid. Life was too fucking short. "Will that make you feel better? If it helps, Liam never got around to it."

"Ally..." Nate reached out and touched my arm, and I had to force myself not to recoil. *Just get it over with,* I mentally commanded, both to me and to Nate. *Get this done and maybe everyone will get over whatever they need to get over.* But I could tell Nate wasn't going to move further. Both the way his eyes raked me up and down before meeting mine and the tent that was just beginning to set up camp again in his tuxedo pants said he wanted to, but I knew he wouldn't. Not without a little push. Or a not-so-little one.

He'd been lying on his side on the bed ever since he'd pulled away. Now I shoved his shoulder so he lay flat and climbed on top of him, rendering my 34Cs unignorable enough to keep him distracted while I unbuttoned his shirt before bending down to kiss him again.

This time, he didn't resist, returning the kiss with a surprising amount of fire while he gripped my waist to keep me balanced. "You really are hot," he mumbled in between kisses, as if the thought had never occurred to him before.

He slid his hands up my back and homed in on the clasp of my bra, which he then proceeded to fiddle with to no avail. After a minute or two of trying to let him get it on his own, I was about to tell him I'd get it when he pulled away, angrily spitting, "Fuck it, I can't do this."

I jolted back, startled by the venom in his voice. "Nate, it's not that big a deal. I'll–"

"No, I can't do *this.*" He swept his arm up and down, indicating the length of my body, and slipped out from underneath me to roll off the bed and onto the floor.

"We need to stop, Duncan," he said, his voice low. I could see his fingers shaking as he started to rebutton his shirt. "You shouldn't be here. Doing this. With me."

I suddenly felt very cold, but I couldn't seem to find my dress. I yanked the covers around myself instead. "Why not?"

"First of all, because you're in love with another guy–"

"Stop talking about Liam," I cut in, shaking, those words crawling down my spine. "I don't want to talk about Liam."

"You think I do?" Nate shot back. "You think I feel good about this?"

"He's out of the picture!" I exclaimed, growing seriously frustrated. "He wasn't even mine! Aren't you the one who was so fond of telling me that?"

"I was full of shit!" Nate yelled back. "I was angry that my date with Vanessa went badly, and I wanted to blame it on actors not being able to date regular people. I wanted things with you and Liam to fail because I wanted to think they had to, that people like us couldn't be with people like them. And I hated seeing him get both you *and* the girl I've been fantasizing about for years. I just didn't want him to have everything when I had nothing. I put those shitty ideas into your head so you'd dump him and he'd see what it's like to be a regular loser for once. I'm sorry, okay?"

"Okay? *Okay*? No, it is not fucking okay!" My head was spinning. Or maybe the room was spinning. I wanted to yell more, but I knew that the next time I opened my mouth, it was going to be to throw up. I gestured wildly for Nate to pass me the garbage can and I promptly vomited several cups of jungle juice and I don't even know how many flutes of champagne.

Nate at least had the grace to hold my hair back, but he stood as far away from me as possible while doing it, clearly terrified of me.

When I was finally sure I was done, I wiped my mouth on the back of my hand and thrust the can away from me. Nate immediately let go of my hair and backed away.

"How could you do this to me?" I didn't yell it—my head had begun pounding with a vengeance—but I needed to know. "You lied about liking me, you made me feel like shit about my relationship and myself, and worst of all, you actually pretended to be my good friend the entire time. What did I ever do to deserve this from you?"

"Nothing," Nate said, his tone a combination of desperation and assurance. "We *are* friends, Duncan. None of that was bullshit. I had a great time with you tonight and I still—"

"Oh my God, *stop*." I held up my hand; I couldn't listen to him talk anymore. "You think we're *friends*? You think friends do this to each other? I can't have this conversation with you right now. I can't even be here right now." I slid off the bed, snatched my dress from where it glittered on the ivory carpet, and pulled it on over my head. "I have to get out of here." I grabbed my shoes but didn't slip them on; wearing four-inch heels now was only going to hinder my movements. Before Nate could protest, I was out the door.

★★★★★

Of course, once I actually got away from Nate, I began to realize just how limited my options were. I couldn't call my parents to pick me up; my father was in the hospital, and I wasn't going to have my mother bring Lucy along to find me reeking of alcohol. Even if Van and I had been speaking, she was in New York, as, obviously, was Liam. Pretty much everyone else I knew was in that room, and nobody had a car. I'd brought twenty bucks in my bra, but that certainly wasn't going to be enough for a cab from Malibu.

Behind me, I could hear Nate emerging from the bedroom, so I quickly dashed down the hall and out the back, onto the beach. Not a chance I was going to come face-to-face with him again that night. I had no idea where I was gonna go, but I couldn't imagine there was anywhere I could end up that would be worse than being at Corrinne's right then.

After the whole mess with Nate, it actually felt good to be walking outside, breathing in the sea air and letting the cool breeze make the spangles on my dress dance and glimmer in the moonlight. As I thought about how the sand must be sloughing off an entire layer of skin from my feet, I couldn't help smiling as I thought of how they probably resembled my dad's now, albeit with some subtle nail polish. Of course, it wasn't long before the fond thought turned to feelings of guilt at how incredibly stupid I was being right now—how stupid I'd been all night, all month, all year. I had no idea where I was going. Hell, the only other time I'd even been to a beach house in Malibu was—

Josh's house. Even in the dark of night I could see the backyard of his house just yards down the beach, the tacky Christmas lights that illuminated his palm trees year-round twinkling in the sky like stars on acid. It was an absolutely absurd idea and I knew it even as I felt my legs carry me up the stone stairs from the sand to the pool area, but I pushed all thoughts out of my head except for getting the hell out of Malibu.

He might have been an asshole, but he was an asshole with a car—or, at least, cab fare.

I'd expected that there would be a party going on, but the house was completely silent, which was definitely *not* good news. I hadn't thought Josh had planned to go to New York this week—he was all movies and modeling, no TV, so there was no reason for him to be at the upfronts—but what if he'd gone to hang out with Liam at the party? My heart hammered in my chest as I slipped into my shoes and pressed on, refusing to turn around before I knew for sure the house was empty.

It was strange to be in the backyard when it was so quiet; it was a completely different place from the one I'd been to weeks earlier. It was even more beautiful, and definitely more serene. I was dying to dip my aching feet into the pool, but I didn't dare. I walked right up to the door and searched for a bell, all the while unable to escape the feeling I was being watched.

"It's just a security camera manning the entrance," I murmured to myself, glancing upward. I didn't see a camera, though, nor did I see a bell, but when I turned, I looked straight into a pair of eyes and screamed.

"JESUS!" YELLED JOSH, pulling open the door to his media room, where I saw now he'd been sitting and watching *The Usual Suspects*. "Do you mind? I'm trying to have a peaceful evening at home."

"I can see that." I glanced past him, but he was clearly on his own, a bucket of popcorn and a six-pack his only company for the evening. "Look, I'm sorry for just showing up like this. I don't know if you remember me—"

"Of course I remember you," he said icily. "I just don't like you."

"What did I ever do to you?" I blurted. "You're the one who walked in on *me*."

"First of all, it was *my* bedroom, and second of all, you dumped my best friend, that's what you did. What the hell are you doing here, anyway? Trying to trade up?"

"Gross! Of course not!" Then I realized that maybe I shouldn't have been so emphatic about that, considering I needed to ask a favor. I shifted uncomfortably as I tried to figure out how to ask. "Um, I mean, not that you're not good-looking and all—"

"Spit it out, Liam's Ex. I assume you didn't come here looking for him since I know you know where he is right now." His expression softened for a moment. "I will say, though, if Liam was upset about not being able to take you to prom before..." He whistled. "You do clean up nicely."

I barely registered the compliment; I was too focused on the fact that Liam actually gave a damn about not being able to take me to prom, so much so that he'd even mentioned it to Josh. "He mentioned prom?"

Josh snorted. "What, you think guys don't talk about shit? I had to listen to him bitch and moan for hours when you dumped his ass." He shot me a look. "*Please* tell me you're not here to do the same. I can't listen to any more of it. I told him getting a real girlfriend was a bad idea, but he was all, 'Nah, Chester, she's special!' Whatever the fuck."

With each word, Josh might as well have been poking me with a flaming stick. Everyone seemed out to hurt me that night, and the worst part was that I obviously deserved it. Maybe Liam and I weren't meant to be, but he'd been as good a boyfriend as he'd been able to be, all things considered. He'd earned more from me than to be ditched at a party and dumped over the phone.

"So, are you going to tell me what you're doing here?"

I bit my lip. "Can I come inside? It's getting kind of weird talking to you through the door."

Josh heaved a sigh like he was doing me the biggest favor in the world and stepped aside to let me in, closing the door behind me. I opened my mouth to tell him I needed to get home, but I ended up spilling out the whole stupid story, from how I'd decided to break up with Liam to how I'd gone to prom with Nate even after fighting about it with Vanessa, and right down to my explosive argument with Nate at Corrinne's.

"Et *voila*," I said lamely, gesturing around me. "No phone, no car, no best friend, no boyfriend, and no available parents. You were the only person I could think of who might be able to help me get home."

"Wow, that is a pathetic story. No wonder Liam hated that little shit."

"Yeah, no kidding," I muttered.

"For what it's worth, I'm sorry about your dad. That part does blow."

"Jeez, Liam told you about my dad, too? Boys really do talk."

"Who do you think gave him the brilliant idea to volunteer so your dad could get a private room?" Josh asked casually, picking up the beer he must've been in the middle of drinking before I darkened his doorstep.

I dropped my head into my hands with a groan. That was the final straw. Liam and Vanessa had volunteered to spend the day at the hospital together to help my dad? How the hell had I not put that together?

"You didn't know he did that," Josh deduced.

"Apparently, I didn't know a goddamn thing about my own relationship," I gritted out. "Why didn't anyone tell me?"

"About the hospital?"

"About everything! Suddenly everyone seems to be coming out of the woodwork to tell me how much Liam cared about me, but where were they—*you*—when I needed to hear it? When I felt like a pathetic hanger-on living in a fantasy?"

Josh raised an eyebrow. "So you're angry because other people didn't tell you your boyfriend was crazy about you?"

"No, of course not! I just..." Oh God. Had I been *that* insecure? Had all the signs been there that Liam was all in while I was just too self-conscious about my non-celebrity status to notice? "Was he?" I asked softly. "Crazy about me, I mean."

He rolled his eyes. "I wouldn't remember who you were if he wasn't."

"Then how could he pretend to date Vanessa? And how could he miss my prom?"

"He thought he was doing what you wanted him to do," said Josh. "He knows how much she means to you—or *meant* to you, fuck if I know. He was just trying to make you happy, and when he realized he could use it to his advantage with the whole double-date thing, it sounded even better. Of course, he had no idea what a douchebag your little friend was."

"He's not my friend," I growled.

"Whatever. And as for missing your prom...sorry, sweetheart. I don't know what to tell you. He's getting paid a fuck-ton of money for hosting the party, and he seemed to think he'd need it to help some chick fly home from college as often as she needed to see her family and her boyfriend, and maybe head over there as often as humanly possible, too. What an asshole, right?"

"Now you're just messing with me." *Please just be messing with me.*

"Why would I bother messing with you when telling you the truth is so much better?"

I gritted my teeth at the evil look in Josh's amber-colored eyes, but I couldn't hold my anger for long. I was feeling too many other things—guilt, regret, sadness, and oh Good Lord, did I miss Liam. I would've given anything in that moment to be able to run into his arms right then, apologize profusely, and then finish what we'd started upstairs in this very house.

But that wasn't going to happen, and it couldn't, as long as Liam was three-thousand miles away.

"When's he coming back?" I asked Josh, not caring how obvious and desperate I sounded.

"I dunno," said Josh, taking one last swig of his beer before slamming the bottle down on his coffee table. "First week of August, I guess? Assuming *Daylight* gets picked up at upfronts tomorrow, which it definitely will."

"I'm sorry, did you just say *August*?"

Josh looked at me strangely. "Yeah, when'd you think? Doesn't make much sense to come back to L.A. for, like, two days before the Gallagher movie starts shooting in New York."

"So Liam got the part," I murmured.

"Jesus, when you cut somebody off, you really cut them off, don't you?"

"Hey, this isn't all my fault. I said I was okay with following *Jade*'s orders, not getting it on for every wannabe gossip columnist with a Wi-Fi connection. Besides, it's not like Liam even came over to try to explain things or get me back."

"After the way you dumped him? Over the *phone*? You can't do that to a guy with trust and abandonment issues like Holloway's and expect him to come crawling back," Josh argued. "You're talking about a guy who had to bribe his fucking father to take him in. When he was *eight*. And then you just disappear, dodge his calls, and eventually tell him you don't want to see him anymore?"

"Stop it!" I demanded, jumping up, feeling the tears I'd worked so hard to keep inside begin to prick the insides of my lids. "I get it! I'm a horrible person, and

I screwed everything up, and there's nothing I can do about it." The tears started to spill, and I couldn't wipe them away fast enough. How could I have been so selfish? I knew how painful Liam's life had been better than anyone; had I really deluded myself into thinking that because he was hot and famous, he was invincible? That because Van always bounced back from rejections, Liam was guaranteed to do the same? "Please don't say any more. I can't stand it." With all the tears I'd shed over my father in the last four months, I hadn't thought I had any left, but it was like a dam had burst. I fled the room, a tearful, snotty mess, and searched for a quiet corner I could truly bawl in.

Josh let me go, but after a few minutes of sobbing in the black marble powder room, I heard footsteps enter and then he handed me a tissue. "You can stay here tonight," he said in the kindest tone he'd used all evening. "It's too late to take a cab back alone, and frankly, I don't wanna pay for it. I'll call my driver in the morning and have him take you back. Your parents aren't expecting you back tonight, are they?"

I shook my head, sniffling. I'd texted my mom from Nate's phone as soon as he'd mentioned the afterparty to tell her I wouldn't be returning until morning. Wordlessly, I let him lead me to a guest room and accepted the spare toothbrush and oversized T-shirt he provided.

"Thanks for this," I barely rasped as he started to leave the room. "And hey, if you speak to Liam—"

"Don't worry," said Josh. "There's no way in hell I'd tell him you were here. Even I know that's no good for anyone."

"Thanks." We exchanged a brief smile, and he walked out, closing the door gently behind him.

I went to the en suite bathroom and looked at myself in the mirror over the sink. I was a disgusting mess of eye makeup and general blotchiness. My hair, which my mom had painstakingly styled into the kind of curls I could only hold with enough product to style the entire Kardashian family, was a frizzy mess. I frowned at my reflection and then washed my face and brushed my teeth in preparation for a night of crying myself to sleep.

24

I WOKE UP FEELING LIKE someone had methodically shoved cotton balls into my mouth one by one, filling it so far that they went up into my brain. I'd completely forgotten Hangover Prevention 101—drink a ton of water before you go to sleep—and now I was paying the price. I couldn't even imagine how much worse it would've been if I hadn't thrown up the night before.

Ugh, the night before. If only that could dissipate like the pleasant effects of alcohol. I blinked myself awake, and when I could finally compose my thoughts, the first one was: *Coffee*. The second was: *Wait, where the hell am I?*

It took another few seconds to remember that I was at Josh's, and as I washed up, I prayed I wouldn't have to face him again this morning. No such luck. The second I exited the guest room and turned the corner in search of the kitchen, there he was.

"Good morning, sunshine," he said wryly. "Or should I say afternoon?"

"Shit," I muttered, grabbing his wrist to glance at his watch. It was almost one. I seriously hoped my mother wasn't freaking out right now. "Can I use your phone?"

"There's one in the kitchen. There's an espresso machine in there too, but I don't know how to use it, so you're on your own if you want coffee."

"I'm okay," I lied. No way was I taking a chance on breaking a fancy kitchen appliance I'd have to spend my whole new college fund to replace. "I'll just take that phone." I took the cordless handset from the wall and dialed my home number, but there was no answer. My mom was probably at the hospital. I tried her cell instead, and she picked up on the second ring.

"Hello?" She was obviously puzzled by the number.

"Hi, Mom, it's me. Just wanted to let you know that I'm okay and I'll be home soon."

"Did you have fun?"

She didn't sound particularly perturbed by the fact that I still wasn't back. I'm pretty sure that was a glaring sign that my own mother thinks I'm boring. "Yeah, I had a great time," I replied, which was true for most of the night, at least. "Are you at the hospital?"

"Yes, with Lucy, and Grandma just got here to visit so I should go. I'm glad you had fun, sweetie."

"Yeah," I mumbled. "Send my love." I hung up and turned to Josh. "Should I be concerned that my mother doesn't seem to be panicked that I've been out all night with strangers?"

"You worry about the weirdest things," said Josh, shaking his head. "If you hand me the phone, I'll call Ronen. He's my driver, and he'll take you back to wherever it is you live."

I nodded dumbly. I didn't want to get in a car with some stranger, but what else could I do? I certainly wasn't going to ask Josh to come with me, not that he would've been all that comforting a presence. The look of hatred that had glittered in his eyes the night before was gone, but I didn't think I'd magically moved into his top five.

"*Daylight Falls* got picked up, by the way," he added dryly.

Ah, the glitter was back.

Still, I was relieved to hear it, although I didn't bother responding. There hadn't been much doubt, especially not with the added buzz generated by the awe-inspiring romance of its stars, but despite my fight with Van, I would always want her to succeed. The same went for Liam, although I imagined that finding out for sure that he'd be stuck in this role for however many years the show lasted would only be bittersweet for him.

Josh and I sat in silence once he hung up on Ronen, but when the black Escalade pulled up in the circular driveway, Josh hopped off his seat and walked me out.

I whistled. "Taking me all the way to the car, Joshua? I had no idea you were such a gentleman."

He rolled his eyes. "I'm getting in with you, smartass," he informed me as Ronen held open the door. "I've got shit to do."

"Right," I mumbled, instantly feeling stupid. For a second, I'd actually thought he was trying to be friendly. Not that I cared if Josh was friendly. The only reason I'd ever want Josh to like me was because he was Liam's best friend, but now that I was nothing to Liam, Josh was nothing to me.

I thought the car ride would be as silent as our non-breakfast had been, but as soon as Ronen had pulled away from the house, Josh asked without so much as a glance in my direction, "What is it about you, anyway?"

"You mean, what did your friend see in me?" I asked wryly.

He smirked, still looking straight ahead, his eyes concealed by sunglasses that probably cost more than my parents' house. He pressed the back of his hand up against the tinted window and tapped his nails against it. "No, I've had to sit through enough of that from Liam, thanks. I mean, what makes you so fucking immune to us?"

I raised an eyebrow. "What's that supposed to mean?"

He turned to glance at me now, his nails still tapping. "I mean, you're not rich, your parents aren't in the industry, and you go to public school, so it's not like you hang out with tons of celebs all day. So why the hell are you so jaded?"

"You don't have to have a parent in the industry to get exposed to it," I informed him. "Growing up with Van and watching her interact with stars and agents and fans and paparazzi—and watching her set herself up to get rejected over and over again for the simple fact of who she is—was really all I ever needed to know that I want no part in anything Hollywood."

Josh snorted. "Everyone gets rejected, girly. Aren't you the one who rejected Liam for who *he* is?"

"That's not—"

"Look, you're still close with Park, right?"

I didn't feel the need to point out that not lately, I wasn't. "She's a good person," I said. "The fact that she's made some choices I wouldn't make for myself doesn't take away from that."

"So the fact that she's a celebrity doesn't define who she is for you."

"It's hard to let that define somebody you've traded Barbie underwear with." He raised an eyebrow again, and I rolled my eyes. "We've been friends a long time."

"We're all people, Ally," he said, his voice bordering on weary as he took off his sunglasses and rubbed his eyes. "If you can separate her from Hollywood and be cool with her choices, then why can't you do the same for Liam?"

"Actually, I *wasn't* cool with this particular choice of hers," I informed him. "Look, I get that they have to do it or whatever, and that's fine for them, but I don't have to have it around me. If breaking up with Liam and cutting off communication with Vanessa is the only way I can deal–"

Josh snorted. "You call this dealing? Bitch, you're delusional."

"Oh, fuck you."

"Whatever. You think you're so much better than we are because you're a 'normal' person." He rolled his eyes as he air-quoted. "You think your morals are so much better, and you're so much more grounded. Except you froze out your best friend; you dumped your boyfriend with, like, two words as if he didn't matter for shit; you went to prom with an asshole you knew would piss off Liam even more; and then you got plastered and stumbled over to my house, even though I'm basically a stranger. Oh, and the two people you seriously hurt have been doing nothing but trying to help you pay for college and take care of your sick dad."

"Shut up. I mean it," I warned, my voice shaking.

"So where in there do you come off like a saint who has her shit together?" he continued as if I hadn't spoken. "Seems to me like the only people keeping you in one piece are the ones you think live a fucked-up, abnormal, immoral lifestyle."

"You're putting words into my mouth." I narrowed my eyes. "Judging what you do isn't judging who you are."

"What we do *is* who we are," Josh snapped. "How the fuck do you not see that? It's not like Liam chose to chill with a glass of Cristal rather than take you to your prom. This shit comes with the job when you're still new to the game—and trust me, no matter how long we've been doing this, we're *all* new until we can stop auditioning and pulling stupid publicity stunts just to get a little attention."

"But Liam doesn't even like this crap."

"No, but it's all he knows. You don't realize that until you came along, Liam never had anything else. It's not like he's got family, and because he hates almost everyone in the industry as much as you do, he doesn't have a lot of friends either. Work is all he's got, and he doesn't know how to stop right now. He's not *going* to stop right now," Josh added emphatically, as if I didn't get it.

Which, until that moment, maybe I didn't.

I looked away, clenching my jaw as I stared out the window, wishing I were sitting on the side with the ocean view. I was tired of these conversations, tired of getting schooled on Liam and what a terrible bitch I'd been, breaking his heart. All I'd wanted was a relationship grounded in the real world. Hadn't that been what he'd wanted, too? Wasn't that part of the draw for him of dating me, of what relaxed him about me?

"Could you imagine Vanessa stopping?"

"Vanessa says no to stuff all the time," I informed him. "And she asks my opinion. She actually cares what

I think about what she should and shouldn't do. Liam never asked me about signing with Jade, or about the party."

"You never asked him about prom," Josh reminded me smugly.

"Oh, shut up. It's not the same and you know it."

"No, and Vanessa and Liam aren't the same either. I know you're all, 'Oh, they're both stars and they're hot and they must be in love by now' and whatever stupid shit jealous chicks think, but Vanessa has parents and a good best friend to help her think shit through. Liam doesn't have that. The guy lives on autopilot."

"Aren't you Liam's best friend?"

"Yeah, but I'm a stupid dick, or haven't you noticed?"

That surprised me enough to turn back in his direction. "I noticed," I said. "I just didn't realize that *you* noticed."

To my even greater surprise, Josh laughed. "I know my limitations. Holloway's my boy and all, but he hates my shit as much as you do. Hates my parties, hates the people I hang out with, hates the chicks I bang. If it were up to him, I'd be living in a one-bedroom condo right next to his and we'd spend our nights chillin' in front of the TV. I'd kill myself in three days."

"Then you really shouldn't try dating him as a non-celebrity," I informed him, "because that's all you get to do."

Josh shrugged. "Hey, if it's not worth it, it's not worth it. It's not like you're even gonna be living in the same state in a few months. I just think you should've let him down easier."

The mention of the fact that I'd be going to New York at the end of the summer while Liam and everyone else I loved remained in L.A. hit me like a punch to the gut. Originally, getting away had been the point, but now...

"Stop confusing me," I blurted out.

Josh looked at me in surprise. "Was I?"

"Yes! I mean, no! I don't know," I grumbled. "Just shut up. It's been a complicated few months."

"Apparently. You have more drama than *Daylight Falls*. Are you sure you're not an actress?"

I flashed him a look that was meant to shut him up but only made him smirk. Apparently Josh Chester had been on the receiving end of so many death stares that he was immune to mine. Fortunately, we pulled up in front of my house just then. I couldn't wait to jump out of the Escalade, but just as I was about to, Josh handed me a card.

"What is this?" I asked, examining it. It looked like a standard business card, black with silver lettering. "Are you trying to slip me your digits?"

Josh snorted. "Not quite, homewrecker. I want you to work for me."

"You've gotta be fucking kidding me." Something about being around Josh made me drop the F-bomb about a million times more than usual.

"Nope. I need an assistant I won't wanna sleep with, and you now have experience and need the money. I start filming next week and go through the end of July. Ten thousand bucks."

Ten thousand bucks. For two months of work. That'd be a huge help; there was no denying it. My dad was doing so well these days—his scans kept coming back showing improvement—and being able to tell him we were going to be fine financially with regard to my tuition would definitely help ease some of his residual stress.

On the flip side, working for Josh sounded like a nightmare.

"Fine," he sighed when I still didn't respond after a minute, "but fifteen is my final offer."

"Fifteen thousand dollars, Josh? Are you out of your mind?"

"You want *more*?"

"I want to know why the hell you would spend that much cash on a barely experienced assistant when there's a massive pool of qualified people you could choose from."

He shrugged. "Like I said, no chance in hell I'll want to sleep with you. Plus, my manager seems to think it'd be a good idea to have someone around to tell me when I'm being an asshole."

"Well, *that* I can do," I said wryly.

"Good. You start Monday. I'll do my best to work around your classes, but you're probably gonna have to do some skipping. Good thing you're already in college, right?" He slipped his sunglasses back on. "Text me your number and I'll text you where to be and when."

I opened my mouth to inform him that I hadn't actually accepted the offer, but he was already done with me, instructing Ronen where to go as he typed something into his phone. They sped off, leaving me standing in front of my house in fuchsia silk pumps and a sparkly gold prom dress.

Working for Josh was impossibly exhausting, but it was rarely ever boring. (Except when I had to wait in line for him for three hours to get his iPad fixed—*that* was boring.) My days were packed with handling his fan mail, buying gifts for people whose asses needed kissing, and tracking down random things he came across that he had to have *now*, whether a scrimshaw-handled pocketknife or an electronic dartboard that spoke in a British accent. I spent hours researching everything from the chocolate and liquor preferences of various assistants to the flower and music preferences of various hook-ups.

Barring having to buy lingerie for Shannah, which made me gag so hard I thought I'd lose a lung, it was actually kind of fun seeing what absolutely bizarre task Josh would assign me next.

Until one day in July, when he managed to come up with something worse than finding a lace 32B corset for a girl I despised.

"No freaking way," I said aloud to Josh's empty bedroom, where I was currently separating the huge pile of clothing he'd pointed me to this morning into smaller piles I'd mentally labeled either *Sell on eBay*, *Donate to Charity*, or *Burn Because No One Should Ever Wear This Again*. A disturbing number of items with unidentifiable stains were finding their way into the third pile.

I looked down at the text again.

Buy 2 1st cls tix 2 NY 4 this wkd 4 LH bday. Sndng u link 4 gift.

As if having to decipher Josh's text speak wasn't bad enough—even autocorrect seemed to have given up on him—I had to buy the plane tickets he was using to fly to New York to celebrate Liam's birthday *and* buy Liam's gift? Was he trying to torture me?

Stupid question.

I went online to buy the tickets. *Is the second one for Shannah?* I wrote back when I got to the part where I had to input the passenger's name for the second ticket, silently praying the answer would be no. The idea of her at Liam's birthday party made my skin crawl.

N, *shes a ho fo sho. Tix 4 u. Nd my asst w/me.*

Oh, *hell* no. There was no way I was going to Liam's birthday party, no matter how pissed it made Josh. I started to text back as much when my phone beeped again.

Chill u cn skip da prty.

My eyes darted around the room. Did Josh have some sort of secret hidden camera in here? Was he watching me go ballistic at the mere mention of Liam's name and the suggestion of seeing him again? I did a thorough search of the room and finally decided that no, it was probably just really obvious that I could not handle the idea of being back in Liam's presence. I took a deep breath and typed in my own name.

"It'll be nice," I reasoned to myself out loud as I proceeded with the ticket purchase. "You'll get to check out Morningside Heights, familiarize yourself with the neighborhood before you move for good, and it'll probably be the only time in your life you'll ever fly first class."

I finalized the purchase and decided to stop talking to myself as I moved on to the e-mail Josh had just sent with a link to whatever undoubtedly overpriced piece of crap he was going to have me buy for Liam.

I clicked, and I couldn't help but smile. It was a framed original poster of *The Godfather*, autographed by the entire cast. Obscenely expensive, but Liam would love it. I ordered it to the Bowery Hotel, where he was apparently staying this summer, as per Josh's instructions, and tried not to ponder who might be keeping Mr. Holloway company at said hotel. Then I did the most pathetic thing of all and looked up the hotel online so I could picture exactly where Liam was sleeping at night. As I clicked through the pictures on the website, I started to imagine my head on one of the fluffy white pillows next to his, and that's when I decided I should probably shut off the damn computer and get out of Josh's house.

But I didn't. Instead, I did what I'd sworn not to do for months.

I Googled Liam.

Pages and pages of results filled the screen. There were fan clubs devoted to Liam, fan clubs devoted to his character in that stupid movie, fan clubs devoted to "Lanessa," and even fan clubs devoted to Tristan Monroe, his character on *Daylight Falls* who had yet to be revealed to the world.

I clicked on one after the other, reading about the perfection of Liam's abs (*But have you ever traced them with your finger or tickled them with the ends of your hair?*), the sexiness of his voice (*But have you ever heard it whisper faintly in your ear about how good you smell, and taste, and feel?*), and the otherworldliness of his eyes (*But have you ever seen them crinkle up when you've made him laugh by doing a terrible Al Pacino impression, or telling him about the time you accidentally mooned a bus of star-seeking tourists, or regaling him with the awful joke about the pirate and the peanut butter?*) (*Or have you ever seen the way they glaze over when he's exhausted from kissing you for hours, or the way they glitter in the dark when you've turned off the lights to watch a movie, whose script he probably knows entirely by heart? Or the way they look at you like their owner forgot how beautiful you were until just this moment?*)

I dropped my head into my hands, groaning. Why had I thought I could handle this? Worse, how had I managed to convince myself that I was over Liam when I so obviously wasn't?

Still, I couldn't bring myself to stop. Instead, I searched for Holly Crenshaw's blog, suddenly burning with the need to read the "interview" with Van and Liam that had precipitated our breakup. Both breakups, really.

I bumped into America's hottest new (or not-so-new? Sources say things were brewing between the couple for months before they made it official) couple, Vanessa Park and Liam Holloway, at yet another one of Josh Chester's infamous bashes. They were every bit as cute as they are in promo pics for their new series, the long-awaited Daylight Falls, *which will be revealed at upfronts next week.*

The young couple was first spotted out on Santa Monica Boulevard, and they've been inseparable ever since.

"It's great to finally find someone who shares a lot of the same values I do," says Liam. "My girlfriend's such an amazing person, and she keeps me really focused and driven but is also really chilled out. She makes me want to be really proud of what I do."

How adorbs, right?? And what does Vanessa Park—Van to her nearest and dearest—think of her man?

"He's such a great guy," Van gushes. "He's kind, he's loyal, and he's really great to the important people in my life."

Does that include BFF Alexandra Duncan, who was rumored to have a fling with Liam? The question makes both halves of the couple laugh.

"Ally's literally the best person I know," says Van. "The idea that she would ever do anything to hurt me is laughable."

The phrases "my girlfriend" and "the important people in my life" were a one-two punch to my gut. Something that felt very much like an icy fist closed around my heart, making my chest ache unbearably. This time, I did shut down the computer, and I got the hell out of Josh's house. Maybe packing would help me figure out how the hell I was going to apologize to them both.

★★★★★

My attempts to talk to Vanessa before I left for New York were nothing but failures. She didn't answer my phone calls, texts, or e-mails, and I'd just decided to suck it up and march up to her door when Josh informed me that we needed to leave for our flight four hours early so he could get his customary pre-flight shave and massage.

I was no more successful at checking out my future neighborhood as I'd planned; I barely had five seconds to text my parents and tell them I'd arrived safely before Josh all but shoved me in the car he'd had me order so we could take off for our day of getting him fitted for new suits, taking him to interviews, and scouting out the perfect outfit for Liam's party from Barneys before heading to the airport. (On the bright side, Josh *did* tell me to use his credit card to "buy myself something pretty." I decided to ignore the fact that he seemed to think I was his hooker and promptly did just that, heading straight for the sale section as was my habit and plucking a gorgeous black Stella McCartney mini-dress off the rack.)

Not that I planned to go to Liam's party. I was dying to see him, but there was no chance the feeling was mutual, not when I'd treated him so badly. Plus, I still hadn't figured out how to even begin to go about apologizing to Van, and I didn't know what I'd do if I showed up and she was there, her arm intertwined with Liam's, acting like the perfect girlfriend.

But my biggest fear of all was that it was no longer acting between them. It'd been weeks since I'd spoken to either one; what if, in that time, the fake relationship became less fake? What if the reason she wasn't answering my calls was that she was by his side 24/7? If only Josh weren't such an asshole, I might've asked him, but I was far too embarrassed, and far too unprepared to deal with it if the answer were yes.

"You sure you're not coming?" Josh asked as he finished buttoning the black shirt we'd bought at Prada earlier that day.

"Positive," I confirmed as I flipped through the channels on the TV in our room at the Mercer Hotel. (Yes, we'd only gotten one room, but Josh assured me about a thousand times that there was no way he'd be sleeping in that bed tonight. Wink wink, nudge nudge.) "Have fun, and please don't come back, especially with any gory details."

"Not to worry," said Josh, picking up the bottle of cologne he'd also bought that day and spraying it liberally while I did my best not to choke on it. "Look at me. Do I look like I'm sleeping alone tonight?"

I just rolled my eyes. Josh didn't need my confirmation that he looked hot, and there was no way I was going to give it to him. "Anything you need me to do tonight while you're gone, boss?"

"Just sit tight by your phone," he instructed. "I'll probably text you with some names to look up."

"Oh, joy," I muttered, but I did make sure the ringer was up on my cell phone, which sat on the nightstand next to the bed.

"That reminds me, I gave that hot chick at Barneys your number. If she calls looking for me, just send her to the party."

"Which is where?"

"Liam's suite at the Bowery. He's trying to keep it small."

"Just you and a hundred of your closest friends?" I asked wryly.

Josh smiled smugly. "If Holloway's lucky."

If I rolled my eyes at Josh one more time, I was pretty sure they'd stick that way. "Have fun."

Josh glanced at the TV; I'd settled on watching Shannah Barrett's stupid show, just to torture myself. "You too," he said, obviously holding back. I threw a pillow at him, and he let it out, the sound of his mocking laughter trailing after him as he exited the room, leaving me alone to wallow in my misery.

★★★★★

I was happily lost in the world of crappy TV when my phone rang. I glanced at my watch and snorted. It'd only taken Josh twenty minutes to find a piece of ass, and now I was going to have to spend equally as long looking her up to make sure she wasn't secretly a paparazza, a gold-digger, or a man. I rolled over with a sigh and grabbed the phone, and was surprised and a little afraid to see that it was my father.

"Dad?" I greeted him hesitantly as I turned off the TV. "Is everything okay?" My dad wasn't much of a phone chatter, even in his healthier days, and every time I saw his picture flash on my caller ID, I was afraid he was calling with bad news.

"Better than okay, AlGal," he said, his voice cheerier than I'd heard it in months. "I wish I could tell you this in person, but I can't wait."

My entire body tingled with a combination of anxiety and excitement. "Did the IL-2 work, then? Is the cancer gone?"

"Almost, honey. I'm down to fifteen tumors, and all but two are benign."

My mouth dropped open. "Fifteen tumors? And that's *good* news?"

He laughed, startling me. "Do you know how many I started with, Al?"

"No," I admitted.

"Neither does anyone else. My chart just says 'too many to count.' This is amazing news. The doctors say that at this rate, they expect me to go into full remission in just a couple of months."

I hadn't even realized that my eyes were filling with tears until one spilled over and landed on my lap. Several others quickly followed, but I couldn't even be bothered to wipe them away. I could feel myself smiling so hard that it hurt.

"Daddy," I just barely whispered, my voice caught in my throat. "That's amazing."

"Yeah, kiddo, it really is." I could tell that he was crying too, and it made me cry even harder.

"I'm gonna come home," I announced, climbing off the bed to gather my stuff. "I'll text Josh that I'm leaving and I'll get on the next flight, okay?"

He laughed softly. "That's okay, sweetheart. Have fun in New York. We have plenty of time to celebrate when you get back. It's just another two days, right?"

"Right," I said, but I didn't feel good about it. "I just really want to see you now."

"I know, sweetie, but you have a responsibility to be there, and besides, you should have fun and get to see the city a little bit. Now that we'll *all* be coming to visit, you'll need to up your tour-guide game."

I laughed automatically, but my head was a whirlwind. My dad was going to live. My dad was going to be able to visit me in college. My mom wasn't going to be alone. Lucy and I weren't going to be down a parent. Next Father's Day wasn't going to be immeasurably sad. It was like everything I'd prepared myself for over the last four months had been for nothing, and I couldn't have been happier.

"Consider it done," I managed, swiping at my runny nose with my free hand.

"So what are you up to tonight, kiddo? Just because you're a few thousand miles away doesn't mean you can't celebrate."

"Watching TV in my hotel room," I admitted. "I suppose I could order room service in your honor."

"Oh, come on. I can't believe I'm saying this, but you're eighteen and you're in New York City! I know my life just got lengthened a little, but life's still short, AlGal. Way too short for wasting on movies you've seen a hundred times when there are brand-new experiences to be had. Now get up and go out, will you? But be safe and no drinking. Or smoking. Or drugs."

I laughed. "Aye aye, father. I'm gonna put on my fanciest jeans and sneakers and head off to McDonald's to get myself a fancy New York City cheeseburger."

"That's the spirit! Love ya, kid."

"I love you too, Dad. I'll see you on Sunday."

We hung up, and I turned the TV back on, but I couldn't focus. My dad was right; I needed to celebrate. He'd been to hell and back and emerged with the second chance he'd been looking for. It only seemed appropriate that, in his honor, I fight for my second chance as well.

★★★★★

Thirty minutes later, I'd successfully washed off any evidence of my crying jag, swapped my lounging clothes for one spectacular mini-dress, and done the best I could with my wavy auburn mass and a hotel blow dryer. My shoes were nowhere near cute enough, my nails were chipped, and I probably shouldn't have so stubbornly refused to entertain Josh's offer to treat me to an eyebrow wax, but I was as ready as I was ever going to be. I grabbed my phone and purse, dabbed on some lip gloss, and went down to Mercer Street to get myself a cab.

★★★★★

The ride to the Bowery Hotel took far less time than I needed to screw up the courage to face Liam and possibly Vanessa.

"Just go in, say happy birthday, and if it's horribly awful, pretend you have a message for Josh and then *run*," I muttered to myself as I stepped into the hotel's beautiful lobby and walked up to the reception desk. "I'm looking for Liam Holloway's room," I said, cringing inwardly as I heard the shakiness in my voice.

The receptionist narrowed his eyes at me. "There's no one staying here under that name," he informed me coldly.

Had Josh lied about where Liam was staying for some reason? Was he trying to make a fool out of me somehow? "Thanks anyway," I said, turning to walk away, when the receptionist's words repeated themselves in my head. *Under that name.* Of course Liam wasn't staying under his own name, and, as it happened, I knew exactly what pseudonym Liam was fond of using; he'd told me on our very first "date." I turned back.

"How about Frank Slade?" I asked, giving the name of Al Pacino's character in *Scent of a Woman*.

That did the trick. The receptionist warmed right up and directed me toward the elevator. A minute later, I found myself standing in front of Liam's door, the sounds of a full-fledged party blasting from inside, the pounding of the music uncannily matching my heartbeat.

I knocked, and with every banging of my fist on the door, I felt my nerves seize. What was I doing? And *why*? What if that door swung open and Liam and Vanessa were standing on the other side, making out in full force? What the hell would I do with myself then?

I didn't have time to figure it out. The door swung open, revealing an extremely smug Josh Chester. "I knew you'd show up."

"I shouldn't have," I said, feeling my cheeks flame. I turned to go, but Josh's hand closed around my arm and pulled me back.

"Don't even think about it," he said shortly. Then he called back into the room, "Hey, Holloway, my present finally arrived!"

"Your *what*?" I tried to wrench my arm back, but Josh's grip was too tight and people were starting to stare. "You ass—"

"Ally?"

Josh and I both looked up at the sound of Liam's voice. God, I'd forgotten how gorgeous he was. Fan club pictures didn't do him justice. The summer sun had added even more golden highlights to his slightly shaggy hair, and his shirt sleeves were rolled up to reveal deeply tanned and well-muscled forearms. The shirt was new—or, at least, not one he'd worn before—and its deep green color turned his eyes the beautiful, mesmerizing shade of wet leaves. Those eyes were currently staring at me as if I'd come to announce that I'd run over his dog. *Crap. I knew I shouldn't have shown up.*

I smiled meekly and waved to match. "Just thought I'd come say happy birthday," I said, my voice barely audible above the music. I could feel heads turning in my direction, and I knew it was time for me to go. I did, however, notice that Van's wasn't one of them. "So, um, happy birthday."

Josh had loosened his grip when Liam had said my name, and now I eased out of it and went back into the hallway. I could feel tears threatening to fall again, and not the happy variety I'd cried just an hour earlier.

I leaned against the wall and took several deep breaths, willing myself to stay calm enough to get back downstairs and get myself a cab, but I'd only gotten two breaths in when the door opened and Liam stepped in front of me, his brow still furrowed in confusion.

"I'm sorry," I said softly. "I shouldn't have come."

"Probably not, but even though it makes me a total chump to say it, I'm glad you did," he replied, the corner of his mouth lifting in a small smile. "I've been wondering how you were doing."

The words were nice, but there was an undertone of *Don't forget why I don't know how you're doing* that made me wonder if a second chance really was in my reach. "I've been all right," I said quietly. "Feeling a bit like a jackass, but all right."

He laughed briefly, and there was no trace of happiness in it. "Well, I certainly know how that goes."

It wasn't quite the opening I'd been hoping for, and suddenly, I felt like I'd shown up at the SATs without a no. 2 pencil. "It's good to see you." It was the understatement of the century, and I immediately felt sorry for saying it. "I mean, you seem good. Look good." *Shut up, Ally.*

"Do I?" he asked lightly. "Because I don't feel all that great." We were both silent for a few moments, and then he said, "You look good too. Really good."

At that, a tear escaped and trickled down my cheek, and I angrily swiped it away. "Don't be nice to me," I demanded.

He stepped back. "Okay. How do you want me to be?"

"I don't—I just—I mean, I came here to apologize. Don't be nice to me until I get to apologize."

A lock of hair fell into his eyes as he nodded, and he pushed it back impatiently. "Okay."

I looked down at my toes for a moment, trying to gather my thoughts, but all the words I'd prepared to say on my way over slipped out of my mind as if they'd never really been there in the first place. I looked up into those beautiful, sad eyes. "I'm sorry."

"For what, exactly?" He sounded genuinely curious.

I opened my mouth to list my sins—not being honest about how much the publicity stunt bothered me, not telling him about prom and how much it meant to me, leaving the party without telling him, breaking up with him over the phone—but then I heard myself whisper, "I just wanted to be enough."

Pain flashed across his face. "Of course you were enough, Al. You were everything."

"No, I wasn't," I said, feeling more tears slip down my face, faster than I could catch them. "And I get now that I couldn't have been, that you were so used to being alone that you never understood that you *had* somebody real in your corner. You didn't need to do that publicity stunt with Van, and you didn't need to hire Jade. It was all a safety net, and I should've told you that you don't need one, that you are great and you are talented and you were going to be fine no matter what happened."

"Ally—"

"Let me finish. Please." I took a deep, shaky breath. "I screwed up, Liam. Or we both did, I guess. I should've let you say no to Jade when you first wanted to. You didn't need her, and neither did Vanessa. And it was so stupid, because my whole life, all I've ever wanted was 'normal,' but then normal wasn't normal at all, and what I had was so much better and I–" My voice broke, and I swiped my tears away, only to feel new ones take their place. "Even after all of that, it wasn't you. I thought it was, that it was because you were a star and had your whole weird lifestyle, but it wasn't you. It was me. I don't think I ever came around to believing that we were possible, that I could be the one when you were surrounded by girls who would've been a better fit."

Liam's broad shoulders slumped, as if the weight of my apology had physically taken its toll. "You know nobody's ever *been* a better fit for me, right? I wanted all the same things you did–"

"I know that now," I said quickly. "I do, and I'm sorry I didn't before. I was so afraid of...being rejected for being me, I guess, that I didn't realize I was rejecting you for being you. You were just living such a different life from me, and it was getting harder and harder to trust that there was a place for myself in it."

Liam smiled ruefully. "I didn't exactly make it easy. I should've known better than to think you'd be cool with everything just because it was Van." He reached out and rubbed away a tear, and I could feel my heart thumping with every moment his thumb lingered on my cheek longer than was strictly necessary. "I think I overestimated just how jaded you were."

"No one's immune to the sight of her boyfriend kissing someone else," I said with a pathetic shrug. "Not even me."

"I know. And what's worse is that I really should've understood that when I realized how much I hated seeing that little weasel Nate touch you."

I smiled, sniffling as the tears relaxed their descent. "So Vanessa was telling the truth; you actually were kinda jealous, huh?"

"Insanely," he admitted with a laugh. Then his face grew serious. "Van mentioned that you and he went to prom—"

"It was awful," I interrupted, desperate for him to know that there was nothing between me and Nate, that there never had been. "All I wanted was to be with you, and all *he* wanted was to mess with you. Don't ask," I said quickly. "Just trust me when I say Nate has never, ever been anything more to me than a friend, and now he's not even that."

Liam nodded slowly. "And you and Josh? Are you guys friends now or what?"

"Or what," I said dryly. "But he *did* fly me here, which was somewhat sweet, even if he always seems to have ulterior motives." I sniffled again. "What about, um... Are you and Van, uh...?" I couldn't even bring myself to ask the question, but I needed to know the answer.

He snorted. "Of course not."

It was amazing how much lighter I felt when he said that, but I also felt...guilty. What if he actually liked her—or they liked each other—and I was getting in their way? Considering how badly I'd treated them both, I certainly didn't have the right.

"You can, you know," I said softly, feeling my insides twist even as I said, "All I want is for you to do what makes you happy."

He smiled and reached out, lightly brushing my tear-sticky face before tucking a strand of wild hair behind my ear. "You're what makes me happy, Ally."

"Then do me," I said in a joking voice. Only I wasn't—joking, that is. I knew exactly what I wanted to do with my night, and what I wanted to give Liam for his birthday. But I wouldn't throw myself at him. Not again.

"Cute," he replied, but the rasp in his voice as he responded suggested he wasn't entirely sure I was joking either.

I didn't respond. I couldn't. One of two things was going to happen now. Either Liam was going to thank me for coming and say he should get back to the party, or he was going to–

His hands cupped my face and his lips pressed against mine before I could even complete my thought. *Thank God.* I responded immediately to his familiar touch, curling my arms around his neck and pulling him as close as humanly possible.

I have no idea how long we spent kissing in the hallway, but suddenly, the hotel room door was yanked open, and we jumped apart.

Of course. Josh.

"You're welcome," he said sweetly to Liam.

"Give me your key," I ordered Josh before Liam could respond to him.

"What? Why?"

"Because I want to be *sure* you won't storm in this time." I held out my hand, enjoying the shocked looks on both guys' faces as Josh handed it over.

"Bro, you're gonna leave your own party?" Josh asked Liam.

"Blame it on your birthday present," Liam answered with a grin as I pulled him down the hall.

26

I'D ALREADY BEEN AWAKE FOR an hour when Liam finally stirred, his arms tightening around my waist as he blinked into the sunshine and yawned.

"Good morning," he murmured sleepily, kissing my bare shoulder. "Glad to see you're still here. I was afraid I was just dreaming the world's best birthday surprise."

"Nope," I informed him, lifting one of his hands and kissing it. "You're stuck with me." I wanted to turn and kiss him, but despite whatever personal strides I'd made, they did not include losing my self-consciousness about my morning breath.

"Mmm, sounds perfect." He gave me a quick squeeze. "Best birthday ever."

"It's only just started," I reminded him. "Your actual birthday is today. So how are you going to spend it?"

"With my girlfriend, I hope," he said, yawning into the back of my head.

My heart gave a little jump at the word. It wasn't that I didn't want to be Liam's girlfriend again, but though I knew now that his intentions were better and our relationship far stronger than I'd known, I still didn't know how best to handle dating him. And did it even really make sense to start something with him going back to Cali and me moving to New York for good?

"Liam—"

"I actually have something I want to show you." He slid his fingers up and down my side, my skin tingling everywhere he touched, and just as I closed my eyes to enjoy the sensation, I felt his mouth join in, his lips leaving featherlight kisses on the back of my neck.

"Not that I'm complaining, but I believe you showed me this last night." I sucked in a breath through my teeth as he found a particularly sensitive spot. "I suppose I could be talked into another 'showing' though."

He laughed, the low, sexy sound making my toes curl. "I'm actually being literal in this case," he said. In one swift motion, he rolled me onto my back and straddled me. "But I'm glad to hear you're so amenable." He bent down to kiss me, morning breath and all.

Totally worth it.

Round two lacked the twinge of pain that had accompanied round one, which made me feel kind of like a seasoned professional. I told that to Liam, and he laughed.

"You're officially a sexpert," he said fondly, collapsing next to me and brushing my hair off my now-damp forehead.

I smiled, but the fact that I had something else on my mind must've been plainly visible on my face. "What's wrong?" he asked. "It didn't hurt again, did it?"

"It didn't," I assured him.

His face took on an even more worried look. "You're not...sorry we—"

"No! Definitely not." I planted a hard kiss on his mouth, as if it would render him incapable of even thinking of asking that question again. "Trust me. I've wanted this ever since…well, pretty much ever since that first time I offered it when I *didn't* really want it."

"That was an interesting day," he said with a smile.

"There were a lot of interesting days, weren't there?"

He groaned. "Don't remind me." He rolled over until he was looking me directly in the eye. "Is that what's wrong? You're afraid to get back into a relationship with me?"

"That's part of it," I admitted. "A big part."

"It'll be different now, you know."

"How's that?"

He reached out and tucked my hair behind my ear. "I think it's time Vanessa and I 'broke up,' don't you? Pull a 'no comment' on my love life, and you and I can finally go to the Getty, and the Tar Pits, and Mongolian barbecue joints? Or, more accurately, since you'll be here—The Frick, the Bronx Zoo, and Ray's?"

I bit my lip, unsure how to respond. I would love that, obviously, but I'd always said I would do what was best for him and Van, and I didn't know if this was it.

"If you're thinking about my career, or Vanessa's, just stop. Upfronts are over, Ally. The show is a go. We both tested well; they're not gonna replace either of us at this point. We'll both be fine. The show is airing in September, it'll look like Vanessa and I had a good run but were better off as friends, and everyone will be happy. You'll be far away from the paparazzi without me, and I'll come here and visit as often as possible." He cupped my cheek in his hand, gently caressing the skin with his thumb. "I know being in a fight with Vanessa is killing you, Ally, and I know it's killing her, too. It's not good for you two not to be speaking."

For the third time in little more than twelve hours, I felt myself getting choked up. "We had a pact," I admitted, shifting my gaze to his shoulder. I couldn't quite bring my eyes to meet his for this, and I could feel a blush creeping into my cheeks. "We always said we'd tell the other one ASAP when we lost our virginity. We even have a code word we agreed to text if we couldn't get away to make an actual phone call."

"Ooh, how James Bond. What's the word?"

"Like I would tell you. Anyway, not telling her feels so weird. Almost like it doesn't really count."

Liam raised an eyebrow.

"Well, of course it *counts*," I said quickly. "You know what I mean."

"I should hope it counts," he said mock-huffily, but then he broke into a smile. "I get it. I do. And while I feel kind of strange advocating that you broadcast our sex life, I do think you two need to fix things."

I couldn't really argue with that, but before I attempted to do so, I had to know something. "Why wasn't Van at your party last night?"

He shrugged. "I was keeping it small. Just close friends and people who were already in New York."

"So you don't consider Van to be a close friend of yours?"

Liam looked distinctly uncomfortable. "Don't get me wrong," he said, "she's a really nice girl, and she's great to work with, but I'm not really interested in making friends with the people I work with."

"Why not? Your best friend—which I still don't understand, by the way—worked with you once upon a time."

"Josh is a special case," said Liam. "I didn't know anything about anything when I met him; I was just a scared kid trying to break into the business so my dad wouldn't vanish and get me tossed into foster care. Most kids, even at that age, would totally have preyed on the fact that their competition was terrified, but Josh talked me through everything and calmed me down. I met him at a fucking audition, and he helped me get the part. Then, after we became friends, he invited me to sleep over at least once a week so I could get some space from my dad. Kinda hard not to stay best friends with a guy like that."

"Wow, it's weird to think of Josh being...nice."

Liam laughed. "Hey, he brought you here, didn't he?"

"He actually did more than that," I said hesitantly. I wasn't quite sure how to tell Liam I was working for Josh, especially considering how it came about.

Liam, however, saved me the trouble. "I know, Ally."

I raised an eyebrow. "You know? Like, everything?"

He nodded.

I exhaled sharply. "Josh is such a dick."

"Yeah, but also not." He traced a line down the center of my body and I closed my eyes, remembering that night months ago when he first did that very same thing and marveling over the fact that it still gave me chills. "I asked him to take care of you and he did. He's a good guy when he wants to be."

I shook my head. "I should've known you were behind him hiring me," I murmured.

"Oh, no, that was actually his idea, if you can believe it," he said, kissing the top of my head. "Now go call Vanessa while I shower." He slipped out of bed and padded over to the bathroom, leaving me alone with my phone and no excuses.

I took a deep breath and dialed her number. It went straight to voicemail; no surprise there. But I refused to give up. I tried her cell two more times, and when she didn't pick up, I called her house. Her mom picked up after the second ring.

"Hi, Mrs. Park, it's Ally."

"Ally! We haven't seen you in so long!"

"I'm sorry about that, Mrs. Park. I've been working. Gotta make money for college somehow!"

"You should try acting," she suggested. "I can't understand why they pay so much money, but they do."

I winced, hoping Van wasn't in the room listening. Her parents never bothered to hide the fact that they thought acting required zero talent. "I'll keep that in mind. Is Van there?"

She must have covered the receiver, because when she shrilly called Vanessa's name and announced that I was on the phone, the sound came through muffled. I could just barely hear a response—obviously Van was home—and then Mrs. Park sighed and informed me that Vanessa couldn't come to the phone right now.

Okay, fine, if that was how Van wanted to play it. "Would you mind just giving her a message for me, then? Can you just tell her I said 'ukelele'? Yes, like the instrument." I waited a minute, and then Mrs. Park came back.

"She says she'll call you from her cell phone."

"Thank you. I'll see you soon, I'm sure."

"I hope so, Ally." We hung up, and my phone started to ring again ten seconds later.

"Is this for real or are you just trying to get me to talk to you?" she demanded as soon as I answered the phone.

"Do you seriously think I'd cry 'ukelele'?" I demanded, genuinely offended. "I'm happy to send you picture messages of the condom wrappers, if you'd like."

"That won't be necessary, thanks." She paused. "So, who was it?"

"Van! Do you really think I'd lose my virginity to some random guy? It was Liam! Of course it was Liam."

She was silent again, and I was afraid that somehow that was the wrong answer. But then, in a voice tinged with a cross between anticipation and impatience, she said, "So, are you gonna tell me how it was or what?"

I laughed as relief flowed over me. "It was really, really good," I told her. "It hurt a tiny bit, but not as much as I thought it would." I dropped my voice. "He is so good at...um, tuning the ukulele, it's not normal. And don't even get me started on how good he is at playing it."

"Alexandra Mabel Duncan, you are quite the scandalous woman! And why are you whispering? Is he there now?"

"He's in the shower," I confessed.

"The plot thickens! So are you in New York or is he here?"

"I'm in New York." I filled her in on my new job as Josh's assistant, and allowed her a minute of fake retching noises in response before we shifted the conversation back to me and Liam.

"Does this mean you guys are back together?"

"It seems that way, although now of course we have the whole distance issue to deal with."

"So you're definitely going to Columbia, then?"

"Of course I'm going to Columbia," I said, even though the idea gave me butterflies, and not the good kind. "When was I ever *not* going to Columbia?"

"I don't know. I kinda thought that between everything with your dad and things working out with Liam, you might stay."

"Ah, but I haven't told you the best news of all yet." I filled her in on my dad's miraculous development, and from there we moved on to talking about how things were with her parents, which transitioned into talking about how work on her movie was going, and then before I knew it, Liam was standing in front of me, wearing nothing but a towel, looking utterly amused and mind-blowingly hot, drops of water dripping from dark hair onto his broad, tanned shoulders.

I lifted my shoulders in a "Yeah, yeah, girls can chat on the phone forever" shrug, but I couldn't help the smile that spread across my face at the sight of him. It felt like everything was finally falling into place...and then it hit me that I was about to leave it all. The smile drooped, and I turned away from Liam.

"Hey, Van–"

"He's out of the shower?"

"Yeah, and we were, um, talking about spending his birthday together. Like, out, maybe."

"Sounds like fun. Enjoy, and wish him a happy birthday for me."

"No, Van, like *out* out, like where people can see us–"

"I got it, A. Like I said, enjoy. We'll figure the rest out later, okay?"

"Okay." I paused as I turned to ask Liam if he could give me another minute, but he'd already disappeared back into the bathroom to give us our privacy. "Listen, Van, before I go, I just wanna say, I really am sorry. For everything. I should've told you immediately when Liam and I got together, I should've been honest about how much I hated the whole publicity stunt the second I realized I couldn't handle it, and I definitely should've taken your advice and stayed away from Nate."

"Eh, let's just say this was definitely not all your fault. Calling you jealous of me and Liam was a really cheap shot, and I'm sorry I said it. I know you're not."

"I don't know, I guess I sort of was, or maybe am. I don't know. Not of your relationship or that you're famous or anything," I added, "but I guess about the fact that you guys...make sense."

Van bit out a laugh. "It takes more than a shared profession to make a couple make sense, A. If I'm being perfectly honest, *I'm* the one who was jealous. Doing the whole fake thing with Liam, especially in front of you, just reminded me how *single* I am. And at the party, you guys were just being so cute and couple-y and happy, and I think it put me over the edge. I'm sorry I kissed him in front of Holly. That was a stupid and bitchy thing to do. Frankly, I'm glad it's all over. Forgive me?"

"Please, like there's really a question of that."

"Cool, so when exactly do I get my best friend back?"

"I'll be back on Sunday; maybe we can hang out then?"

"Sure, as long as you come armed with many more details." She paused for a moment, and then she said, "And hey, A?"

"Yeah?"

"Congrats on mastering the ukulele."

I laughed. And it felt really, really good.

AS IT HAPPENED, THE tabloids caught wind of the fact that Van wasn't with Liam on his birthday, and from there, it was only a matter of time until their public relationship slowly unraveled. Neither of them confirmed it, of course–their days of publicly discussing their private lives were done–but after that, the "date" appearances stopped and the public began to fill in the blanks.

With *Daylight Falls* coming in September and both of them filming movies over the summer, it didn't really matter; there wasn't much that could bring them down. When Liam *finally* came home at the end of July (okay, *finally* might be a little unfair, seeing as he flew me back to New York for a long weekend, with Josh's blessing), we actually managed to venture out in public without anyone trying to throw eggs at me. Okay, so it was only semi-public–mostly movies in dark theaters, dinner at restaurants like Burger King that were almost never plagued by paparazzi, and drives up PCH protected by the tinted windows of his Range Rover.

It was incredible.

No, it wasn't necessarily "normal" by the strictest definition of the word, but who said normal was a good thing? If my dad were "normal," he'd have been on his death bed. If Van were "normal," who knows if we'd still be best friends? And if Liam were "normal"... Well, let's just say that the idea of Liam being anything other than what and who he was didn't really appeal to me anymore.

"Ally? Are you almost ready?" my mother called up the stairs.

I took a deep breath and looked at myself in the mirror. We—me, my family, Van, and Liam—were going out for dinner to celebrate my father's upgraded status of "No Evidence of Disease," as well as the fact that I was off to college in a little less than a month. I was wearing a new dress and carefully applied makeup, and I'd spent no less than an hour on my hair. I had something of my own to celebrate tonight, but I wasn't quite sure how everyone else would feel about it. At least if my announcement was met with lots of anger and yelling, I'd look good for my public stoning.

"I'll be down in a minute," I called back. I smoothed down my hair and took another deep breath, willing my hands to stop shaking. "It's show time."

★★★★★

Sitting in the car with my parents and having to keep my mouth shut was torture, but I didn't want to say a word until Liam was there as well. Van was the only person who knew what I was up to, and I prayed she wouldn't spill the beans to Liam, who was driving her, before I had a chance to.

Van and Liam were already at the restaurant when we arrived, sitting at a table in the back corner and obviously doing their best not to draw any attention to themselves. I squeezed into the seat next to Liam, accepting a warm kiss on the cheek upon my arrival, and watched as Van excitedly hugged my parents like the third daughter she basically was.

A busboy immediately came over, filled our drinks, and handed out menus. Before we could even check out the appetizers, my dad clinked his fork against his glass.

"I just want to say how grateful I am for each and every one of you," he said, smiling around the table. "This is not the kind of thing you can survive on your own, and it takes a really strong support system to be able to sit where I am now. And a big part of that is making sure that your support system has a support system." He winked at Liam, whose cheeks turned the tiniest bit pink at the acknowledgement. I squeezed his hand under the table.

"And, of course, I want to make a toast to Ally, who'll be going off to New York soon..." He blinked, and I could see his eyes start to mist over. "I can't believe what a big girl you are," he half-murmured, as if talking to himself. "Going off to college already, all the way across the country–"

I couldn't take it anymore. "I'm not," I burst out, jumping up. All eyes turned to look at me, except for Van's; she was studying her menu so hard there was no way she could read a single word. "I mean, I am," I amended, "but not yet. I was going to tell you all tonight. I deferred admission to Columbia."

My mother's mouth dropped open. "You did what?"

"Ally!" My father didn't seem too pleased either. "How could you do that without telling us?"

"I wasn't sure I'd be able to make it happen," I said quickly. "I missed the deferral date, and I didn't even realize I wanted to defer until..."

Until Liam took me to look at an apartment he was considering buying in New York so he could be near me as often as possible, then took me back to his hotel room to make love to me again and whispered "Je t'aime" in my ear as I fell asleep. And then I came home and saw my family looking like a happy, healthy family, which we haven't in months. And then I had dinner with Van at the Lunchbox, and I realized we've just entered this weird and cautious new phase of our friendship and I can't leave like that, can't leave anything just like that, can't leave everyone behind.

"Um, recently," I finished, shrugging meekly.

"Let's just say, this past year didn't exactly go as I planned, but right now, things are good. Really, really good, actually. And I know I was dying to leave everything behind and go to New York, but now, that's the last thing I want." I took a deep breath and looked around, grateful that everyone was still listening calmly and no one was looking at me with an expression of horror. "If there's one thing I've learned this year, it's that you have to work at making your own happy ending. So that's what I'm doing. Columbia will still be there next year, and until I go, I really just want to spend more time with all of you."

"How did you manage to defer if you missed the deadline?" Dad asked with a furrowed brow.

Vanessa timidly raised her hand. "Um, I might've had something to do with that." She glanced past me at Liam. "We have to make an appearance at the drama school at some point, by the way."

He looked up at me and smiled, revealing his rarely seen dimple. "Well worth it," he replied, reaching for my hand to intertwine his fingers with mine.

"And what are you going to do in the meantime?" Mom asked, sounding less angry but still a bit confused.

"Actually," I said slowly, "Josh offered to extend the assistant job through next year. Apparently, I don't suck at it, and I'd rather take orders from someone who already gets on my nerves than my best friend. Much as I'll miss seeing you guys on set," I said to Van and Liam, "I feel like this is probably a better arrangement."

"I'm not sure anything that requires you to take orders from Josh can be classified as 'better' than anything," Liam said wryly, "but whatever keeps you here is okay by me."

"So you see," I said to my parents, "I'll be making more money, still get to go to Columbia if I want to next year, get to spend more time with the people who matter most, *and* I'll still be around to drive and babysit Lucy. Doesn't get much better than that, right?" I said hopefully.

My mom smiled despite herself, shaking her head. "We're happy you're sticking around, Ally. Next time, maybe just give us a little advance notice? Now we'll have to wait a whole extra year to turn your room into a gym."

"You *what*?"

She and my dad exchanged a grin and laughed. "You deserved that," said my father.

"Maybe," I grudgingly agreed. "So, are we toasting or what?"

Everyone raised their glasses in the air, and my dad announced, "To happy endings."

My mom smiled and kissed him on the cheek. "To happy beginnings, thank you very much."

"To happy beginnings," the rest of us chorused, and as our glasses clinked and everyone in the restaurant turned to stare in our direction and whisper, I simply smiled.

ACKNOWLEDGEMENTS

IT'S EMBARRASSING TO SAY THIS as a writer, but I don't have enough words in my vocabulary to adequately express my gratitude to my wonderful editor—and friend—Patricia Riley. Thank you for loving Ally and Liam just as much on twelfth read, for making them and their story stronger, and for giving them the perfect home.

Major Spencer Hill thanks are also due to Lauren Meinhardt, for all her editorial insights; Lindsay Smith, for her meticulous line edits; Linda Braus and Traci Inzitari for all their help and support; Christa Holland at Paper and Sage, for my beautiful Hollywood cover; Cindy Thompson and Patrice Caldwell, for all their work on the publicity side; Jenny Perinovic, Sydnee Thompson, and Rachael Kirkendall for making this look like an actual book; and my brilliant copy editors and friends, Becca Weston and Sarah Henning, who do so much more for me on a daily basis than fix my typos.

This book probably wouldn't exist if not for a few amazing people guiding me along the way. Utmost thanks to Christopher Koehler, for teaching me that writing is not a solo effort, and for so much more than that. To Arielle Kane, thank you for ripping this manuscript to shreds so I could learn how to piece it back together. This would be half a story if it weren't for you. And to Andrea Somberg, thank you for placing so much faith, time, and effort in this book.

To my critique partners—Marieke Nijkamp, Gina Ciocca, Maggie Hall, and Erica Chapman—you light up my life. You are constant support, and brilliant notes, and all-important commiseration, and endless patience, and glorious gifs, and you make me love doing this every day. Thank you for more than I could possibly fit in this book, let alone on this page.

I also owe major debts of gratitude to the following:

My agent, Lana Popovic, the warmest, most brilliant, most supportive mama bear anyone could ever dream of having in her corner;

The teachers who made me feel like this whole writing thing was something worth doing, and taught me how to do it well (or at least with proper grammar), especially Mrs. Helene Fechter, Dr. Steven Milowitz, and Ms. Melissa Jensen;

Team Cupid, for all your support and page-polishing efforts—especially Melanie Stanford, for great-under-the-wire notes—and, of course, the lovely Cupid herself;

Sarah Benwell, Cait Greer, Valerie Cole, Phil Siegel, Jen Malone, Diana Peterfreund, and Leah Raeder for early reads and/or general wonderfulness at various points in the process;

YA Misfits—my sisters in argyle—for being there through everything, always;

OneFourKidLit, for sharing your wealth of knowledge, experience, and battle scars;

Ali Rosenbaum Grange, for graciously lending me "AlGal";

Gawker, WordSmoker, Crasstalk, Twitter, and all the "invisible friends" I've made within, for being my homes away from home and making me feel I had a voice worth listening to;

The fantastic book bloggers out there who work their butts off to promote authors and share their love of the written word, and especially those who went out of their way for this one;

And all the other amazing writer friends who are always willing to hold my hand (or my hair back) through this world, especially Rick Lipman and Heidi Schulz, who've had to do it a lot more than most.

I'm incredibly blessed to have the most supportive constants in my life a dreamer could ask for. Thank you to my wonderful family-in-law—Debbie, Jerry, Eric, Orly, and Simona—for everything, plus bonus points to Eric for setting me straight on LA roadways.

To Mom, Dad, Aytan, Tamar, and Jonathan, I am eternally grateful to have grown up in a family that always made me feel achieving this particular dream was not an "if" but a "when." Thank you for that, your patience, your constant support and pride, and all the ways you inspired this particular story.

Finally, the biggest thanks of all goes to my husband, Yoni, for making all of this possible in everything he does, for being my biggest fan, and for giving me unwavering faith that teenagers can have a happily ever after.

And Liz, happy 30th. Thanks for sharing your day.

ABOUT THE AUTHOR

DAHLIA ADLER is an Assistant Editor of Mathematics by day, a Copy Editor by night, and a YA author and blogger at every spare moment in between. She lives in New York City with her husband and their overstuffed bookshelves. *Behind the Scenes* is her first novel.